HOW WE DEAL WITH GRAVITY

a novel

by ginger scott

For every parent of a child with autism.

PROLOGUE

Avery

The looks on their faces—that's the worst part.

Nobody tries to help. They never do. They just rush by with their own children, hiding their eyes so they don't see *the woman causing the scene with her kid*.

They scoff at me, judge me. They make grand assumptions.

"She needs to learn how to control her son," I hear them whisper.

Or, "I bet she lets him walk all over her. It's her own fault, really."

Sometimes, I actually feel ashamed. I mouth apologies, as best I can, and I cry. Sometimes...I *cry*.

Then there are other times—the ones where I grit my teeth, and I stare back into their eyes, with laser-like precision. I bite my tongue, fight against my grain, wanting to shove them, swear at them—make them feel small.

But most of the time, I just count. I count and I pray—not that I've stepped foot inside a church once in my life, but I pray anyway, because if someone's going to be heard, Lord, it *has* to be me.

I've made it all the way into the thousands before the counting stops. I've had security step in, try to *calm* the situation. I've broken displays in the grocery store, set off car alarms in parking lots, and toppled tables in restaurants.

That's part of the reason I don't go out much. It just...well...it just isn't easy. Hell, it's *far* from easy. It's barely possible. And some would argue it isn't.

But it's only Max and me in this world—and sometimes, he and I have to conquer its cruelty together.

His teeth are locked on my arm. I felt the skin break minutes ago, and I know when I finally pull his mouth away, there will be blood.

Four hundred seven. Four hundred eight. Four hundred nine.

I'm clutching Max to my body, our grocery bags splayed around us near the store's entrance. I keep staring at the lone red apple that rolled furthest away. Even the damn produce is abandoning me—hiding.

Four hundred sixteen. Four hundred seventeen.

I shut my eyes, tired of the furrowed brows and the sneers from the old ladies pulling out their carts. If I don't see them, they won't exist. I won't hear them. There's no way I could over the shrilling scream Max has kept up for at least 15 minutes straight. His body relaxed in my arms a few minutes ago. But I made the mistake of thinking it was over—that we were done. I tried to walk him to the car, leaving the groceries where they lay. And that's when he got me with his teeth.

My arms are so tired. When Max is like this, it's like he's possessed with super strength, and it takes all I have in me to keep his arms down, to keep him from hurting himself. This little boy, barely five—I don't know what I'll do when he's ten, fifteen or…

Sometimes I can send my dad out for these errands. But he almost always gets something wrong, coming home with strawberry pastries instead of cherry. Getting something wrong is almost worse. But today? Today, I don't know. I think I'd pick the pastry meltdown.

I had to park far. Not in *our* spot. He was edgy then, shuffling his feet more than normal, and bouncing on his toes. Then the bread aisle was blocked because we were later than normal, and the deliveryman was stocking the shelves. We always go down the bread aisle first.

Always.

But today we couldn't. And somehow, through a miracle, Max accepted that. But his feet began moving faster, and his arms began swinging more, his hands reaching to *almost* touch everything, careful to come within a millimeter without actually pressing his skin to anything foreign.

We gathered our small list into the basket. We paid. We bagged the groceries. And we were almost out the door.

Almost.

I felt the handle slipping. Like slow motion, I saw it all play out in my mind before it really happened. The bag tore open, and

2

the apples—Max's apples—all rolled onto the ground—the dirty ground. And Max had met his match.

"What a spoiled brat!" the woman says as she shoves her plastic purse in the top basket of her shopping cart.

All I can do is smile, and meekly, at that. *"I'm sorry."* That's what I'm saying with that smile. That I'm sorry my son has autism, and that I don't know how to hide it from you.

Max's grip is loosening even more, and my lungs finally fill up.

I look back at the apple.

Four hundred sixty-one. Four hundred sixty-two.

Today, I will make it home before dark, but without apples. I can't do this again...not *today*. I'll send my dad for the apples tomorrow. And I'll give him pictures so he gets it right.

But I've got nothing left. Today is one of those *sometimes*. The ones when I cry.

Mason

I can't believe I'm back here, in this *shit hole!* At least I'm not staying with my mom. She's been shacking up with a new guy, some rich asshole she met at the big car auction that comes to town.

He's hung around longer than most. I think it's been a few months, not that I pay attention to the pointless stories she tells me over the phone.

She hasn't given up the apartment, which is good. She did that the last time she met the guy that was going to be *the one.* She had to move all our crap into storage and back out again a month later. She lost the two-bedroom, too. Just one more reason to be glad I'm not staying with her while I figure things out—I hate sleeping on the fucking couch.

Calling Ray Abbot was really my only option when the label dropped the band. Ray's taken me in most of my life. He taught me my first chord and gave me my first Gibson for my sixteenth birthday. He's the reason I love rock & roll and the blues. Ray put me—scared shitless—on a stage in front of a mic and a drunk-ass crowd of locals when I was ten, maybe eleven. Changed my life.

I still remember climbing up to sit on the stools in the back of his bar after school while my mom finished her shift. When I called, Ray told me she quit again after she started dating the new guy. But her locker's still there, along with all her shirts and her apron. He even made a joke about how he doesn't peel off the "Barb" sticker from her nametag anymore because he knows he'll just be printing a new one out in a few months.

Thank God for Ray Abbot. I swear, with the amount of times Barb Street walked off the job during a shift, if it weren't for that man and his forgiving nature, I'm pretty sure I wouldn't have had food on my plate when I was a kid.

I didn't tell my mom I was coming home. She would baby me, tell me it was the band's fault, and that I needed to find someone new. I've been with the guys for years, and she still doesn't know their names. I'll call her in a few days, when I have something to say—when I can tell her I'm hitting the road again and getting the hell out of Arizona.

Ray's bar looks exactly the same. You would never believe the talent that's passed through this joint by looking at it from the gravel parking lot out front. The metal sign that reads *Dusty's* is banged up and crooked, and the spotlight that shines on the marquee is dim. I don't even know why Ray bothers to put up the names and show times—there's no way a car passing by out here in the desert would be able to read it. Hell, I'm standing seven feet out, and I can't make out a goddamned word!

The people come anyway. Ray could post on that sign out front that the world was ending, and he'd still have a full house by 8 p.m. on a Friday. It's because the music is *that good,* and you can count on it. It's simple—if you're a hack, Ray won't put you on.

There's a new band jamming tonight. I scope them out when I walk in and slide through the crowd lining the tables in the back. They're pretty tight. A country band...a little bluegrass maybe? I like their sound.

"Well, are you just going to stand there, numbnuts?" I hear the gruff voice say from behind me. Ray bumps into my arm with his elbow, hard enough to knock me off balance.

"Hey, old man, just cuz my ma quit, don't go thinking I'm picking up her shifts. You can bus your own tables," I joke back, following him into the kitchen.

Ray dumps the bin of dirty glasses into the sink, and nods to a couple of the guys working in the back before drying off his hands on the towel tossed over his shoulder. He settles his gaze on me with a tough-guy sigh, but I know he's just giving me shit. He lets it go on for a couple of seconds before he starts laughing and pulling me in for a hug.

"Damn, Mason. How long's it been?" he asks.

"Five years, Ray. Five years," I say, both sad that I haven't come to visit, and dejected that I'm right back where I started.

"Wow, man. That long, huh?" Ray says, nudging me to follow him to the back office. Just like the rest of the bar, Ray's office looks like time stood still. The layer of dust on all of the framed photos is thick, and I zero in on the one of him with me right away.

Five years—five years ago I took a picture with Ray on that stage, celebrating my big break. Some fuckin' break. The boys and me have played nothing but shit-small towns and tiny venues without as much as a month or two off in between, and I don't even have an album to show for it—at least, nothing anyone's playing.

"So, label bailed, huh?" Ray says, kicking his feet up onto his desk and gesturing for me to take a seat on the old sofa.

"Yeah, it was time, though. They weren't doing anything for us," I say, falling deep into the worn cushions.

"Hmmmm," Ray says, chewing at the inside of his cheek, and twisting at the end of his graying mustache.

"Oh, come on, Ray…you know we're good. You *know* it!" I start to protest, leaning forward, ready to stand on my feet. Fuck this, I didn't come here to get a lecture. I called Ray because I thought he would understand. He's the one who pushed me to fight for this, and he's half the reason I want it so damned bad. If he's going to tell me I can't make it now…

"Sit your ass down, hot head," he halts me. I roll my eyes at him, but I sit back, giving him the respect he deserves. However, I'm not opposed to walking right out of here and slamming his door in his face if he starts to get high and mighty.

Ray leans forward and reaches into his desk drawer, digging through piles of notebooks and papers before finally coming up with a giant envelop full of clippings. He unfolds the top and dumps six or seven newspaper articles on his desk, spreading them out like a winning poker hand. I keep my eyes on him the entire time—I don't dare look down at the papers, because I know what they are, and I hate that he's read them.

"Let's just take a look, shall we?" he says, pulling his glasses from his front pocket just to be melodramatic. This is going to be *way* more painful than I thought. I should have known—Ray doesn't lecture. He doesn't need to. He can put you in your place in an instant just by pulling at the threads of your skeletons and weaknesses.

"This one's from two months ago. Says here Mason Street and his band left a crowd of nearly 3,000 ticket holders waiting until almost 11 p.m. before finally taking the stage in Oklahoma City," Ray says, flicking his eyes to mine for a brief second, just long enough to burn in his disappointment. "Oh, wait…there's more. It goes on to say that when the band finally took the stage, they only made it through one song before the drummer passed out. And then…wow, really? And then Street broke his guitar over his knee and punched his bass player, starting a brawl that police had to break up."

"Yeah, yeah…I get it," I say, but Ray's quick to cut me off.

"No, Mason. I don't think you do. Let's take a look at this one," he says, unfolding the one that's going to hurt to hear. I'm not going to get out of here without letting him say his piece—so I sit back again and get comfortable. I still won't look at him, though, so instead I stare at the wall of photos.

"The Mason Street Band was arrested for disorderly conduct after trashing—*trashing!*—a Reno hotel suite. Damage was estimated at $250,000 and included two windows," Ray pulls his glasses off and rubs at his forehead. He doesn't need to finish. "Damn it, Mason. You really don't know why the label dropped you? You and those…those…those clowns that you call a band. Jesus, boy! It's a good thing you've come home, but I don't know—"

I turn to him now. If he's about to say what I think he's going to say, I want to look into his eyes while he crushes me. "What, Ray? What don't you know?" I ask, throwing my shoulders up in defeat.

Ray's slow to respond, spending his time folding up the sad scrapbook he's kept on me. The worst part…I don't think there's a positive article in the mix, and I wouldn't know where the hell to find one. He slides the folder back into his drawer and leans forward on his elbows, cracking his knuckles while he studies me.

"Kid, you sure made a mess of things. You're the most talented thing I've ever put up on that stage. But your goddamned head is thick, you know that?" he says, mouth tight, and showing only half a smile. "I don't know if you can fix this, that's all. But we'll try, okay? We'll sure try."

Ray stands up and walks over to reach for my hand to pull me up to my feet. He pats my back as he guides me back out to the bar. I just shake my head, because I really don't have any answers. I get how Ray sees things, but he also doesn't understand what it was like to play, night after night, in some of those joints. Every month there was promise of a bigger ticket, of coming in for an album, recording something new. But then another month would pass, and nothing. The guys quit believing about a year ago, and I just couldn't keep it going anymore. I quit writing, too.

"Hey, Ray," called the waitress from behind the bar, "we're getting hammered out here already. What are we doing about Barb?"

"Avery's coming in early. She'll be here in a few," Ray says back.

I can't help but chuckle at the thought of Avery working the bar. Ray's daughter has always been mousy. We all called her Birdie when we were younger, because when she talked it sounded like chirping.

"Avery actually works here?" I half laugh to Ray as I join him behind the bar. Out of instinct, I start grabbing glasses and drying them. I did a lot of dishes at Dusty's before I hit the road, and if Ray's going to put me up for the next few weeks, the least I can do is help out until Birdie shows up.

"Yeah, she works the night shifts. She's going to school, too. Girl works her ass off," Ray says, either not picking up on the humor I see about Avery in a bar, or just ignoring it. "Hey, will you take these to the back and bring in the clean ones?" Ray asks, handing me a bin full of dirty glasses.

"Sure," I say, lugging them with me to the back. Sal and Manny are working the kitchen today, so I spend a few minutes with them. Those two have been working here almost as long as my mom has, and they're like uncles to me. Hell, Sal taught me how to throw a punch when I was getting picked on in fifth grade. And Manny taught me how to take one in high school. My mom was pissed when he punched me in the face, but when she found out it was because I was dating his daughter, she never brought it up again.

Ray yells through the swinging door. "Hey, Mason! Avery's here, so why don't you take my keys on over to the house and get settled?"

"Ah right, boys. I'll catch ya later. I'm going to see if I can talk the old man into letting me play a night or two," I wink. I dry my hands, and then shake theirs before heading back into the busy bar, where the crowd is starting to build. Ray's manning the tap;

8

it's at least two-people deep, and most of the tables are full. I recognize a lot of the familiar faces, but there's always a batch of new ones, too—tourists and college kids looking to party.

"You sure Ray? I can stay, help out?" I offer, but Ray just pulls out his keys and tosses them to me.

"Nah, this is nothing. Just another Thursday night!" he says, topping off a beer and going right in to fill the next one.

I grip the keys in my right hand, nod *thanks* to him and turn around, but before I make it a full step, I slam into one of the waitresses. Trying to stop myself, I accidentally grab her tit with my free hand.

"Ugh, asshole!" she pushes me to the side as she flies by and whips through the swinging door into the back. All I see is her long, straight, strawberry-blond hair as she disappears. I'm probably going to see this girl for the next few weeks, so I follow her back past Sal and Manny into the small locker room, chuckling a little and looking at my left hand with fondness.

"Hey, wait...hey, I'm totally sorry. I really didn't mean to grab...shit; I mean...I didn't mean to do that. Damn, I'm sorry," I say, lightly laughing and waiting for the girl to turn around.

"Whatever," she says, clearly unimpressed with me. She pulls one leg up to tie her shoe on the bench, and then tucks her hair behind her ear. I'm about to give up and go when I realize just *how bad* this is.

"*Birdie?*" I say, my mouth moving toward a big grin. She tosses her head up when I say her name, and the fire in her green eyes pretty much knocks me on my fucking ass! This is not the Avery Abbot I knew in high school. I know I'm walking on thin ice, but I can't help but let my eyes wander down from her soft face and pink lips to what might just be the tightest goddamned body I've ever seen. I can see every inch outlining her bra under the thin, white Dusty's T-shirt; the black shorts hug her hips so well, I'm wishing like hell she'd turn around and drop something just so I could watch her pick it up.

"Mason," she says, forcing my gaze back up to her eyes. She isn't smiling when she looks at me. *Shit,* I need to fix this. I can't have Ray's daughter this pissed at me.

"I'm so sorry, Birdie. I wasn't looking, and I totally didn't know that was you," I say, trying to make my tongue work in my mouth, while I search for something else to add, something *smart.* I've got nothing, so instead I just lean to the side and watch her push past me again. I breathe deeply when she walks by, and the girl actually smells like vanilla—like a fucking dessert!

I stumble back out to the bar and look at the keys in my hand, then back up to Avery as she ties the green apron around her tiny waist and pulls her hair back into a ponytail. She always wore her hair like that, but I don't know—it's somehow *very* different now. The tiny freckles on her neck have me in a bit of a trance when Ray bumps into me.

"You headin' out?" he asks. I feel the teeth of the keys against my fingers. There's no way I'm leaving, no matter how bad of an idea it is to flirt with Ray's daughter. I know the line, but I won't be able to get my mind straight if I don't just straddle it a little tonight—get inside her head.

"In a bit. Let me just help out for a while, so I know you've got this handled. It'd make me feel better since you're putting me up and all," I smile at him, and hand him back his keys.

"Alright then, you can start mixing," he says, pushing the keys in his pocket and going back to work. I pull a ticket and start mixing on the other end of the bar, but I keep my attention divided on Avery the entire time, just waiting for her to come over. She keeps heading to the corner of the restaurant area—probably to avoid me.

She's almost in front of me when she locks onto my gaze, and spins around on her heels toward her dad. I'm not gonna lie, I take a good look when she leans over the bar to talk to Ray, and I'm half-tempted to race around to the other side of the bar to check out the view from behind. But something she says catches me off guard.

"Dad, you know he can't stay with us! Max isn't going to like it," she protests, crossing her arms. Her dad waves his hand telling her to calm down, and she spins around and walks back to the corner. Who the hell is in that corner? And who's Max? Shit, is she married?

Avery doesn't return to this side of the bar for the next 20 minutes. I saw her hand her orders to another waitress to bring them over a few times, and she actually had her dad bring out some of the plates, just to avoid passing by me on her way to the kitchen.

What the hell? It was just a boob grab, and it was a damned accident. If this girl was going to get that bent out of shape, then I don't need to waste my time with fantasies.

"Pain in the ass," I mumble under my breath, focusing once again on the drink orders.

"Hey, Cole. That's Mason, go on in and relieve him," Ray hollers, nodding in my direction. A big burly dude heads my way, pushing the sleeves up on his one-size-too-small black shirt. He must be the new bouncer. Hell, he's big—with my luck, he's Avery's husband, or boyfriend or...whatever.

"Hey, man. Mason, nice to meet you," I reach over to shake his hand, hoping like hell he doesn't crush my fingers.

"Oh yeah, you, too. It's funny, I feel kinda like I know you, the way Ray talks about you around here," he smiles, shaking my hand and holding back—*thank God!*—then taking over on the next drink order. I'm a little surprised by his words, though I don't know why. I know how Ray feels about me—like I'm his own son. There's just something about hearing someone else say it.

The crowds are getting thick now, getting ready for the headliner. Back when I was in high school, Ray started pushing Thursday nights, and when I turned eighteen, I was one of his first performers. He fought like hell with the town council over his liquor license requirements when he put me on stage. But Ray's got a lot of friends in high places in Cave Creek.

I can't help but look over at Avery's corner a few more times before I leave. Maybe it's the challenge, but I just want her to give in once, to come over here before I leave. That way, I can ask her what crawled up her ass and why she cares if I stay at Ray's house. Or maybe not, maybe she'll just motivate me to hit the road sooner.

"You know her?" Cole says, leaning into me.

"What, Avery? Yeah...we went to high school together. She hung around the bar a lot when I was here, too," I say, my eyes glued to her like a stupid tracking beam. I'm so weak.

Cole bends down to get something out of the mini fridge, and comes up with a small glass of chocolate milk. He puts it on a tray with a napkin and two straws and pushes it toward me.

"Thanks, man, but I'm not thirsty," I laugh. Does he seriously think I'm lame enough to offer to split chocolate milk with some girl? I could go down the street right now to the next bar, and leave a half hour later with three chicks ready to ride me until I kick them out in the morning—and they wouldn't care that I didn't know their names. They never do.

Cole nudges me again and nods back in Avery's direction. "Nah, man. It's her order. Take it," he winks.

Well, damn. I've been waiting for an *in* all night, and now that I've got one, my hands have turned to jelly, and my heart rate is keeping time with the band—pulsing out of my head.

Cole nods one more time, so I take the tray in my hand and head to the back corner. Only, when I get there, Avery is gone. I roll my eyes at my own luck, and head to the corner booth. There's a kid with curly blond hair sitting in the farthest corner. He looks about five, and his legs are pulled up underneath him, his attention completely focused on the iPad in front of him. Looks like some sort of space game or something.

"Whatcha playin' there, buddy?" I ask, but the kid doesn't break his concentration. He just keeps playing his game, like he didn't even hear me. Maybe he didn't.

"One chocolate milk," I say, putting the napkin down and then placing the glass on top. I wait for a few seconds, but he doesn't say anything. I was never a video-game nerd—I just don't get the appeal. I roll my eyes, and start to turn when a strange voice stops me.

"Straws," he says, the one syllable word somehow sounding as if it has two or three, the way he pronounces every *individual* letter.

"Oh, yeah. Sure," I say, pulling one off the tray and tossing it next to his glass.

"No," he says, before I can leave. "That's not right. That's not right. That's not right. Two straws. Two straws. Two straws."

I look back at the tray, notice the second straw, and immediately put it down by the other one. His eyes are wide, but still focused solely on his video game. I wait for a few seconds, and he finally puts the tablet down, his fingers very methodical as they place it perfectly in line with the rest of the table. He then reaches for his glass, and moves it closer, looking into the milk a few solid seconds like he's inspecting it, before reaching for the straws and unwrapping them slowly. He puts them both in at the same time. Sipping long and deep through them both together, his eyes focus on the small bubbles in the milk, oblivious to the clanking of glasses and loud noise of the crowd of two hundred or so people building just a few yards away from him.

"So…anything else?" I ask, wondering if this kid even realizes I'm still here. He doesn't say a word, and he doesn't stop drinking. I'm background to him—irrelevant.

"Okay, then…" I say, shaking my head and blinking as I turn to walk away. "Weird fucking kid."

"Hey!" Avery says, charging closer to me. "What'd you give him? Leave him the hell alone!"

She's almost to me, looking past me, when I reach out and grab her wrist. "Hey, calm down. I just delivered your order. Relax, would ya? Cole gave it to me," I explain, suddenly wishing I just went to Ray's an hour ago, like he told me to, instead of acting stupid over a pretty girl.

Avery's posture slumps, and she lets out a heavy breath. She snaps her eyes to my hand, which is still on her wrist, and then quickly shirks it away. I'm almost offended, but she doesn't give me time before she's grilling me. "You're sure? Cole gave that to you? He made it?" she says, almost manic.

"Yeah, I'm pretty sure I can remember simple things like who gave me milk," I shrug.

She brings her hands to her face, rubbing her temples, and I take a minute to scope out her left hand. No ring. Damn, she's been nothing but a big pain in my ass, and I'm still making sure she's not married. What the hell is wrong with me? Suddenly, she stops, and her eyes soften when they land on mine, and then she actually smiles. *Oh hell, that's some smile.*

"Thank you," she says, leaving her gaze on me long enough for me to memorize every fleck of gold within the green of her eyes.

"No problem. Least I can do. That kid's a real weirdo," I say, tilting my head in his direction. Without warning, her smile is gone, and her hand hits my cheek with such force, I fear I may have actually swallowed a tooth.

"What the fu—" I'm about to question her, but it's too late. She's gone. I don't even know which direction she walked, so I just rub my face and make my way back to Cole, no longer sure if I want to thank him or punch him.

"What the hell? I give that kid milk, and she slaps me," I say to him as I reach into the ice bin and fill the center of one of Ray's towels. "Shit! That stings! I think I have a shiner."

Cole chuckles a little to himself, and starts shaking a martini. "Sorry, man. I really was trying to help you out. I didn't see how that could go wrong," he looks back at the corner where Avery is standing once again. I'm thinking about walking over to her and calling her on her bullshit, but then she slides into the booth and points to something on the kid's iPad.

"That's her son," Cole says—short and sweet. Fuck, I'm an asshole.

My face must clue him in at how shocked I am, so he turns around and leans on the back of the bar to give me his full attention for a few minutes.

"I thought she wasn't married? Is she divorced?" I ask, moving the ice a little lower and wincing.

"Something like that. The dude married her, and then bailed right away. Some guy from your high school, I think. Some *Adam* or something?" Cole says, and I know immediately.

"Adam Price. He was our student body president. He and Avery were into all that honors class shit," I say, remembering what a smug asshole Adam was back then.

"Yeah, that's it. Adam. He left when Max was one. Ave's been doing a damn good job with that kid on her own, though," Cole says, turning back to his work, and not realizing how much he's kicking my ass with every single word. Shit! I just mocked the kid of a hard-working single mom because he didn't thank me for bringing him chocolate milk.

"Oh, this is bad. I should apologize. I was kind of a prick to her," I say, looking over at the booth where she's sitting next to her son, my stomach turning over and over with guilt and shame. Who the hell am I? I'm just some loser musician who got dropped from his label, thrown out of a club in Tulsa for drinking too much, and sent home to lick his wounds.

"She'll get over it," Cole says.

He says that now, but I think if Cole knew half the shit I've done, he'd take it back. In fact, he'd probably have a good long

14

talk with Avery warning her to stay away from men like me. And he'd be right.

CHAPTER 2: PEOPLE DON'T CHANGE

Avery

"Claire, it's been an hour. When are you going to get here?" I ask, hiding in the back locker room, away from those damn stalker-eyes of Mason's. I feel like he's watching everything I do, just waiting to judge me or laugh at me. I swear, all it took was him calling me *Birdie* to make me feel seventeen again. I had to check the mirror to make sure my braces were, in fact, gone.

"I'm pulling in the lot. I just need to find a spot, okay? What's the big deal anyhow? You've brought Max in before. Your dad doesn't mind, and Max is always good at Dusty's," she says. I can hear her keys jingle, followed by the beeping of her door, and I'm immediately filled with relief that she's here.

"Just meet me around back," I say, sprinting through the kitchen, hoping not to get stopped. I make it to the back door, and prop it open with my foot to let Claire in.

"Okay, I see the door. Be there in a sec," she hangs up, and a few seconds later I feel her pull the door completely open.

"Hey, Manny. Hey, Sal!" she says, walking over to hug the guys. Claire works at Dusty's, too, but she's usually on the morning and early afternoon shift and doesn't get to see the guys much. I don't know how I'd survive without my best friend. She works all morning, and then spends the evening with Max so I can get a few shifts in during the week. She's gone through a lot of training, and she's amazing with Max. She's the one who finally got him to put his own socks on—in under a minute.

Max has a hard time focusing on things he doesn't want to do. In fact, lately, unless it has to do with the moon or the stars or how the earth rotates, it doesn't have a place in Max's world. But Claire's managed to find ways around the distractions.

Basically, we bribe him. And I used to cringe at it—felt like I was treating my son like a puppy. But Claire has taught me that it's really just human nature to work toward goals, to seek rewards. So when Max does something I want, or something Grandpa wants, he gets something he wants—simple.

My pockets are always full of tart candies. Max likes sour things. But he can't eat certain foods, and most candy upsets his stomach. There's only one store in Cave Creek that sells the gluten-free tarts, and if they ever discontinue them, I will throw a one-woman protest of epic proportions.

"Okay, so where's Max? And what the hell has you so worked up?" Claire says, pushing her purse back up her shoulder and leaning on the prep table in the kitchen.

"Remember Mason Street?" I say, my mouth watering with the need to vomit just saying his name.

"Ave, the whole state remembers Mason Street. Wait, is he…here?" she's already bolting for the swinging door and cracking it open. I love Claire to death, but subtlety is not one of her strong points. "Where is he? What does he look like in person? Is he still hot?"

"Claire, we've known him since grade school. You know what he looks like," I roll my eyes.

"Yeah, but that was before he went on tour with a band. Did they hit it big? Is that why he's here? Is there a concert somewhere? Can he get us tickets?" Suddenly, my friend has gone full-groupie.

"No, Claire. He didn't hit it big. He's a loser, and my dad's taking him in," oh god, I was going to regret saying that. She backs away from the door and flashes that mischievous smile she's famous for—the one that's been getting me grounded since fifth grade.

"Mason Street is *sleeping*…at *your* house?" she says, her eyebrows bobbing up and down just to annoy me.

I sigh heavily and sit down on the small step stool behind the door, folding my hands around my face and leaning forward. "Yes, Claire. Mason Street is sleeping at my house. At least, until I can get him to leave," I say, standing back up and forcing myself to have a little backbone.

"Why would you make him leave, Avery?" she's already pulling out her compact to check her makeup and touch up her lipstick. I can't believe how predictable she is.

"You know Max won't like it, Claire. And because, frankly, I think he's a goddamned selfish asshole!" I say.

Claire just lowers her brow and studies me before answering. "You're not being fair, you know. You still think Mason Street is the same guy he was at eighteen. But if you think about it, Ave, you're nothing like the Avery Abbot of Cave Creek High School," she says, sneaking a look back through the crack in the door.

Claire's partly right—I'm nowhere near the girl I was at eighteen. That girl was hopeful and innocent. That girl didn't have a little boy who depended on her for everything—a little boy who she wasn't sure would be able to survive kindergarten, let alone this world. And that girl had fantasies about getting married—in a church, with a big puffy dress, and violins playing from a balcony—to a man who would help her raise their three kids and live happily ever after.

Yeah, I had veered far from the course *that girl* was on six years ago. Instead, I became the girl who got knocked up in college, who dropped out to have a baby, and who's raising her son on her own, while she lives with her dad and tries not to drive off the bridge on her way home from work every night.

"Damn, Avery. Did you get a good look at him? I swear, girl—watching him talk to Cole is putting ideas in my head about those two," she says in her teasing voice.

"Claire!" I slap at her arm.

"What? Do you know the last time I went on a date? And I mean a real date—not TV trays in your living room with your father," she jokes. I smile and laugh softly, mostly because I feel a little guilty. Claire has given up her social life over the last three years just to help me get through school. Sadly she's the husband Adam never was, and I wish like hell I could tell her to live her life, set her free. But I can't, because some days she's the only thing holding me together. And Max—oh, Max—he responds to her more than anyone else.

"Seriously, Avery. Come look," she pulls me close to her by the door. I feel ridiculous, but I indulge her. "That—that man right there—is going to be down the hall from you...*tonight!*"

I squeeze my eyes shut at first, mortified that the boy whose name I used to doodle on my papers as a teenager might run into me late at night when I sneak to the bathroom in my pathetic T-shirt and sweatpants. Mason is in the middle of laughing when I open my eyes to look. He's so much older, but god is he familiar.

18

His smile was always my favorite; the way it dimples at the corners and stretches the width of his face. His hair has somehow gotten better, just long enough to split down the middle and curl over his eyebrows. He's still wearing the white V-neck T-shirts and worn out jeans, but his body seems to fill them out more. He's gotten a tattoo on one of his arms, and I'm dying to know what it says, but I don't dare let Claire know that. She's right. Mason Street is hot as hell. But that doesn't matter, and it doesn't matter for lots of reasons—the biggest being Max.

"I get it Claire. Mason is good looking," I say, backing away from the door and lifting my palms to show her she wins, and her grin says she's about to brag and tease me, but I cut her off. "But so what? There's a reason he's landed back here, Claire, and it's not because he has his shit together."

Claire offers me a conceding smile instead, and nods once. "Okay, I'll lay off. But you totally have to give me the details on anything juicy tomorrow. Let's go get Max so I can take him home," she says, pushing through the door.

When we pass through, Mason is right there. He wasn't coming in, but rather stopped, and I know he heard us, and that's what halted him. I feel bad for a few seconds, knowing I judged him like he's done to me so many times. But when I see the floppy blond curls on Max's head as he slides from the booth, I forget all about Mason Street, because in my reality, he's nothing.

"I'll have him in bed by eight thirty. What time are you off?" Claire says, her eyes wide as she looks at me because she sees Mason standing right behind me. I ignore it all.

"I should be home by eleven. I just need to get Dad through the busy part. I'm on again tomorrow, so I don't want to work too late tonight," I say, bending down to try to look Max in the eyes.

This is always a struggle, but the therapists say it's something I need to practice with him every chance I get. Max doesn't make eye contact. He never has. It was the first clue we had that something was wrong. By Max's one-year appointment, he wasn't doing any of the things on the checklist for parents—no sounds, no emotional expressions, no pointing or acknowledging things around him at all. I was terrified he was blind, or deaf—or both. Adam and I fought about it—we fought a lot. I had to drag Adam with me to Max's pediatrician, because he thought I was just overreacting.

But then our world was rocked. The doctor said the word *autism*, and the next day Adam was gone. I tried to find him for months, but eventually, I just gave up. A year later, I started to get money deposited into my account, and when I did a little investigating, I found out it was from him. Seems my father had a few words with his parents, and they forced Adam to do the right thing...*financially.*

The money's nice, but when I'm piecing together my life with help from my dad and best friend, just so I can work as a waitress and take two classes a semester, I kind of wish Max had a father instead of some state-mandated child support stipend.

I can feel Mason's stare behind me while I try to look Max in the eyes, and it makes me remember the sting on my hand from slapping him earlier tonight. I hate that he's watching this, because I know he'll have questions.

"Max, you need to look at me. I know you don't want to, but you have to do it, just for a second, okay?" I say, my hands putting light pressure on both of his shoulders, just enough to keep Max still on his feet. He doesn't like affection, so I try not to touch him too long. "Aunt Claire is going to take you home, and then she'll go through your books with you, okay?"

Max nods *yes* once, so I know he heard me, but I really want him to use his words.

"I need to hear you. Can you say your words, Max?" I ask, my voice breaking a little, because I hate that I'm begging, and I hate that a stranger—at least in terms of my life—is witnessing this.

I look up at Claire, and she's on the verge with me, hopeful, but sad all at the same time. She flicks her eyes to mine for a few seconds, and gestures with her chin to my right side. I reach in and pull out two candies.

"I need to hear your words, Max. And you need to make eye contact, just for a second. And then you can have two candies, even though it's almost bedtime," I say, and instantly Max's pupils are square with mine. He holds my gaze for two full seconds, and then looks back down at the corner of the floor. "We need to read *Planets*. The page is marked," and that's all Max says.

20

I can't help it that I cry a little—I do every time. Every little thing is such a huge milestone. Claire understands, and I'm so happy to see her smile when I stand back up and give her a hug. "Sure, pal. Auntie Claire will read *Planet*s," I say, also whispering, "Thank you," in Claire's ear.

"My name is Max," I hear him say from below, already walking through the kitchen door.

"You're right. Max, not *pal*. I'm sorry," I say, laughing while I wipe my eyes with the tissue from my back pocket. Max doesn't respond to anything but his name. Sometimes it's a cute idiosyncrasy, but I worry that some day someone's not going to find it as cute as I do. But I'll worry about that hurdle another time. Today was a success—today, Max looked at me…for two whole seconds.

I don't even acknowledge Mason when Max and Claire leave. Instead, I pick up my tray, and head to the back to bus a table that's cleared. He doesn't follow me, but he's still hanging around. I can't avoid the kitchen forever, so I finally pass him with a full tray and a bin of dirty glasses. I back through the door and he follows. *Damn.*

"Here, let me help. If there's one thing I'm good at, it's washing dishes," he says.

"Yeah. Clever," I say, fighting against my need to look at him after I speak to see if my words cut just a little. His prolonged silence lets me know they probably did.

Mason is reaching for the glasses as fast as I can pull them from the bin. He's working so fast that it's almost like he's trying to impress me with his dishwashing work ethic. I dump the last few in before he can catch up, then slide the bin over and reach for my tray to head back out to the bar. I make it almost to the door before he stops me.

"Birdie, wait!" he says, and I cringe. My shoulders literally fold into my spine, I hate that name so much, and just hearing it now—after he called Max a *weirdo*—snaps something deep within.

"I'm not twelve anymore, Mason. My name's Avery, for fuck's sake—*Avery*," I say, my hand on my hip, and my lips pursed tightly. Mason looks down when I finish my mini-tirade, and draws in a deep breath before squaring back up with me. He's always gotten away with his flippant remarks because he's so damned good looking. And that might have worked when I was sixteen. But I don't have time to take shit now, and the twenty-five-year-old me isn't really impressed with his perfect-ass teeth and scruffy chin.

"Avery. Sorry. Some habits die hard," he starts, and I'm already turning to leave. I can't bear any more *cleverness* either.

"No, seriously, please...hear me out," he says from behind me. I give him one more chance, and when I turn around, he's walking over, his hands dripping from dishwater so much he has to pat them on his jeans. I can't help but watch them when he walks. I used to stare at those hands in high school, when he'd sit up there on that stage and strum his guitar for hours at a time. I had goddamned fantasies about those hands, but I learned to hate them pretty quickly.

"Go on," I say, keeping up my tough stance, and finally looking away from his hands to his face.

"I'm sorry about what I said...you know...about Max? I didn't know he was your son. I never would have—" I butt in before he can get the last offensive word out.

"You never would have what, Mason? You never would have made fun of him if you knew he was mine? But if he's someone else's child, someone else's son, then he's fair game to call names?" I can tell I've backed him into a corner, because the shameful look on his face is the same one I've imagined putting there millions of times.

"He's five, Mason. He's just a kid. But there you go, swooping right on in and exploiting whatever makes him different," I'm on a roll now, and Mason is getting a lifetime of my pent-up resentment. "Gahhhh, you are *exactly* the same person you were when you left. No wonder you ended up back here. Some fucking music career, Mason—why don't you go back and tend to your dish soap?"

I spin around so fast, and leave him standing there alone, I don't have time to take in what I know is a crippling look of shock. For once in my life, I said the exact thing I would have pretended to say when I relived the day in my shower. And it feels wonderful.

CHAPTER 3: SPEAKING MAX

Mason

Getting slapped by Avery Abbot was enough to make me change my entire opinion of her being weak. But getting put in my place, and being called a failure? *Ooooph*—that one stuck with me all night and well into this morning.

I left the bar after she ripped me apart, just glad that we were alone when she did so no one could give me shit for it. I gave myself enough shit. Feeling guilty was strange for me. I'm starting to wonder why I thought staying with Ray Abbot was such a good idea in the first place—he's done nothing but tell me what a disappointment I am, and his daughter thinks I'm a complete jerk.

I am a jerk—who am I kidding?

I travel light. When I left home the first time, five years ago, it was with my giant football bag stuffed with every piece of clothing I owned. I still have the same damned bag, and the clothes inside haven't changed much either. I dragged that and my guitar into the house last night, and into the small spare room with the blow-up mattress. I slept here a few times in high school—when I wasn't getting along with one of my mom's boyfriends.

Ray's always been my escape plan. It's funny; when I look back on it now, I think Avery kind of liked it when I stayed at her house. She used to sit in the hall when I sat on the spare bed and played a song. She'd never come all the way into the room—too nervous. But she would sit there, with her skinny legs folded up into her chest, hugging them to her body.

We're the same age, maybe a few months apart, but she's always seemed younger, like a child that I had to be careful around. She was good at school—student council, honor society…shit like that. I scraped by. Football, basketball, and girls—that's how I spent my time. And damn, when Ray started putting me on stage, the *girls* part got really easy.

By the time I was a senior, Avery wasn't interested in listening to me play any more. I didn't really care because she was never my type. Somehow, though, she's the only thing on my goddamned mind this morning.

This house is so quiet. I think Ray's awake; I swear I can hear something happening in the kitchen downstairs. Everything in this house is old, but the kitchen is from the fifties. The cabinets have been painted yellow a few times, so much so they stick when you open them. The stove has coils, and they smell when you turn it on—burning off whatever was cooked last. The fridge vibrates when you open it because the suction is so strong you actually need to brace part of it with your foot when you tug on the door.

It's almost eight in the morning, and I've been up for the last two hours. I pull my guitar onto my lap and strum it once, just to see if anyone notices.

Nothing.

I'll play lightly. Avery and Max's bedroom is on the other end of the hall, so I don't think I'll wake them. I loop the strap over my head, and position myself with my knee bent on the corner of the mattress. It's not ideal, but I haven't touched my guitar in days. I start to get scared I'll forget what it feels like, where to put my fingers, if I don't at least play for a few minutes.

This guitar has always been home. As soon as I touch the strings, I'm gone—there's this melody I've been trying to work out for weeks. I haven't written in months, but this one phrase seems to keep repeating every time I play. There's something wrong with it, but I just can't seem to work it out. It's kind of like my life.

My eyes are closed when I hear the sound of someone's breathing. It's not Ray, because his is heavy—labored. I'm hoping—*damn it, I'm actually hoping*—that I'll see Avery at my door, when I peel one eye open and look right at Max.

He's not surprised to see me. Avery must have explained to him that I'd be in their house. He doesn't even seem to be nervous around a stranger. He's just staring intently at my hands, watching my fingers move up and down the length of the guitar. It's like he's memorizing every movement, the way his eyes twitch a little with every motion.

I don't know what to say to him. Fuck, I'm shit with kids. I've never really been around them, except for my friends when we were growing up, but I don't think that counts. I just keep playing instead of talking, and Max seems to be fine with that.

24

I start to change up the melody a little, and Max clearly notices, his eyes flashing wider for a fraction of a second—like a computer memorizing more data. He hasn't moved a single step from his position in the very center of my doorway. His hands are limp at his sides, and he's swaying a little. I've played for a good five or six minutes under his watch, and at this point I'm not even being quiet anymore.

"Do you want to try?" I say, my hands still making music.

Max doesn't answer, but just continues to stare. I'm not sure what's wrong with him. I know he doesn't like to look people in the eyes—I got that much from last night. And I know he doesn't like to talk much. Hell, I don't either—I *get* him more than he knows.

The sounds downstairs start to pick up, so I stop strumming and pull the guitar strap from around my neck. Max is still looking at it, but not moving from his spot. I lean it against the edge of the mattress, there and available, while I leave the room. Maybe it's just a weird fantasy, but part of me feels like maybe if I'm not looking, Max will pick it up and start to play.

I'm halfway down the stairs when I lean back to peek to see if Max has gone into my room, but he hasn't. I can still see his feet, his body swaying in the doorway. He probably doesn't want to get in trouble with his mom—I can see Avery being strict with him, telling him not to touch stuff that isn't his.

As soon as the smell hits my senses, I'm suddenly fifteen again. Ray's skillet is bubbling with bacon and sausage—and I swear it's swimming in the very same grease it was when he used to make me breakfast years ago.

"Now that's how a man likes to wake up," I say, pulling my arms over my head into a wide stretch and patting Ray on the back.

"Breakfast ain't free, ya know. Take the trash out, would ya? There's old eggs in there," Ray says, nodding toward the trash bin by the door.

I salute him and run up the stairs quickly to grab my shoes so I can haul the trash outside. Max isn't in my doorway anymore, but his own door is now closed. I wonder if he just went back to bed, or if his mom is awake? Who am I kidding—I just want to know if Avery's home, and if I'm going to get to see her this morning.

I skip back down the stairs and grab the bag of trash by the door and walk it around to the side of the house. It's funny how very little has changed. Ray's GMC pickup is still pulled up on part of the lawn, and it looks like Avery's taken over the Buick; I can see a booster seat in the back.

Avery's mom used to pick her up from school in that car, but after she died from breast cancer, Ray just let it sit in the driveway—untouched. We were seniors when Ruthie passed away—I remember Avery changed after that, too. Not that we talked much then, but she always had this light in her, this fire. She was a go-getter, the one who was going to leave this place to change the world, make it better. But after her mom died, she sort of slipped into the background. I guess Adam was there to pick her up.

I kick the tire on the Buick out of fondness—I'm glad to see the tires full again. I take in the rest of the outside of the house on my way back inside, too. The paint is chipping, and the siding is slipping in a few spots. If I stay here long enough, I'm going to have to put in some work on the place. That's the least I could do for Ray.

By the time I'm back in the kitchen, Avery's made it downstairs. She's wearing a gigantic long-sleeved T-shirt, and a pair of black leggings, her hair all twisted on top of her head. She looks like sunshine in the morning. She's pouring a glass of juice, and mouthing something in a whisper to her dad. She hushes as soon as she sees me, and I feel like even more of a fucking loser than I did just an hour ago.

"Hey, Ray. You know, I've been thinking—I didn't realize you had such a full house and all. I can just stay at the apartment. Mom's still up on the rent..." I start, and I notice the fraction of a smile curl on Avery's lips. She's relieved, and it makes me feel like shit—but it's short-lived, because Ray squashes my idea the second I suggest it.

"Shut it. You're staying here. Now eat your breakfast," Ray says, sliding a plate to me. I sit down and prop my elbows up on either side before grabbing a fork and digging in. I sneak a glimpse at Avery again, and the smile that started seconds ago has been replaced with a look of pain.

26

This entire trip back home is torture. My mind is spinning, trying to come up with an idea—a way out. But I'm broke. I mean I have a small amount in savings, but the label barely paid me a dime, and the guys are all sorting out their own shit, just as broke as I am. I'm stuck here. And as long as I'm not kidding myself, I'm probably stuck here for a while—at least until I can book myself some gigs and earn enough to try and make a go at this on my own.

Avery won't even look at me. I try to open my mouth, start a conversation with her, at least a dozen times—but every time I'm left with my mouth agape, nothing to say. I could apologize, but I've done that. She doesn't want to hear it. I could ask her what's wrong with Max, but I'm not going near that conversation. That's what earned me the *asshole of the year* honor in the first place.

"Max coming down?" Ray asks as he slides into his seat with a full plate of sausage and eggs. I'm so grateful he's picked up the conversation.

"He should be. He was writing something upstairs. I couldn't get him to stop," Avery says, looking back to the stairs.

"I can go get him? Tell him breakfast is ready?" my words come out anxious and desperate, leaving my mouth so fast that I didn't have time to think. Avery's just staring at me with disgust, her brow pinched, as she slides out of her seat and heads upstairs. *Fuck, I'm an idiot.*

Ray chuckles to himself at my expense.

"Shut up, old man," I say, shoveling a forkful of eggs in my mouth.

Avery is back seconds later, and Max is trailing behind her. He's clutching a stack of notebook paper in his hand, and he won't let go, even when Avery tries to take it from him so he can eat his breakfast. It's kind of funny to watch the stand-off as she holds onto one end of the papers and Max the other, his opposite hand already working the fork to cut into a toasted pastry Ray put on a plate for him. I can't help the small laugh that escapes me, which only fuels Avery even more as she shoots me a death glare.

I just shrug at her. I can't win with this one, and I'm already in a hole so deep that I might as well just keep digging.

"Sorry, but my money's on Max," I laugh, causing her to huff and sit back in her chair, defeated.

Avery finally stands from the table to fix her own plate, and as soon as she does, Max puts the papers down flat next to him. I shake my head in amusement, kind of proud of him for winning this battle, when he slides the pages toward me across the table. I can feel *everyone* stop *everything* the second he does.

"Me?" I mouth to Ray.

Ray shrugs and raises his brow, no help at all. I turn to Avery next, and her hands are gripping the edge of the table, her eyes fixated on the papers, squinting at them like she's trying to sort through a puzzle.

Max hasn't moved the papers any closer, but they are now in the very center of the table. I don't know what to do, and I'm so afraid of doing the wrong thing, that I'm almost stuck. I look at Ray again, wincing, just hoping that he'll see how lost I am with this kid and help me out. Thankfully, he does, as he wipes his hands on his napkin and leans forward, moving his hand toward the papers.

"Max, mind if I see what you've got here?" he waits, and Max doesn't respond. "I'll give them right back."

Ray slides the stack closer to him, and Max seems to be okay with that. He pulls a pair of glasses from his shirt pocket and puts them on, crinkling the papers and stacking them neatly together in front of him so he can read. He's half smiling as he flips through them, nodding. Finally, he starts to hum, and when I begin to hum along, we both freeze and look at one another.

"That's a pretty song, Max. Did you just write that this morning?" Ray asks, his eyes locked on mine and a faint smirk on his face.

Max remains silent, his gaze fixed on his plate, but he nods *yes.* Avery comes back to the table, and she reaches slowly for the papers, not wanting to start another round with Max over them. Her dad slides them in front of her and tilts them so she can see, and I lean forward to look along with her. I would say it was unbelievable if I weren't looking right at it. Max charted every note that I played for him this morning—every mistake and every improvisation that I strummed less than 30 minutes ago. Everything—*exactly.*

"Max, did you learn this from Grandpa?" Avery asks, her eyes finally coming to meet mine. She's looking at me with surprise, but I'm *looking* at her. I'm looking at her because it's the first time since we've come back together that she's letting me, and I'm embarrassed that I never really saw *her* before. Her eyes—they're fucking unbelievable.

Max finally puts his fork down and looks up from his plate, though not at any of us directly. "I heard Mason play it this morning. I wanted to see what it looked like, so I copied Grandpa's music books," he says, standing abruptly and heading for the stairs.

"Uhm, Max? You forgetting something?" Ray calls after him. Max stops at the bottom step, and looks up and to the side.

"Thank you for breakfast. I am excused," he says before climbing the rest of the way up the stairs and back into his room.

The room is silent for the next few minutes while we all sort of put together our own versions of what just happened. Ray interrupts us first, standing, and sliding out his chair to begin clearing the table. I stand up to help.

I'm sliding scraps of food off a plate into the trash when I turn back and see Avery standing next to her father, whispering again. Her eyes are wider this time, and she's smiling. Add her smile to my ever-growing list of shit I find drop-dead gorgeous about grown-up Avery Abbot. She catches my stare, and flushes—and the fact that she does makes me nuts.

"You heading to therapy this morning?" Ray asks over his shoulder, stopping Avery just before she starts up the stairs. She just nods *yes* and gives her dad a wink.

I wait until she's out of earshot before I ask Ray. "What's Avery in therapy for?" I'm so damned curious, and suddenly all I want to do is spend my day gathering facts and putting together Avery's puzzle.

"It's not for her. It's for Max," he says, running a washcloth under the water and turning to wipe down the table. I grab a dry towel and follow after him.

"Oh. I get it," I swallow. I'm dying to know what's wrong with Max, but I feel like nobody wants to come right out and tell me. Unable to stand it any longer, I finally break.

"What's wrong with him? Max? I mean…what does he go to therapy for?" My words are jumbled, and on instinct I brace myself for Ray to knock my teeth out. Last time I talked about Max I got slapped—hard!

Ray pauses at my question, refolding the washcloth a few times on the table before knocking his fist on the wood lightly. When he looks up at me, his lips are tight—serious. "Max is an amazing kid," Ray starts, his smile full of conflict—pride and sorrow. "Avery...she lives her life for that boy. He's her center, her sun and moon all rolled into one."

"Yeah, I get that. It's plain to see," I say, trying to show my respect. I've only witnessed a little, but Avery has my vote for mother of the year the way she defends Max. My jaw hurts just from memory.

Ray finishes wiping down the table, chewing at his top lip and nodding, like he's working out what to say in his head before he fills me in. He pulls out a chair finally and leans back, folding his arms across his body, not really looking at me, but more looking beyond me, before finally coming back to meet my eyes.

"Mason, Max has autism," he says. I nod like I understand, and I try my best to match the face he's making, but I have no idea what the fuck *autism* really means. I know the word, sure. And I've heard about it. But I don't know if it's something in your brain or if it's something that happens over time. Isn't it, like, mental retardation?

"Oh, okay. I...I didn't know. I'm sorry. How...how do you fix that?" I ask, raising a brow, wishing like hell I understood more than I do.

"You don't, Mason. You don't," Ray says, and I can tell by the crack in his voice that *this*—Avery's life with Max, Max himself—is what real-life problems look like. Ray stands to turn away, and I let him. He walks back to the sink to rinse out his cloth and to regain his strength. I sit down now myself, and try to understand what Ray is saying.

"So...how?" I start to ask, but I realize immediately that I don't even know what to ask. I bury my face in my hands and rub my eyes, just trying not to sound like an insensitive ass more than I already do. "Was Max...born with it? What...I mean...I'm sorry Ray, I don't think I really know what autism is."

Ray's slow to respond. He finishes cleaning up the kitchen, and then paces over to the stairway to make sure Avery and Max are still in their room. He leans against the banister before beginning, just to keep an eye out for them—probably to stop our conversation before Avery overhears.

"Max was one when we found out. Autism...well, it's sort of like a really big linebacker in Max's brain. It works against him, not letting certain things in and not letting certain things out. He didn't talk for the longest time, and even now, his speech is...strange. It's like he knows the words and when to use them, but the meaning isn't quite right. He sort of doesn't understand emotion," Ray sighs, looking down and kicking at the bottom step.

"But what about the music? Those notes he just charted? How can he do that?" I ask, knowing that it would have taken me hours to figure out how to put all of that on paper.

Ray smirks, curling one side of his mouth up a little and tilting his head to me with a squint in his eyes. "Pretty cool, huh?" he starts. "He does stuff like that sometimes. Max memorizes things. You should see him put together a Rubik's Cube."

I don't understand. I don't get how Max can't make eye contact or have a conversation, but can hear me play something for five minutes and then memorize every single nuance. "How?" is all I can ask Ray, and he chuckles at my response, probably because he's thought the same thing himself.

"Damned if I know," he says. "Avery says his autism makes it hard to do some things but easy to do others. She's that kid's champion, you know? She's all he's got. Me? I'm just the old man who lives here with him, who he lets talk to him...sometimes. Ha! But Avery—she's the one that goes to battle. And Lord help anyone or anything that gets in her way."

I let Ray's words soak in. I have so many more questions, but I can hear Max and Avery making their way down the stairs, and I get the feeling by the way Ray was acting that having this conversation with me wasn't something Avery wants to happen.

"Okay, Dad. We're heading out. I'm off tonight—Claire's got my shift. Too much homework," Avery says, leaning over to kiss her dad on the cheek. I don't move from my seat, careful not to startle her or draw her attention. I feel like I shouldn't know the things I know, and I feel like knowing about Max has made me look at things differently. And for some reason, it's all making me want to be around Avery even more.

Avery Abbot. *Shit, I'm in trouble.*

Avery

Some days start on a high note. Today was one of them. I was so sure I was going to get a full-on meltdown from Max over those papers. Normally, I would have bribed him to give them to me with a candy. But with Mason watching the whole thing, I just felt foolish. I don't want him to think I bribe my son to do everything…though, some days, it feels like I do.

When I saw the music, what he wrote—uh! I was blown away; that kid has this power to move me, I swear he does. He's always flipping through my dad's old music books, but I know no one's ever explained it to him—how notes work, what the lines and dots mean. He just figures some things out.

I bet Mason thought *that* was weird, too. I bet he can't wait to get together with his band, sit around and talk about the weird girl he went to high school with and how she has this *weird* kid. Whatever. Fuck Mason Street! His *weird* is my *amazing*!

Max has been asleep for hours. It was a long day for him. We met with two doctors, and it was a double-therapy day. Jenny, our head therapist, has been working with me for weeks, maybe months, to get Max ready for kindergarten. He'll be joining the class a little late—he's been learning one-on-one, and he's actually doing really well with the academic side of things. That's never been Max's problem. In fact, he learns some things really fast. Memorization—that's his gift. It's the social part that scares the hell out of me. I don't make friends easily, how can I expect him to? Add on top of that his lack of patience for anyone slower to *catch on* than he is, and a schoolyard disaster won't be far behind.

This is what we've been working on the most. Patience—keeping his frustration in check. Eye contact and socializing will be skills Max works on every day at school, but he'll never get there if he makes enemies out of his classmates first.

Today has wiped me, completely. Just imagining my afternoons when Max starts school in a few days is daunting. In many ways, it will ease some of the burden. But I carry Max with me, even when we're physically apart. It's the worry—constant, painful, without remedy. But I've survived today, and I've earned tonight.

I take my basket of bath products and set myself up for a little relaxing reward after the long day. It's my first evening off—truly off—in...*I don't know how long*. The bath water hugs me, and the bubbles crackle softly, almost lulling me into a light sleep. I can feel the pull within my chest, my eyes falling shut, but my mind reminds me that my fingers are pruning and that I have a warm bed and—*gasp!*—a book waiting for me down the hall.

My toes are toying with the drain, trying to convince the rest of me to leave the water, when I hear Mason's guitar softly filtering through the wall. It's faint, and...beautiful. His playing was always perfection. I used to listen to him with my dad, just in awe. I have no musical talent—zero. I wish I did; I've learned music can be a great calming therapy for kids like Max. It's not calming when I sing, however. Things just feel out of order, so I stick to reading him stories instead. Good thing I'm majoring in English.

I wait through four or five iterations of the same melody. It's the one Max wrote down this morning—I recognize it. Mason was never happy with his music, always trying to find the *better* way to play something. That's what he's doing now—he's obsessing, and catching him makes me smile.

Stepping from the water, I leave the drain in place, careful not to make any noise as I dress so I don't interrupt his playing. I pull on my soft cotton shorts and one of my dad's old T-shirts for bed and flip off the light before I step quietly down the hall to Mason's door.

His back is to me, so he doesn't notice when I slide down to sit in the doorway. I can still see his fingers from here, as they work their way up and down, pausing right when they should and gently grazing the strings when it's called for. I think that's what made me fall in love with Mason Street in the first place—long before I really *knew* him, before I fell right back out of love with him. Watching him play, the way he *loves* that instrument, the way his brown eyes shut and his lips whisper small phrases, ideas for lyrics. That's the reason women love musicians—it's all right there in Mason's hands, his eyes, his lips. Mason is the perfect package...on the outside. I could almost forget everything watching him now.

He stops playing for a few seconds, and I catch my breath. The small noise causes him to turn around, and I can feel my cheeks heat up with embarrassment. Maybe it's dread. This moment—the one that was so nice before he began talking—is about to be ruined. I just know it.

"Oh, hey Birdie. Sorry, didn't see you there," he says. *Birdie.* Still with the fucking *Birdie.*

"Avery, Mason. My name's Avery," I say with a heavy sigh. I'm about to get up and leave when he swallows and nods, not putting up a fight. Thank God, I don't have it in me tonight.

"Sorry. Old habit, like I said," he turns away again, focusing back on the guitar propped up on his leg. "Sorry, am I too loud? Max is probably sleeping, huh? Shit...I didn't think."

"No, it's fine. He doesn't wake easily. It was nice," I can feel my eyes flair open when I realize I'm complimenting him, and my pulse speeds up. I decide to let it go, smiling and playing friendly.

Everything feels suddenly awkward, so I look down at my fidgeting fingers and bare feet. I'm smirking to myself when Mason notices.

"What are you smiling at?" he asks, tucking a pencil behind his ear and flipping a page on a small notebook on his mattress.

"Oh, it's nothing," I'm embarrassed he caught me, but I can feel him urging me on, so I continue. "It's just...I was just thinking...here I am, twenty-five years old, and I'm in the same exact place, you know? Like, literally! I'm probably even wearing the same thing I did when I was fourteen or fifteen and I used to listen to you play."

I look down again immediately, because I feel foolish, like some groupie. I used to get so jealous over the girls that would come see Mason play at Dusty's, like they didn't have a right to him. They would go on and on about how talented he was, how much they loved his music. But they didn't really. They liked the *idea* of Mason—the sexy guy playing a guitar.

It was always more than that for me, though. For me, it really *was* the music. And then slowly, the older we got, the more it became about the boy *playing* the song. That boy disappeared though, and I don't think he's ever coming back. But sometimes…sometimes when I see Mason play—for himself, not for a crowd, like he is tonight—I start to think that maybe that boy is still in there. And maybe he's growing up.

I look back up when I realize how long we've both been quiet. Mason is hugging his guitar now, his legs turned to face me, and he's looking at me differently. *He's going to ruin this.*

"You never come in," he says, his brow pinching and his lips shut tightly, considering. I don't know how to answer him, so I just shrug.

"I don't like interrupting. You're being…creative," I say, averting my gaze again because I can't take the attention. Mason is so damned confident. It's off-putting.

"Ha, you're funny," he starts with a chuckle. I raise an eyebrow, not really following where he's going with everything. "I'm being *creative*. Haven't you been listening? I can't figure out a simple bar. I'm just wavering all over the place, and nothing feels right. I don't even know why I thought I could do this in the first place. Bir…I mean, Avery—there is *nothing* creative going on for you to interrupt. I'm not sure there ever was."

Now it's his turn to look away. He kicks his guitar case open with his foot and leans forward to place his guitar inside and close it again. He lets his hands linger on the case for a few seconds before he flips the locks in place and then slides the case over to the wall. His eyes are locked on it, and for the first time ever I swear I see a look of disappointment on Mason Street's face. Maybe it's my motherly instincts, or maybe it's how much Max has changed me as a person, but suddenly I'm on my feet and stepping inside Mason's room, sitting down beside him.

"You wanna know something?" I say, my heartbeat racing in my throat. My voice is shaky, and I can feel actual nerves starting to build in my belly.

Mason leans forward and buries his face in his hands, rubbing at his eyes and smoothing back his hair before turning to look at me—and when he does, my heart stops suddenly. I've only been this close to Mason Street once in my life, and his eyes are the same gold they were then. I'm pretty sure my body is covered in sweat now, but I ignore it. I remind myself I'm an adult, and Mason Street doesn't have any power over me.

"Sure, I wanna know something," he says, his lips twitching into that faint cocky smile permanently etched into my mind. *Even his smile is the same.* Why am I sharing this with him? Why do I care? Why can't I just let Mason Street suffer a little?

"Oh, it's stupid. Never mind, I'm sorry…" I start to get up, forcing myself to remember that I put Mason Street and all of my girlhood fantasies about him in a box—a box I locked up with an imaginary key and threw into the depths, never to be dug up again. I've almost convinced myself to leave when his hand grazes mine, urging me to stay.

"Please. I want to hear," he says, his smile gone, and his eyes locked on the place where his fingers are barely touching my skin. My brain is totally confused by his touch. I've hated him for so long. But I loved him before that. And now, with him here, in our house—I'm not so sure I can keep hating him. But I'm also kind of mad at myself that I don't want to. I feel…weak.

"Okay, this is a secret," I sit back down and let out a deep sigh. I can feel his eyes on me, and I give myself a short glance to decide if he deserves this. Maybe I'm imagining it, and maybe I just want to make it be there, but there's a desperation I see in his face that tells me he does. So I give in and share a little piece of me, let him see himself through my eyes. "One time, when you were staying with us for a weekend—I think you were sixteen? You were messing around with some old songs that you could cover. Do you remember?"

Mason takes a deep breath, almost like he's giving up. "I guess. I don't know, Avery. I used to do that shit all the time," he says, almost deflated.

"Okay, yeah. But this day was different. You were putting together a list of cover songs, stuff you wanted to play at Dusty's—just *you*. No band," I wait, and he nods, remembering. "You were toying with 'Wild Horses' by the Stones. You kept slowing it down, even more, changing it up and playing around with the melody. You worked on it for almost an hour. I swear…you sang that song maybe a hundred times."

"Yeah, I remember," he says, the corner of his lips pulling up into a fond smile. "I never did play it. Couldn't get it right."

"That's just it, though," I say, looking away, afraid that if I have to look at him I'll chicken out. Instead I focus on the small string hanging off my shirt, twisting it around my finger.

"You had it right, Mason. You had it *so* right. Every single time you played it—it was right. And when you weren't looking…" *Oh god, oh god, oh god. I'm really going to do this.* "I, uh…I sort of recorded it."

I don't even have to turn my head to feel the full force of his smile. I don't know if I feel giddy or mortified—either way, I just made Mason Street's entire fucking day. I'm biting my lower lip with enough force that I'm sure my teeth are going to puncture it when I finally get the courage to look at him again, and sure enough—he's grinning ear-to-ear.

"Look, I didn't tell you that to make you get all goofy on me," I say, standing and smoothing out my shorts so they hang a little lower on my legs. Suddenly, I feel vulnerable even having my bare feet on display in front of him.

"I know, I know," he says with a light chuckle. He follows me to his doorway, leaning on the frame as I step into the hallway, to safety. He says he knows, but his damn smile is still in full force.

"It's just…" I purse my lips, trying to find a way to say something to him that might make a difference. Something that will penetrate him—not the usual gushing and flattery he's used to from women. "It's just you're so goddamned talented, Mason. My dad always believed in you. And so did I."

When I see his body twitch, I know my words were right.

"Goodnight, Mason," I say, punching him lightly on the arm, like we're old pals. It feels stupid, but it's the only way I can think of leaving. He doesn't say anything back until I'm almost to my door.

"Hey, Avery?" he whispers, and I turn to find him looking at the floor, hands stuffed in his pockets. When he looks up, it's almost as though I'm looking at that sixteen-year-old again, the one who used to matter.

"Yeah, Mason?" I say, my stomach an absolute mess with nerves.

"Thanks. Just…thanks," he says, shrugging his shoulders up and smiling with tight lips.

"Sure, Mason. Anytime," I say. I close the door and let my forehead fall flat on it, and I stay there, frozen, for a good two minutes. I think I may have just made an enormous error in judgment. I promised myself I would never fall for Mason's charm again. But something seems so different. Maybe…maybe it's me.

Max is bundled in his weighted blanket, fast asleep. He's always been good at falling asleep, and I feel lucky. Many kids with autism struggle, and I don't know how their parents survive. I need these few hours in the evening—alone. I need the *me* time to let my brain stop, though I often spend those hours finishing up homework or researching something for Max. But that's my choice—and at least I can put my headphones on and just be.

Max and I sleep next to one another in a set of twin beds. The separate mattresses make it a little easier—this way he won't be disturbed when I crawl in and out of bed. I grab my headphones and my laptop and nestle into my pile of blankets. I was planning on reading, but that course changed the second I heard Mason playing the guitar.

It only takes me a few minutes to find the file—I converted most of my old recordings to digital files last year. I never listened to the ones of Mason, though. I was too afraid of how it would make me feel, and I'm pretty emotionally spent as it is most days.

I double click the folder open and pause, not sure if I'm ready for this. It's like my hand has other plans though, because in seconds, I see the "Wild Horses" file open up on my play screen and Mason's guitar is filtering in my ears. It's more beautiful than I remembered—his voice sounds so young, but his playing was perfection. And even though he was just a teenager, there was so much emotion to every word that left his lips.

His band website is still up, even though the label dropped them. The links are to personal email addresses, so I decide to take a chance and open one to him. I attach the file and then stare at it for about 20 minutes…starting, stopping, and deleting until I find the right thing to say.

You know me, always have to prove I'm right. Thought you might like to hear what I hear.
-A

38

Send. It's done. The adrenaline pouring through my veins now is thick, and I swear I could run a marathon. I just opened a door that I'm pretty sure can't be shut. I just hope it's a safe door, and doesn't come with regret. I push my laptop to the side and shut the screen before snuggling deeper into my covers. I'm going to be getting up early in the morning and doing my best to leave the house before anyone else—*Mason*—is awake.

CHAPTER 5: CALLUSES

Mason

Two hours, if I'm lucky. That's how long I slept last night, AKA this morning. I sat there on the other side of my door thinking about Avery Abbot until the sun was almost up. I thought about Avery Abbot because she thought about me. And I liked that she thought about me.

I didn't get her email until this morning. That's probably good, because now my head is all kinds of fucked up trying to figure out what to think about it. She has wanted to do nothing but stick a staple through my neck since I ran into her at Dusty's my first day back in town. But last night...I don't know. Maybe I'm reading into it, but I think somewhere, deep down, Avery Abbot cares about me. And I think maybe I care about Avery Abbot.

At first I was just fantasizing about having a little fun with her, maybe getting her drunk and fooling around. But now I kind of just want to kiss her—like a real kiss, not the kind I usually give out just to make some chick think I'm into her so she'll sleep with me.

I've listened to the clip she sent me a dozen times. The first six, I rolled my eyes, not even letting it play all the way through. But something kept calling me back. My young hands didn't even know what they were doing back then, picking around the strings trying to make something sound good—sound different, unique. But there was something there, underneath my inexperience.

Somewhere along the way, I lost my passion, and Avery was right. I hate that she's right. Or maybe I love it. Fuck, I don't know. But it had me watching out my window this morning, just waiting for her to get in her car with Max and leave the house so I could pull out my guitar without her thinking she had anything to do with it.

She had *everything* to do with it. But she doesn't need to know that.

By the time noon rolled around, I had played through everything I'd ever written, and covered about twenty of my favorites just trying to find myself again somewhere in this mess

I've made. And now I just need to convince Ray to let me go on tonight. I need to see how it feels—in front of an audience. See if my heart kicks again...like it used to.

I'm a disheveled mess, my hair wet from the thirty-second shower and my shirt half tucked in when I walk into Dusty's. I always liked the lunch crowd. It was nothing but locals and regulars, people who actually came here to get drunk early and eat the food. I look like I fit right in.

"Thanks for hanging on to my stuff, Ray," I hear a familiar, grating voice say from the other side of the swinging door. If I could wish myself to have one super power right now, it would be invisibility. But since that's not an option, I do the next best thing and duck behind the counter while Ray and my mother walk around the other side.

"Sure thing, Barb. You know you've always got a place here," Ray says, holding the door open while my mother follows him through. I can see the top of her copper hair as I crouch and slide my way around the opposite direction of the counter. "So, you good startin' back up tonight then?"

"Honey, I'm always ready," she says, her overt flirtation like a wet fish slapped in my face. My mother always threw herself at men—doesn't matter that she's known Ray for years. He has a penis, no wife, and a decent job. That made him fair game. At least until some millionaire shows up.

"You can't hide here forever, ya know," I hear behind me as a foot kicks my ass lightly, just enough to push me off balance and onto my hands and knees. I turn around to see a tiny brunette with short bobbed hair and her hand on one hip, her tray balanced against the other. "That's your mama, Mason. She's going to know you're back in town eventually."

"Yeah, I know..." I say, studying her face and looking for recognition.

"You don't remember me, do you?" she says, popping a giant bubble with her gum. I know I know her, but damned if I could remember her name right now. She's one of Avery's friends—I saw her the other night, and I'm pretty sure not recognizing her now is not going to do me any favors when it comes to Avery. *Shit, I hope I never slept with her!*

41

"I remember you…it's just…been a while," I say, standing up and dusting off my jeans, racking my brain…*nothing.*

"Uh huh. Sure you do," she says, walking past me with a smirk on her face.

"Carrie," I take a stab in the dark. The look she shoots back at me tells me I'm not even close.

"*Claire*, Mason! Good lord, at least you got the first letter right. I've known you since sixth grade?" she says, loading up her tray with drinks, straws, and napkins. I decide to help her, hoping my gesture might just earn me some points.

"Yeah, that's right. Sorry. I knew you…I just couldn't get the name to come up. Sorry," I repeat, sheepishly. It's better to just own up to this.

She gives me a short half-smile and pauses for a second or two before shrugging and lifting her tray. I follow behind with a stack of menus. "So, Mason. What are you doing back in town?" she says over her shoulder, dropping off a few drink orders before seating a group of construction workers at a booth.

"You know, just figuring some things out. Not sure if I want to tour any more or maybe work on some solo stuff," I say, not really ready to lay my failures out for her.

"Uh huh," she says, her smile just dripping with condescension.

"I'm not with the label any more, so it's a good time for me to take a break," I keep going. Fuck! Why do I feel the need to justify myself to this chick?

She just keeps going about her business, dropping off napkins for one table and bussing another, and I keep following her, like some new kid who doesn't fit in. That's me—somehow, I'm the new kid! I used to kick my feet up at the corner booth, and skip school until it was time to go on—college chicks lining up just to sit on my lap. And now here I am, begging for approval from a waitress, who clearly couldn't give a shit who I am.

I finally drop the menus I've been carrying around into the bin at the hostess desk and sit at one of the nearby stools, pulling out my phone so I can look busy and find a way out of this sudden feeling of inadequacy. Then I hear the stool drag closer, and seconds later Claire is sitting right next to me, leaning on one elbow—staring. I squint at her and grimace, probably a little rudely, but I'm done trying to impress her. So what if she's Avery's friend.

"Avery told me you blew it," she says, completely deflating me and annoying the fuck out of me at the same time.

"Yeah, well, what does Avery know," I say, flipping through my ESPN app just trying to find something *else* to occupy my attention. Funny how many times I've asked myself what Avery knows over the last 48 hours. Turns out she might just know me better than anyone.

"My god, Mason. Are you really that clueless?" Claire asks.

"Apparently," I sigh, continuing to flip through some story on human growth hormone lawsuits and baseball. Claire's not taking the hint though, so I close the app and push my phone back in my pocket to give her my reluctant attention.

"You, like…really have no idea, do you?" she says, with this faint, cocky smirk. I'm starting to hate this chick.

"Nope," I say, folding my arms up a little defensively now.

Claire's smile gets a little bigger, and now she's scooting closer. She starts looking around, making that face chicks make when they're gossiping. For some reason, it's starting to make me nervous as hell, so I start looking around, too. Finally satisfied that we're alone, she props her chin up on her hand, cupping it a little for even more privacy. I'm starting to think she's about to tell me that she's a transvestite, she's acting so strange—when she drops an even bigger bomb.

"Avery was totally in love with you," she says, a half-whisper. She says a few other things after, about how Avery used to write my name on her notebook and shit, but all I keep hearing—over and over—is that Avery Abbot loved me. Avery Abbot…*loved me?* Where the fuck was I?

"Wait…wait. What? Avery can't stand my ass! And in high school, she barely talked to me. Even when I stayed at her house, she'd always run away, hide in her room. That's why I called her Birdie, because she was so chirpy and mousy all the time," I say. I'm pretty sure Claire is full of shit on this one.

"True. And she never liked it when you called her that. In fact, the first time you did, she came over to my house after school and cried her fucking eyes out," Claire says, instantly sticking a knife through my gut.

"Damn, I never knew that. I thought she always liked it when we called her that. She never said anything..." I say, looking down, a little embarrassed that I now have *ASSHOLE* stamped across my forehead.

Claire laughs lightly and nudges me to get my attention. "Don't beat yourself up over that. She had pretty low self-esteem back then. Not the same girl that will tell you where to stick it today," she says, with a wink.

She's right, too—my first few days with Avery since I've been back in town have been nothing but her telling me *exactly* what she thinks of me, no matter how harsh, which is precisely why I can't believe Avery ever *loved* me.

"Alright, I get it. I teased her. And you say she loved me, which...whatever, I'm not buying that. But why the hell is she so anti-Mason now?" I ask. I want to get to the heart of Avery's beef with me—if for nothing else to make the next couple weeks a little more bearable.

"You are unbelievable!" Claire says, letting out a piercing laugh just to punctuate how stupid she thinks I am. I just stare at her blankly—I've got nothin'. "Mason, don't you remember Nikki Thomas' party our sophomore year?"

Yeah, I remember that party. That's the night I slept with Nikki Thomas, pretty much the hottest piece of ass in our high school. And that was the night I realized exactly all of the doors being a musician could open. It was the night I decided that the second I had enough money I was leaving Cave Creek and heading straight to LA. But something tells me those aren't the things Claire—and more importantly, Avery—remembers about that night. So I just nod slowly and wait, hoping she'll fill me in.

"Everyone was playing that drinking game, and you and Avery got dared to be locked in the closet for 30 minutes. You remember that?" she asks, and I have a vague imprint somewhere in the back of my mind. I'm pretty sure I wasn't sober that night—always one of my regrets about sleeping with Nikki Thomas; I only remember bits and pieces about sex with her.

"Sort of," I say, scratching at the back of my neck. This isn't going to be good—I can tell.

Claire just sighs and shakes her head. "Jesus, Mason. You sat in that closet with her for 30 minutes. That was like...her dream come true. And you just sat in there, with your feet crossed out in front of you, like you were taking a nap. You didn't even talk to her! You practically lived at her house, and you just ignored her so you could endure some goddamned bet you lost!"

Fuck!

"When they opened up the door, you walked out and told everyone she kissed like a bird, too. You said she just pecked at you, and you had to push her off of you. Then you said she begged you to go all the way," Claire is even ashamed saying this shit out loud. The worst part is I can't deny any of it. I don't really remember it—actually, I kind of do, just not clearly. But I can picture it—it's exactly something I would do. And I haven't changed a goddamned bit.

The bar is starting to fill up, so Claire kicks back from the bar and scoots in her stool, patting her hands on the counter a few times before speaking. "I gotta get back to work. But whatever you're trying to *figure out* while you're here, Mason? Make sure you don't have to tear Avery down just to get there, okay?"

I nod at her, my breath pretty much knocked out of my lungs. I thought Ray held up a pretty brutal mirror when he showed me those articles the other day. But Claire just trumped that. Avery might have loved me—once. But I pissed all over that, just like I do everything that's good in my life.

"Hey, Claire?" I catch her before she heads into the kitchen.

"Yeah?" she asks, pausing halfway through the door.

"You think I can fix any of that? I mean—I know I'm *way* beyond saying sorry now. But, I guess…you think maybe I can get her to *not* hate me?" The words sound pathetic as they leave my lips, but I'm all right with that. Turns out, I *am* kinda pathetic. And the fact that Avery said the things she said last night makes me an even bigger asshole—because I don't deserve them, but she's a fucking saint for saying them anyway.

"You can always fix it, Mason," she says, her lips curled into a half smile. "That girl—she'll always see the best in you. Even when she doesn't want to."

The door swings shut behind her, and despite sitting in the middle of a crowded restaurant, I feel completely alone. I have to find Ray. And I have to get him to let me go on tonight. Because I have to go back to the beginning and see if I can get shit right this time around. And I'm pretty sure it all starts with Avery Abbot.

CHAPTER 6: THE SOUND OF THAT

Avery

Somehow, I made it out of the house before anyone saw me this morning. And somehow—*somehow!*—I got Max to cooperate. He didn't like the change in routine. And he dug his heels in hard with me this morning. But a few extra candies, along with the promise of more time with the planet books tonight, and I managed to stave off any meltdowns.

Once I sent that email to Mason, I didn't sleep much. I even got up to Google how to retrieve it a few times, but all of the answers seemed fairly technical, so I gave up. I wanted to send it to him. I'm just afraid it will come back to bite me. Being nice to Mason Street always does.

For some reason, though, Max seems to be taken with him. Max doesn't really notice new people. Besides Dad, Claire, his few therapists, and me, everyone else is just a cameo player in the play of Max's life. He remembers names, though. He always remembers names. But people who haven't worked with him, who haven't earned that spot in his circle, are just associated with the job they do. Cole is the guy who brings Max his chocolate milk at the bar. And Bill, the older man who checks out our groceries, is the guy who sells Max his apples. I've tried to explain to Max that those people have full lives too—bigger than just that one thing they do for Max. But he doesn't really listen or care to know them more than he has to.

That's not the case with Mason, though. This morning, on our way to his one-on-one kindergarten session, Max asked me about Mason's guitar. He asked me what kind it was, and how hard it was to learn how to play. I didn't know the answers, so I told him he should ask Mason, and he said he would. Our entire exchange was surreal—no bribes exchanged, no rewards needed to be dangled to get Max to want to talk to Mason. He has a question, and Mason has the answer—and Max made the connection on his own.

Maybe that's why my heart sank a little when I pulled into Dusty's and saw Barb's car parked out front. I knew she'd be back—she always comes back. But I know as soon as she realizes Mason is staying with us, she'll insist that he stays with her, now that she's back in her apartment on her own.

I scan the lot for Mason's Dodge Challenger, but it isn't here. I'm instantly relieved. I know I'm going to have to be a big girl and face him sometime, but the longer I can put that off, the better.

I hurry inside with Max so I can get to my locker and change before anyone comes in. Cole gets Max set up with his chocolate milk in the corner booth, and I take a few minutes to jot down a short reminder list for the homework I need to get done this weekend. Saturdays are hard, only because we've been building in so many therapy sessions with Max, so I've been pushing all of my homework to Sundays. A lot of people burn the candle from both ends, but sometimes I feel like I just threw my candle in a skillet to melt the entire damn thing at once.

"So, you hear Barb's back?" Claire asks from behind me.

"Yeah, I figured. Saw her car in the lot," I say before putting my books away and flipping the clip on my locker to shut it tightly.

"She's a hoot! That woman gets more action than I do, and she's almost fifty!" Claire says, pulling her Dusty's shirt from over her head, and swapping it out for a blue tank top from her locker. "She's going to be on with you all night. It'll be nice to have the help. There's gonna be a bit of a crowd."

There's always a crowd on Saturdays, but nothing I can't usually handle, so I wonder what Claire means. Someone big must have been added last minute. When I finally turn to square up with her, she's sitting sideways on the small bench next to me, smirking. And I know that smirk—she's up to something.

"What is that face for?" I ask, pursing my lips and not sure I'm ready for her answer.

"Mason's coming in," she says.

"Yeah, I figured. He's been helping Dad out, because he's staying with us," I say, hoping she just nods and tells me I'm right, and that it turns out it's really no big deal at all.

"No, I don't think you're following me. Mason's coming in...to play!" my friend instantly squeals and grips my forearm like a love-struck teenager.

48

Mason is playing. Live. Tonight. After I gave him that recording. After I told him I believed in him. After I bared a little of my past to him. And there is nowhere for me to hide; I'm going to be here, and I'm going to have to hear it. My heart is beating a million times per minute, and I have to wipe my palms on the sides of my shorts because they're sweating so much.

"If it's okay with you, I thought maybe Max and I could stick around, just for the early part?" Claire asks, snapping me from my trance.

"Huh? Oh, yeah…I guess that's fine. As long as Max is okay with it. He's had a long day, but he has a lot of his things with him, and I brought my iPad," I notice mid-sentence that the smirk is still full-force on Claire's face. She's got more—I don't know if I can handle more. "Okay…what else has you all gushy?"

"Oh, nothing. Just…" she's torturing me with this, and the feeling in my stomach gives me the sense that I'm going to want to bury my head in the ground after tonight is done. "I might have had a little conversation with Mr. Street today."

"What *kind* of conversation?" I ask, my tone clipped. I'm getting really nervous now. And frankly, I'm starting to get a little pissed off at my friend:

"Oh, the kind where he talks a little bit about how he doesn't know why you hate him so much and then your friend maybe tells him he was a douchebag in high school. That kind of conversation," she says, her lips now in a tight, proud smile to match her folded *I-told-you-so* arms.

Shit! I know Claire meant well, but I also know she doesn't really get how much the way Mason used to treat me around his friends bothers me. "Claire?" I sigh.

"Relax. I didn't go into too many details. I just reminded him about Nikki Thomas' party…" she starts.

Fuck!

"And I told him how you hated it when he called you *Birdie*. Oh, girl…you should have seen his face when I told him how the first time he did it, it made you cry," she's still going, and my heart has officially run out of rhythm now. I'm no longer dying, because I've just ceased to breathe. Claire has officially embarrassed me to death.

"Oh, and…well…this part you're going to be a little mad about…" she's biting her lip. *This part*—whatever she's about to tell me—is what has her thinking I'm going to be a *little mad*?

"Oh god, Claire…what did you do?" I ask, letting my face fall forward into my hands. I can actually feel the heat radiating off of my cheeks.

"I sort of told him that you used to be in love with him," Claire says, standing up immediately and backing away. Smart, because she knows I want to smack her. She raises her hands up quickly, signaling there's more. "But, before you get all angry, I only told him because I think he's got a little thing for you."

I let my face fall right back into my hands. There's no way Mason has a thing for me, not even the tiniest of little things. And after the stuff I said to him last night, and the secrets my best friend just unlocked for him today, I'm pretty sure he thinks I'm some crazy, obsessed girl from his past.

"Claire?" I say, shaking my head at her.

"Avery, don't overreact. I promise I didn't give him anything that would embarrass you. I swear!" she's waving her hands emphatically, like she's tossing magic in the air that will somehow make me okay with all of this.

"I want to go home and throw up, Claire! But I can't, because I need Saturday night tips. And now I have to walk the floor, while Mason is perched up on that stage listening to half-dressed bimbos scream at him, getting in line just to see if he'd be willing to use them for the night. And he'll have this perfect goddamn view of me—the stupid girl from high school, who's *in love* with him!"

"I told you, I told him you *used* to be in love with him!" Claire tries to correct.

"Used to be…still am—it's all the same to him, Claire! He's not going to believe I'm over him? Especially after…gah! Whatever. He's just going to taunt me with it—make it all into some game until he has someone else to amuse him. Hell, I hope he moves back in with his mom now," I turn to lean back on the bench, and let my head fall flat against the wall so I can stare at the ceiling. One day. One day! That's all it took for my friend to rip open every wound from my adolescence and give all my secrets to my enemy.

"He's not going to do that, Ave. Listen to me—that guy...he felt bad. I mean, horrible! He even asked me if I ever thought you'd forgive him," she's sitting next to me now, shaking my arm and trying to get me to give in. I think she's probably sugarcoating it all now for my benefit. But maybe, just maybe, somewhere in Mason's selfish-ass brain, there's a little hint of guilt. I stand up and let out a big sigh before plastering a pretend smile on my face.

"Okay, Claire. If you say so. But you're definitely staying tonight. For as long as Max will let you," I drop my smile when I look at her, making sure she understands my tone while I tie my apron around my waist, and flip my head over to toss my hair up in a bun. I'm not messing around tonight, and I'm not going to do anything that will make Mason think I'm concerned in the least about what he thinks about me.

I open the swinging door and walk through, promising myself that I won't look up at the stage once tonight. And I had every intention of keeping that promise—right up until my eyes landed on Max...sitting next to Mason...and talking, while playing a game on the iPad. Max is talking. And Mason is listening. And I'm frozen at the door, just watching my son have a semi-normal interaction with a man he just met.

Not wanting to interrupt, I slip through the door quickly and walk over to where Cole is lining up the glasses for the night.

"Hey, how long's that been going on?" I ask, motioning to the corner.

"A good ten minutes, I guess. He seems to really like Mason. Kid's said maybe a dozen words to me ever, and two of those are *chocolate* and *milk*," Cole laughs.

I lean forward, keeping my head low so Mason doesn't notice I'm watching. Max is pointing to things on the iPad, and Mason is just watching and nodding. Max is talking. He's talking *a lot*. He never makes eye contact. There's still a barrier. But he's engaging Mason—without a single reward waiting for him in the wings, other than the pleasure of talking to someone else.

Unable to take it any longer, I pick up a stack of menus and walk to the corner booth, pretending that I need to bus and prep a nearby table. I catch Mason's eyes on me for a brief second as I approach, but he quickly looks back at the iPad. I can tell he's uncomfortable that I'm getting closer though; I see him noticeably shift in his seat. His eyes dart to me again, and on instinct, I flash a friendly smile, just like I would any other patron in the bar. Mason's eyes widen a little at my reaction, and I can see the start of a smile curl at his lips, but he quickly brings a hand up to his chin, propping his weight on the table while he settles his concentration back to Max.

"This is how you add the instruments," Max says, his voice very serious while he slides his fingers rapidly around the iPad screen. "You have to know the numbers. The instrument numbers need to match the ones on your lines."

I have no idea what Max is showing Mason, but he's rapt with it. Once I set the table, I move closer to the booth, stopping right next to the edge where Mason's knee is sticking out. I see him physically tighten up to get smaller when I'm there, pulling his leg in and tucking it under his seat. He actually seems nervous, his leg bouncing up and down under the tabletop while his hands fidget in front of him.

"So, what's so exciting over here?" I ask. Mason's leg bumps hard into the underside of the table when I speak, and the saltshaker tips on its side, spilling granules in front of both of them. I hold my breath at first, knowing how little Max likes messes. My son moves the iPad from his view, but only for a moment before moving it back and continuing with his lesson on whatever app he's showing Mason. I slowly reach forward with a napkin to wipe the mess onto my tray, amazed.

"It's called Garage Band," Max says, always only giving me just enough to satisfy the question.

"Are you teaching Mason how to use it?" I ask, leaning a little closer so I can see the screen. Mason leans forward as I do, like he's trying to maintain some force field between us. He's so uncomfortable, and I could kill Claire for this bucket of awkward she threw in both our laps.

"I am. He is a fast learner," Max's choice of words makes me giggle. He's heard us say the same words to him during his therapy sessions. Funny that he's paying a twenty-five-year-old the same compliment.

"Good. Well, it's nice of you to teach him," I say, then force myself to leave. As much as I want to stay and watch, I also want to pretend that it's normal that Max is showing something to Mason—and I don't want to do anything to screw it up.

I head back through the kitchen, to the locker area, just to catch my breath. Saturdays usually fly by because this place gets so busy, but I have a feeling that tonight is going to seem a lot like *forever*. I have been dreading seeing Mason again after sending him that recording, but I didn't think I would feel so lost for words around him. To say I'm uncomfortable in his presence would be an understatement, and I'd like to blame Claire for it all, but honestly, I think the anxiety I'm feeling around him is just as much my fault as it is hers.

It was so easy when he was this memory from my past—a story I pulled out of the air when I was out with the girls, reminiscing about the douchebags from our past. He's always been part of my pity party—the girl who was rejected publicly by her high school crush, and then knocked up and abandoned by her husband. My sad story always won the bet, especially when I got into the details. Imagine how sad it would be if I let myself fall for Mason again.

Funny how I can't stop imagining.

I shut my eyes and lie back on the bench for a few minutes, taking deep breaths to ease the anxiety I can feel gripping at my lungs. Once my head feels clear, I sit up and adjust the knot of hair atop my head. I can't hide in here all night, and at least I've broken the seal of silence between Mason and me—and I feel like I won the first round. He's weak. And I'm stronger.

Yes. I'm stronger.

Mason

I hear words. That's all I hear—words, words, words. My mother has been talking for a good fifteen minutes, but I haven't heard a single thing she's said other than, "…how could my own son come home, and not even call to let me know!"

She caught me by surprise. I was all mixed up, sitting next to Max, having him want to talk to me—like I was his *friend.* And then Avery came over, and for some reason my throat closed up, and I couldn't think of a single thing to say to her. Hell, I couldn't even look at her! And she seemed perfectly content with me not looking her direction.

And the second Avery left, my mother was standing in the spot she'd just abandoned. Max didn't even flinch when my mother started berating me with a string of choice words. In fact, Max just kept right on teaching—sliding his fingers around and building a song on the digital timeline. I envy that kid and his ability to focus—or maybe it's his ability to tune out.

That's exactly what I'm doing to my mom right now, only instead of an iPad, I'm obsessed with figuring out Avery. She didn't seem angry when she saw me tonight, and she even left me alone with Max—something that two days ago she would have died before she let happen.

Talking to Claire earlier dug up a lot of old memories, and a lot of shit that I'm not proud of. Looking back, yeah...I knew Avery liked me. I never thought it was anything serious, but that's only because it wasn't serious to me. It was this funny joke that I had, and I'd roll my eyes to my friends about how I liked going over to Ray's, but that his daughter always followed me around like a puppy. I didn't think I was ever mean about it. Honestly, I was always actually kind of jealous how easy school and shit was for her. But I also never wanted anyone to get the wrong idea about the amount of time I spent at Ray's house, never wanted anyone thinking Avery was my girlfriend.

Then one day, out of nowhere, she stopped hanging around, and I always wondered what I did wrong. It didn't keep me up at night or anything like that, but sometimes, when I'd see her with her friends at school, I'd think about it—she'd always look away, completely uninterested in me. Guess that great mystery is solved now.

"Honey, are you listening to me?" my mom's teary words snap me back to the present. She's crying, but it's that fake cry she does when she wants to get attention. I hate it. It used to work on me when I was a kid, but by the time I was in junior high, I could see right through it.

"Yeah, ma. I'm listening," I say, leaning forward and rubbing my face. "Look, I didn't know how long I would be here. It happened suddenly, and you were talking about letting go of the lease, remember? I didn't want it to be a big deal."

54

"But you're my baby, Mason. You're always a big deal." If I had a dime for every time my mom said that to me. I know she loves me, and I know that if I *really* needed something from her, she'd do her damnedest to come through. But I also know she's not the first, or even the second, person I'd turn to.

"I know, Ma. I know. And I love you. But I just wanted to figure things out. Besides, it's a music business thing, and you know I've always gone to Ray for help with that," I say, hoping that'll be enough to let my mom off the hook.

"He's so good to you. I owe that man, Mason. I know I do," she's switching to guilt mode, and I've got to steer her back before she starts with the tears again.

"No, you don't, Mom. He's a family friend. He's *my* friend. That's why I came to him, and that's all," I say, and she seems to be willing to let this one go...for now.

"Okay, but I'll get the sofa bed ready for you—you can come stay with me when you're done with Ray," she's insistent on this, and I let it be, just standing and giving her a hug, like a good son.

I'm not leaving Ray's. I'm not leaving Ray's because staying with my mother would only make me resent her, this town, and my failure even more. Barb Street is lonely—she's always lonely when she leaves a relationship. But she'll find a new one; she always does. I'll visit and call now that she knows I'm in town. But I'm not moving my crap into her apartment and sleeping on the sofa bed. And I'm not leaving Ray's house.

And damn. I'm thinking about Avery again.

I'm actually nervous. I haven't been nervous since the first time Ray threw me up on his stage. But I'm nervous now. I keep telling myself it's because I'm doing something different, going up on that stage without a band—just my guitar. And I'm playing some cool covers—the kind of shit I always wanted to try. I'm just nervous because I haven't practiced them much, because I'm going in a little cold.

The place is packed. Word got out fast. I know Claire's responsible for about half of the people in here. She overheard me talking to Ray about performing. I didn't know she was such a fan of my music—shocked the hell out of me, actually, considering just a few hours earlier she was busy trying to suffocate me with guilt. Her mood toward me turned around really fast when she found out I was playing tonight.

"You ready, kid?" Ray says, patting my back once and squeezing my shoulder. I let out a big breath and smile. "All right then, I'll go let everybody know."

Nothing was ever very formal at Dusty's. That's what people loved about it. Even the stage was nothing to look at—a two-foot platform with a black curtain behind it. Once, a while back, Ray talked about fancying it up, but all of the bands begged him not to—it wouldn't be the same. Playing at Dusty's was like playing in your best friend's garage. It's where you try things out and see how they sit—without all the pressure. Tampering with the environment would just ruin it all.

"Hey there everyone. I'm sure you all heard, but our boy's in town. He's trying out some new stuff, and of course, he came home to do it," Ray says, and I thank him internally for finding a way to spin everything for me. I make a mental note to tell him later. "I'm not gonna make y'all wait for him. I told him he could play as long as he wants tonight, so let's make him feel real welcomed, all right? Mason...come on up."

The whistles still get to me, and I can't help the embarrassed smile on my face. I climb up and take the stool at the front of the stage while tonight's crowd screams for me. It's just the stool and a mic—that's how I wanted it tonight. And even though it's a crowd for Dusty's—probably 150 people—it's small compared to some of the places I've been playing.

"Hey there," I say, my voice echoing a little, and more whistles coming back up in response. I laugh lightly, my cheeks hurting from the embarrassed smile filling my face. The people here have always been so good to me. It used to be the adoration that got me off—the girls thought I was sexy, the guys thought I was man enough to not want to kick my ass in the parking lot after the show. But coming back—playing here tonight—has my eyes wide open. These people don't love me because I'm some hotshot musician. They don't care that I have some stupid ounce of talent that sets me apart from them. They love me because I'm theirs— because this is home, and I'm family. The feeling that sinks into my chest is strange, but it's good.

56

"First off. Thanks, Ray, for letting me hang out up here tonight," I say, nodding my head to the edge of the stage where Ray's still standing. Once Ray gets a few whistles, though, he stands up and heads back behind the bar where he feels more at home.

"So, I've got a few favorites I'd like to play for you guys tonight. Nothing new, just some songs that have always been kind of a big deal to me, if that's okay?" I ask, hearing a few more squeals from some of the girls in the audience.

Normally, I'd scan the crowd, zeroing in on exactly where those screams are coming from to decide which girl—or two—I'd be talking into coming back to the hotel room with me. But my gaze doesn't stray an inch tonight. I saw Avery the second I took the stage, and I can't seem to look away. She's floating from table to table, her hair piled on top of her head with a few lone strands kissing her neck. She's keeping her back to me. And something tells me it's on purpose. I was planning on starting out simple, to get my chops warm. But I'm man enough to admit that Avery's part of the reason I'm doing this in the first place, and if she's not willing to look at me, I'm willing to work for it.

"This first one is a song I never thought I got *quite right.* But a good friend…well…she told me otherwise. She's pretty stubborn," I laugh lightly as I set the song up, my insides just begging Avery to turn around. I can see her back at the bar, and she's alone. I know she's just listening, waiting to see if I'm going to do what she thinks I'm going to do. "This one's 'Wild Horses'. "

When her tray falls, my heart speeds up. I know I'm in trouble. But I've been in trouble before. I *love* trouble. So I start to play, and when I sing, I keep my eyes on her the entire time, just waiting for the moment she turns around. She never does. But she doesn't move from her spot, either, and I think maybe she's in trouble, too.

Avery

I don't know what I was expecting. I'm not surprised Mason is playing this song. I practically challenged him. But I didn't think it would make my entire body feel numb hearing it. I haven't looked at him all night, not since I saw him talking to Max. I didn't see his

57

face when he took the stage, and I can't say for sure that he was looking at me when he introduced his first song. But he was definitely *talking* to me. I can feel it deep down, and it hurts a little.

Mason Street is going to crush me—he's going to rip open my heart...again. He's going to completely destroy me, unless I can stand here and convince myself that my heart isn't pounding out of my goddamned chest just listening to his perfect voice.

Every flick of his fingers on that stupid guitar sends a new wave down my body. Every crack in his voice—his voice that is suddenly so much older, so much...sexier—gives me shivers. I'm so thankful that no one has come near me, because if they did they'd see the flipping goosebumps all over my arms. But no one has ventured anywhere near my spot at the bar. They haven't moved because they're frozen stiff. Mason has everyone captivated; he's just that amazingly good.

I wonder if he's looking at me. I want to turn around to check so badly, but I'm terrified I'll meet his eyes. That would be it—I don't have many cards left to play, and my defense is weakening. If I look at Mason now, I'll be lost. And I don't have time to be lost—I have too many things on the other side of this fantasy that depend on me.

When the crowd stands and starts to whistle and yell at the end, I take my opportunity and race to the kitchen, heading right for the safety of my locker. By the time I get there, I have my shirt untucked, and I'm pulling it in and out from my body just to get the air flowing around me. I'm so hot I think I might pass out, and I lay back on the bench with my knees pulled in.

"So, that was kind of intense," I hear Claire say over me. I could lie, tell her I'm not feeling well, but Claire's always seen though my bullshit. I can't pull any punches with her. Besides—who else would I talk to?

"Yeah...that was," I say, flopping my head to the side and meeting her eyes. She's already smirking, and I just keep my stare on her, hoping she gets that I'm not ready to be teased. I'm overwhelmed right now.

"I'm not going to brag that I was right...*but I was right, huh?"* she starts.

58

"Right about what? That Mason Street is hotter than ever? Uh…yeah, check. That he's gotten sexier? Uh, yes…he has. That my stupid girl-crush is going to come raging back like a case of the shingles?" I fold my arms over my head while my ears pick up hints of Mason's next song. He's singing "In Your Eyes" now—*fucking Peter Gabriel!*

"Well, yes. I was right about all of that," Claire says, lifting my feet and putting them on her lap so she can sit down. "But that's not what I meant."

I squint at her, and my chest feels heavy; I'm having a hard time filling my lungs with air.

"I meant about him having a little thing for you," she says, and I roll my eyes immediately in response, and cover my face again.

"Claire, Mason does not have a *thing* for me. He likes to get to me, he likes the attention—that's it!" I say, swallowing hard, probably with a bit of disappointment.

"*Right.* So that's why his eyes were glued to you the entire time he sang that song, huh?" she says, and I sit up quickly in response to this. "Yeah, I thought that might get you to see my side. Aves, he stared at the back of your head, and the only time he wasn't looking at you was when his eyes were closed, probably imagining your face. Dude is a little smitten, that's all I'm saying."

My mouth betrays me, and slides into a fragile smile. Claire notices—I can tell because her eyes light up a little. But she doesn't call me out on it, probably because she knows how quickly I'll retreat back into hiding.

"Maybe…and just hear me out, okay," she starts, swinging my legs to the floor to force me to sit up. "Maybe you can just go out there, do your job, and…I don't know…stop when you have a minute, and just think about it. Just see if you get any *vibes.*"

I can't help but snort-laugh at her suggestion. I'm pretty sure the only vibes I'm going to get are the ones that travel all the way down my spine. But I guess it can't hurt anything to indulge a little—I've always loved to listen to that man sing. And pretending he's singing to me isn't anything new to me either.

"I can do that…but I'm not doing any *vibe testing,*" I say, tucking my shirt back in, and pulling my hair from its tie so I can rebuild the bun on top of my head.

"And Aves? How about you leave it down?" Claire says, reaching her hands around mine and urging me to let go of the small band holding my hair up. "It won't look like flirting—I know that's what you're worried about. It's just a hair tie."

I hold her gaze for a few seconds. I'm not sure I want to do anything *different*. It feels like giving in. But, it is just a hair tie—something I take out and put in every day at work. No big deal. I finally nod *okay*, and shove it back in my pocket before straightening out my work clothes and marching back to the kitchen door. I turn to Claire one last time for reassurance.

"Max is happy, so we can stay as long as you want," she says, knowing what I need to hear. I smile softly, and take in a deep breath before I head back out to the crowded bar, hoping I blend in with the sea of prettier girls out there and fly under the radar. Or maybe I hope I don't. Maybe I hope I stand out, and that I'm all Mason can look at. My heart is sputtering at the thought—it's fear. I fear the pending disappointment, and I know it's inevitable.

He's finishing up "In Your Eyes" when I get up the courage to walk to the tall tabletops that line the back. They're right in view of the stage, and if there was ever a time to sneak a look at Mason, this was it. I load my tray with empties, sliding my hair behind my ear so I can see better, and that's when I take my moment.

Max is always telling me about gravity, and how it pulls two masses together. Gravity. That's what I'm feeling right now. I'm sure I'm flushed, and despite Dusty's being filled beyond fire code, I can't hear the crowd. I'm completely locked to Mason, his eyes squared to mine, and he's the only thing I see. The background...gone. It's just Mason.

Sitting on that stool with a small spotlight on him, he's wearing a worn-out pair of jeans and a tight black T-shirt that hugs his biceps; the tattoo on his right arm finally showing enough to let me know it's a tiger. Dusty's is never formal. It's not a place where performers dress up—but tonight Mason is making that look so unbelievably sexy. His hair is twisted in all different directions, and he keeps brushing away the long strands that fall in his eyes.

He licks his lips and bites his tongue before letting a smile slide up into his cheeks. I actually have to catch myself on one of the chairs when he does. A few faint whistles from the women in the crowd break through my tunnel.

"I've got a few more, if you guys don't mind," he says, toying with the audience. They eat him up—they always did. "Good, good," he chuckles.

Adjusting the mic a little, he props one knee up on the top ledge of the stool, letting his guitar slide to the side and fall on the strap. The whistles start again—I get it, he's downright dreamy right now. But I still roll my eyes. It's annoying when Mason gets this kind of attention, and I'll admit that I'm probably a little jealous.

"I bet you're all wondering what I'm doing back in town," Mason says, his eyes leaving mine for just a moment before coming back to find me. I give in and set my tray down, sitting in one of the seats to fully take him in. "I blew it."

The crowd laughs, but I know Mason's not really joking. He's dead serious, and when the audience realizes this, too, they start to get quiet.

"No, it's okay. Y'all can laugh. But it's the truth. I tried doing this all on my own, but I wasn't ready. I'm sure some of you have read about our failed concerts, fights in clubs, shit like that. Sorry, Ray…I know you don't like it when I swear on stage."

My dad just waves a bar towel at him and goes back to his business.

"You see, I was ready to leave this town when I was sixteen. And I don't think my head ever matured beyond that, even though I was twenty when I finally left to tour. In my head…I was still sixteen. Sixteen and stupid," Mason laughs at himself now, and the crowd starts to relax and join in. He has them—he has us all. He could tell us to vote for him for president right now, and we'd all mail in our ballots.

"Anyways. This isn't about me messing up my tour. I wanted to get up here tonight to see if I could remember why I ever made this my dream in the fist place. I was so focused on success, I forgot about the ride. And I missed some pretty great things along the way."

My breath held, I fight against my instinct to run—just to hear Mason out, to see what he says next. I'm terrified, because my heart is begging him to make this about me. But I know that, if anything, it's about how badly he feels. It's pity—for making me cry years ago, and for every other painful bit of my past that Claire gave away. My legs are aching to retreat, and I'm pushing my weight to the balls of my feet, readying myself to get back to work, when Mason absolutely floors me.

"If I could do it again…" he pauses, his eyes unmistakably on me now. "I would definitely kiss the girl in the closet."

Oh. My. God.

CHAPTER 7: AND THEN THERE WERE FOUR

Mason

That wasn't planned. I mean I did want to say *something* that would let Avery know how sorry I am. But that last part? That came from somewhere else entirely. What's weird is that I don't regret it. Hell, I felt unbelievable the second the words left my mouth. Maybe it's just the chase…but I sorta don't think that's it.

I saw something in Avery's eyes. I'm not going to say it was forgiveness; I'm not naïve to believe I've even come close to earning that yet. But I think there is definitely a part of her that wants to forgive me.

She was gone by the time I wrapped up my set. *Gone*! I had the usual crowd waiting around to talk to me, buy me drinks, and all that shit. All I wanted to do was talk to Avery though; ask her what she thought. I saw Claire talking to her briefly, and then I watched Claire leave with Max. I was pretty excited that he stuck around too. But Avery was the one I *really* wanted to talk to. And she was already asleep—or hiding—in her room by the time I made it home.

The house was empty this morning. Ray always works long hours on the weekends. He goes in early to set up for Friday and Saturday nights, and Sunday crowds are usually pretty full, too. Sunday is always country night.

I notice Avery's car in the parking lot when I pull in to Dusty's. She must have gotten up early to get out of the house before I woke up. I wonder how she talked Max into getting up early too?

They're all sitting at the bar together when I walk in. Ray's the first to notice me, and he slides a stool out next to him, waving me over.

"Mason, come on over. We're having pancakes for breakfast. Made them myself on the grill," he says, giving me a wink.

I climb onto my seat, and give Avery a sideways glance, but she's looking only at the plate in front of her, nowhere else. Max is busy working with his fork to get his pancake into his mouth. His is cut into perfect squares, and his plate seems free of syrup.

"Hey," Ray whispers to me, urging me to lean in. "Just so you know, these are gluten-free, and they pretty much taste like crap, so be generous with the syrup, okay?"

I nod once, and grab the syrup, making a layer of sweet, sugary goo on the plate before I add my pancake. I catch Avery's reaction when she snickers at me, and I use it as an opening.

"What? You never syrup the bottom?" I say, cutting a huge bite, and stuffing it in my cheek. Ray was right—these are bland as hell. I reach for the syrup and add more to my plate.

"No, I'm pretty sure that's unique to only you," Avery says, laughing lightly. She seems nervous, and damn if it isn't the cutest thing I've ever seen.

"So, you took off last night. I didn't get to ask you, what'd you think?" I really want to have this conversation with Avery alone, but I don't get a sense that she's going to let that happen anytime soon, so I dive right in.

"Oh, yeah. Sorry. Max was up late and Claire took him home. I kind of wanted to get home, too—you know, so I could be with him," she says, and I'm sitting at the edge of my stool, just waiting for her to say something about my song, my *choice* of song. And that damn bomb I dropped in front of everyone.

"Sure, I understand," I say, smiling with my eyes wide. Still waiting. She senses my prodding, and I feel like a jerk that I have to beg her to tell me I was good.

"You were great, by the way. I knew you would be. See? I told you," she says, picking up her plate and walking it to the kitchen. That's it? I was great, she was right? No reaction to the fact that I pretty much publicly asked her to let me kiss her?

"She's right, Mason. You were *you* last night. That's the Mason I remember playing here, the kid I rolled out there for the world to see," Ray says, standing behind me and giving my shoulder a squeeze. "Whataya say? You wanna try that again, say next weekend?"

"Uh, hell yeah!" I respond. I'd do it every night if Ray would let me. But I know he has a pretty long waiting list. The fact that I get the prime spot whenever I want says something about how the man feels about me, and I'm honored.

64

It's just me and Max, and our pancakes now, so I take this opportunity to see what Max thinks.

"I'm glad you were here last night Max. What did you think?" I ask, hoping that this progress he and I have made keeps moving in this direction. I'm still surprised when he puts his fork down and acknowledges me.

"It was a Saturday, and I like when I get to sit up later. It was good," he says, before picking up his fork to finish his last few bites. Sometimes I think Max isn't so different from other five-year-olds, he just doesn't have the filter that blocks out the honesty. Sure, Max thought last night was great—he got to sit up past his bedtime. The fact that I happened to be playing music in the background is meaningless to the fact that he got a couple extra hours of iPad game time. And I don't blame him a bit.

"Yeah, last night was pretty awesome," I say, smiling to myself, and stuffing the rest of my tasteless pancake into my mouth.

I pick up my plate and ask Max if I can take his. I figure he doesn't mind when he pushes it to the side toward me then goes right back to the iPad. I sort of wish his mom was just as direct. Might make figuring out where I stand a whole hell of a lot easier.

Avery's washing up the plates in the kitchen. I pass Ray when I take mine over, and I could swear he gives me a signal with his glance, urging me to talk to his daughter. There's also a good chance I'm imagining Ray's approval—truthfully, disappointing him—*again!*—scares the hell out of me. And I can't think of anything that would disappoint him more than me chasing after Avery.

I start to help with the plates, but she just grabs mine from my hand and smiles curtly. It almost felt…hostile.

"Okay…uh, thanks," I say, taking a few steps back to the door. I stop, though, mid-stride and close my eyes. *Come on, don't be a pussy.* I come back and lean on the edge of the nearby counter, close enough to make her noticeably shift her weight. "So…what did you *really* think? I heard what you said. You thought it was good. And thank you. I appreciate that. But…now that we're not at the bar…with your family…"

She finishes the last plate and turns the faucet off, but she keeps her gaze focused on the damn soapy water, her hands wringing the sponge dry. She looks so uncomfortable that it has me just wanting to retreat—but I'm in too far. And I'd regret turning back.

"I want to know the things you can't say…in front of them," I lean in closer while I ask this, and her breath halts. I swear her fingers are trembling, and it's making me want to reach out and touch her, just to let her know it's safe.

It feels like forever until she finally exhales. And just when I don't think she's going to acknowledge it—*directly*—she does.

"Don't do this, Mason," her eyelids flit, almost as if it's with exhaustion. I'm so taken off guard with her response, I react immediately.

"Don't…do what? Say 'I'm sorry?'" I spit back, probably a lot harsher than I mean to.

"Yeah," she says, tossing the sponge in the sink and wiping her hands dry on the front of her jeans while she walks past me. "Don't say you're sorry."

Shit!

I follow her back though the kitchen door. Max is still sitting in his place, playing on his iPad, and Ray has moved on to business already, loading in some crates from the back. I look over and think about helping him just so I have an excuse to leave *this* conversation. But it's really my fault I'm having it in the first place, so instead, I decide to be a prick about it and slide up on one of the stools next to Max.

"What are you guys doing today?" I ask, knowing Max will probably answer before Avery. I can actually feel her dig her heels in behind the bar while her eyes roll.

"Mom says I am to get a haircut," Max says, his voice almost robotic, and his eyes not leaving the screen of his tablet.

"Haircut, huh? Okay, that sounds good," I fold my hands and smile smugly at Avery. I'm totally tagging along for the haircut. And hell, I might just follow along for groceries, and watch her do her damn homework just to piss her off at this point.

"I don't like having people touch my hair," Max's eyes flair when he says this, and his tone seems more irritated, so I don't tease anymore. I don't want him to think that I'm teasing him.

She leans forward now and forces Max to acknowledge her gaze. "But you are starting school next week, and part of that means getting a haircut. We've been over this, right Max?" She seems tense again, so I decide to back off. I'm about to let her off the hook completely when Max becomes my unexpected wingman.

"Can Mason come?" when Max asks, Avery's eyes almost leave her head. I can actually hear her swallow in response, and she quickly turns her attention to me, her lips barely open, but her face saying everything. She doesn't want me to come—I don't even have to ask. But she *needs* me to come—because Max asked. I haven't known him long, but I know enough to know this is a big deal.

My eyes lock with Avery's, and I do my best to smile, genuinely. "I'd love to, Max. I'd love to," I say, and Avery's shoulders instantly relax.

I understand why getting a haircut was such a big deal the moment we pull into the parking lot in front of the barber. Max seemed fine for most of the car ride, his mind occupied with his game for most of the way. Once we pulled in, and Avery took the iPad from him to store in her purse, everything about Max began to change.

It's not a normal tantrum like I'm used to seeing. My mom used to babysit kids Max's age, and when they didn't get ice cream or to watch their favorite cartoon, it was hard to convince the neighbors that my mom wasn't beating them.

But Max is different. It's clear he's uncomfortable. Something is suddenly off, and his eyes are darting in all directions, not able to focus on a single person or place. It's almost panic, but yet it seems so much worse. He's unsettled, like he doesn't belong.

When Avery opens the back door, rather than exiting, Max starts to kick and rock, each time his movements gaining more power. I want to help, and I feel like I'm intruding by just standing behind her, but honestly, I don't know where the hell to even begin. When she reaches in, just hoping to get his hand, he smacks it away, repeatedly, and starts humming anxiously.

"Max, you need to use your words. Tell me what's wrong?" she sounds so desperate, and I can't help but join in.

"Yeah, Max. I was excited to come along with you. What's wrong, buddy?" I say, but Avery just shoots me a death stare over her shoulder when I speak. I shrug my shoulders with frustration. I know she's trying to dissolve this situation, and I know she's embarrassed, but *fuck*! I'm just trying to help. I have no idea what to do.

Avery gets in the car next to Max and shuts the door, locking me on the outside. I'm left to do nothing but lean on the nearby light post and watch. I can't hear them, but I know Max is still humming. Avery's eyes are closed, and she's sitting calmly next to Max, just waiting. Her lips are barely moving, almost as if she's talking to herself. After a few minutes, Max seems to be relaxing, and that's when I see Avery's eyes open. She unbuckles her purse and shows Max a bag of something that looks like candies, and she pulls one out and hands it to him before putting the rest in her purse. Finally, after at least ten minutes, Max turns his head in her direction; his eyes are almost on hers when he talks, before he suddenly turns back to the front.

I look away when the door opens, mostly because I don't want to make things worse. Max follows Avery into the barber, and I trail behind, noticing how he's dragging his feet and fidgeting with his hands. He's terrified.

"Hey, Nick. Thanks for opening up for us," she says, her smile soft and utterly defeated. Nick opened up special…just for them. I get it. And I wish I could tell her. But she doesn't want pity. She just wants the next two hours to pass, and me to never bring them up to her. And I get that, too.

"Sure thing, Avery. You know Max is my favorite customer," Nick says, his overgrown, graying mustache dusting the top of his lips. "Max, can you sit on the special chair for me? I'll let you decide how high it needs to be."

I can tell that Nick has done this before. I can also tell that he's not sure if it's going to work today. Max is still rocking a little from side-to-side, and his hands have started tugging at one another harder. I'm so goddamned heartbroken for him that I just jump in with both feet, and try something completely unwelcome, but that I think just might work.

"Hey, Nick. I'm Mason," I reach over to shake his hand, and Nick smiles at me with a hint of surprise.

"Yeah, I know who you are. You're Barb's boy," he says, and I cringe inside a little, hoping like hell he's not one of my mom's conquests.

"Yes, sir. That's me," I say, half-squinting, and holding my breath, waiting for the lecture on my mother, or worse—me, and what a douchebag I am.

"You were good over at Dusty's the other night. You planning on playing there again?" I'm pretty sure Nick notices my huge sigh of relief, but I don't care, because I also notice that Max has stopped swaying.

"I do. Next weekend, in fact," I say, looking to Avery next, and making a mental note of her lip tucked nervously in between her teeth. "I've got a few more songs I'd like to try out."

"Good, I'll be there with the wife. She loved your show," Nick says, his eyes darting between Avery and me now. I manage to give him a silent shake of my head before he asks if we're together, so he lets it pass. Thank god, because I think that would pretty much do Avery in for the day.

"So, I was thinking, Nick. I probably need a haircut, too," I say, and Nick is nodding in full understanding. Avery's eyes are wide with surprise, and I take this opportunity to wink. I'm proud when it makes her blush. "You know, it's what you do, when you start something new. And now that I'm playing at Dusty's, I probably should look my best."

Nick takes my lead perfectly and pats the seat next to the one meant for Max and invites me to sit down.

"Max, you mind if Mason gets his hair cut too?" Nick asks, and Max shakes his head *no* slightly. I see his eyes shift to my feet while I step up on the seat, and he leaves them there while I work my way into my chair. Nick fluffs the cape out next, shaking it out to lose the wrinkles, before swinging it around my body and fastening it around my neck.

"So, what are we getting?" Nick asks, scissors in his hands. Honestly, I hadn't thought things through this far. I wasn't planning on cutting my hair for a long time—I sort of liked the length. But…this was more important. And I was coming to terms with the fact that I was going to be in Cave Creek longer than I originally thought, so my hair would probably grow back by the time I hit the road again.

I look to Avery, prompting her to help me answer this—I wanted whatever Max was getting. Her eyes are still wide, but she curls the edges of her lips slightly when she starts to speak, and I swear I can feel my heart kick at the sight of it. "An inch off the top, and shorter on the sides," she says.

My hand runs through my hair one last time on instinct, almost like I'm saying goodbye. "Yeah, that's right. I'll have that," I say, noticing that behind Nick, Max has now climbed into the seat. I tilt my head to Nick so he notices, and when he looks back at me, his smile says it all. *Thanks.*

Avery hasn't said a word about my shorter hair, but I caught her looking at it in the mirror during the drive home. I decided to ride home in the back, next to Max. He let me, and I felt sort of honored by that. He showed me some more details of the music program he was working on the other day. Since the last time, he had composed an entire song. The instrument choices weren't the best, but the intricacy of the song he built was impressive. Every rhythm and count matched perfectly, and it made me wish I could get a *real* guitar in Max's hands.

Max's blonde curly locks look nice, and I'm glad Avery let Nick style things for the kid. She mentioned that he's starting school, and I know from the small bits from Ray that she's nervous about it. Max walks ahead of us up to Dusty's, eager to get inside and count out the candies he earned from finishing his hair cut.

I start to talk at least a dozen times, but I choke on my words every time, so I just follow Avery up the steps to the front door. We're almost inside when she pauses with her hand flat on the door, her damn lip back between her teeth.

"Thank you," she says, her voice so quiet, I almost don't hear it. But I do.

"Don't mention it," I say, shrugging off the attention. I don't like to feel intimate attention, I'd much rather be the person giving it.

"No," she says, turning to face me. I'm suddenly aware of the small distance between us, and I can tell from her quick breath that she is too. She's boxed in by the door, and I know I could back up and give us some room, but I'm having a hard time getting my feet to move. Avery looks down at her feet, her nerves literally radiating from her body.

"No, Mason," she says, her breath hitching slightly, and I realize then that she's trying not to cry. "Thank you. You have no idea...just having someone else there. Just...thank you."

Her eyes crawl up to meet mine slowly, and the look on her face breaks my heart. The tears are pooling just above the faint freckles on her cheek, and a single blink forces them to slide down her face. Without even thinking, I raise my hand to her right cheek and stop the trail of one with my thumb, slowly sliding it away, but leaving my hand there on her face, probably longer than I should.

I start to think that I would be perfectly content just to stand right here, right like this, for the rest of the afternoon, when the door swings open behind her, and the face that greets me is suddenly the last one I want to see.

"Hey, fucktard!" shouts Ben, the drummer in my band, breaking apart any moment I was possibly having with Avery. In the brief second before Ben pulls me inside, I notice the painful look on Avery's face as her eyes shut tightly, and all I want to do is punch my best friend in the gut and run away with her.

She's gone within seconds, and so is Max. My band mates are on their second pitcher of beer, and talking about our set next week at Dusty's—and inside, I want to protest and tell them I'm going on alone. But I just sit there and stare at the place where Avery was standing minutes ago, just nodding and smiling and pretending I'm glad to see them.

And two days ago, I would have been.

Avery

I'm glad Mason's band showed up. When Ben opened that door, it probably stopped me from doing something really stupid. I'm sure I'm going to fail the "lit" paper I worked on Sunday afternoon, because I can't remember a single thing I wrote. My head was too busy being stuck on Mason, and what he did for Max. And I don't have time to be stuck on anything other than what it takes to start and finish my day.

Claire called me during her shift to warn me that the entire band was there. They started drinking at Dusty's earlier this afternoon—all of them. She said they weren't too rowdy, but that one of them offered her $100 to sleep with her. I laughed—that sounds like Ben. He's the only one of the group other than Mason that I know.

Ben went to our high school. He was a bit of an outsider at first—played in the school band and was always into theater, but usually kept to himself. He was a great drummer, though—and that's why he and Mason hit it off. Ben was the first member of Mason's band, and our senior year, he used to play with him at Dusty's. When he started hanging out with Mason, he started going to more parties and dating more girls—his social status sort of shot through the roof.

He was always the first one to laugh when Mason called me *Birdie*. What's sad is before that, Ben and I were kind of friends.

Max starts school tomorrow. We had his final one-on-one session today with Jenny, and she spent most of our two hours together reassuring me that Max is ready. I don't know, though. I don't think Max will ever be ready. But I guess I have to try, right? I have to let him *try*.

I took tomorrow off. I knew I wouldn't be able to focus. I let my English professor know, too, and she gave me an advance of the assignment so I don't have to go to class—not that I'll be able to gather my thoughts enough for that, either. Great, that's two failed assignments I can count on.

I can hear Mason's laugh before I even open the door. It's the loudest and most obnoxious he's sounded since he's been back in town, and my entire chest constricts in anticipation of having to talk to *this* version of him. I swing the door open and move quickly through the restaurant; I'm almost behind the bar without being noticed when I hear Ben's voice.

"Heyyyyyy, there she is. You're right—it is Birdie! Hey, Birdie!" He's hammered, and it's barely four o'clock. I can't bring myself to look at him, but I won't let him get to me either, so instead, I raise my right hand and flip him the middle finger while I walk the rest of the way through the door.

"Dammmmmmmn," I hear the other guys teasing him while the door shuts, and I'm glad I made a dent. I just hope I didn't provoke them to give me more shit. I'm strong—and I've worked hard to get strong. But even I have my limits. And if they all pile on, they'll break me.

"Where's Max?" Claire asks when she joins me at the back lockers.

"I just let him stay home. Dad's with him; he's coming in later, so I figured you could just meet Max there. Is that okay?" I hate how much I rely on Claire. She always says she doesn't mind. But my life has become her life—and she didn't really sign up for all of this.

"Of course. I'll pick up something to eat for your pop on my way there. Max need anything?" she asks, but I'm so lost in my thoughts, I don't register her words. "Avery? You in there?"

"Oh, uh...yeah. Sorry..." I shake my head, and strip my shirt to put my Dusty's one on. "I'm just so stressed. It's school tomorrow—Max's first day."

"That's right," she says, sitting down on the bench next to me, pulling her shoes off, and replacing them with flip-flops. "It'll be good, Avery. You knew this was coming. And Max...he's ready. He's been so good for me in the evenings."

"Yeah, but no offense, Claire. I'm not worried about how he is at night. It's the four hours in the beginning of the day in a classroom full of other five-year-olds that scares the shit out of me. What if he has a meltdown? What if he doesn't make any friends? What if..." I can't help the crack in my emotions when I think about this, and I have to pause to wipe my eyes on the inside of my shirt. "What if he can't do this, Claire? Where do we go from that?"

My friend slides over to me and pulls me in with her slender arm, tugging me close. "Then we figure that out...*if* that's what happens," she says, and I start to protest, but she's quick to hold up her hand. "Ah ah ah. I said *if.* Don't be so quick to discount that boy of yours. He's mighty capable—and you should know that."

I smile at her when she says that. I smile because I can tell she believes Max is capable, too. She's right—I'm his advocate, his fighter and his hero. And if anyone believes Max can do this, it's me. And if I have to burn Rome just to get him through kindergarten, than that's what the hell I'm going to do.

"You're good at this, you know. This best friend gig?" I say, swatting at her with my apron while she stands. She just laughs and runs her fingers through her hair a few times before grabbing her bag and purse.

"I'll read with him tonight. And we'll get to bed early, just so he's rested. But, hey...listen," she says, peeking out the kitchen door at the cackling group of four sitting near the pool tables. "If you need to call me...you know, just to get through *that?* I'll be up, okay?"

Pursing my lips into a tight smile, I just give her a nod. Yeah. *That.* I'm not sure how I'm going to get through *that.* But if my son can head bravely into a classroom full of kids he doesn't know tomorrow, then the least I can do is survive a six-hour shift with a bunch of drunk, washed-up musicians.

I follow Claire out and wave goodbye while I start to set up glasses with Cole. I'm glad he's here. He's been bouncing and bartending for my dad for the last three years, and I'm glad my dad has someone he can count on. Cole moved here with his brother, and they share a small house on the far north end of town. They're into horses. They even do riding lessons during the week. I've always wanted to set Cole up with Claire—I know she'd be up for it. But, he's just sort of this mystery. I might just try though...once Max gets school settled, and I can start to focus again.

"Sorry about that," Mason's voice startles me, and I end up dropping the glass I'm drying.

"Job opening!" I hear one of the guys from his band shout. I just roll my eyes at it and bend down to start cleaning it up.

74

"Shit, now I'm double sorry," Mason says, his body now right next to me, helping me pick up the shards that have scattered along the floor.

"It's okay. It's my fault. Butter fingers," I say, not sure why I'm making excuses. I should have said *yes, it is your fault. You and those thugs you call friends.*

"Hey, I told them to knock it off with the Birdie stuff," Mason says as we stand. I sweep my glass pieces into his open hand and he turns to toss them into the trash.

"Why'd you even bring it up," I sigh.

"Don't worry. They won't call you that again. Ben's grown up a lot—and they got my point when I told them not to," he says.

"Oh yeah, and what point is that?" I ask, going back to drying the stack of glasses in front of me.

"That I'll kick their ass out in this parking lot if they start shit with you. That point," Mason says, reaching over and popping a pretzel in his mouth before heading back to his seat, giving me one last grin.

He defended me. And damn it, I like that he defended me. I can feel Cole's stare, but I ignore him, and keep working on the glasses until I run out and need to load in more.

"Cole, can you bring in another rack? Last thing I want to do is drop more," I say. Cole chuckles and smirks at me before heading to the back, slinging his towel over his shoulder. He's back with more in seconds.

"So, just curious," he says while he drops the new bin in front of me, and I immediately go to work drying and loading. "Are you helping me because you wanted to help out? Or…are you hiding?"

"I'm not hiding," I answer fast, my tongue pinched between my teeth while I concentrate on a spot on one of the glasses.

"Uh huh. Sure," he says, laughing softly while he walks back to the other end of the bar.

All right. I'm hiding. But no one needs to know that other than me. And so far, it's working out for me. The bar is filling up, and I'll be busy with customers soon. Barb just got here, and I know she'll want to wait on her son and his friends, so I can keep to myself. It's my survival plan.

The first hour flies by. It's open mic night, so the acts are starting to arrive. I always like open mic—it's the best and the worst of karaoke. And sometimes, the bad acts are worth more than a dozen great ones. There's a guy with a violin who took up the corner booth, and I can't *wait* to hear his story.

Barb's been handling Mason's friends, and true to his word, no one has uttered a single *Birdie* since he told them to stop. I must be cashing in some karma, because my tips have been over-the-top tonight, too. The last table left me thirty bucks!

I take my break in the back for a few minutes, and pull out my phone to check on Claire and Max. It's barely seven, so I know he's still awake. She usually sends me a quick note when he goes to bed, but she hasn't yet.

Super busy tonight. Say goodnight to Max for me. I probably won't see your text until late.

I wait a few seconds, and Claire quickly responds.

Good. Hope the tippers are generous, LOL! I got a marriage proposal from an old man today. Can you beat that?

One day, Claire is going to say yes to one of the old ranchers who hit on her. She always jokes, but I think she's thought about it before. I want my friend to find love—probably more than I want to find it myself.

No, you got me there. But Ben did call me Birdie!

I roll my eyes remembering his voice. I think the nickname bothers me more now than it did back then—probably because I've had years to really think about it, and build it up in my head.

He's an ass.
How's Mason?

I stare at her text for a full minute, because I don't know how to answer that. Mason has been taking up a lot of my mental space. What he did for Max at the barber was so unexpected. I don't know why my son is so taken with him, but I guess apples don't fall far from their trees. I just can't help but feel like the other shoe

76

is going to drop soon, so I keep him at an arm's-length. I'm willing to be friendly. But I won't call him *friend*.

Oh, you know...he's Mason. He's not as drunk as the other guys, so that's good, I guess.

I wait for her to write back, but she doesn't. I know it's almost time to start prepping Max for bed. I hate that I don't get to tuck him in most nights. But Claire always reminds me that I'm only missing the routine. Max has never been an affectionate kid. He'll hug me, when forced. Sometimes, when I'm holding his arms down after an anger episode, I imagine that I'm holding him and rocking him to sleep. It's similar—I'm calming him. But he doesn't seek my touch out—ever. I used to cry over it, but I buried those feelings when I realized there were some things that Max's autism was never going to let us overcome. He loves me. He just doesn't say it with words or embraces. And that's okay.

The crowd is pretty steady over the next three hours. That's how open mic night usually goes. The first few acts aren't much to brag about, but the later the evening gets, the more likely it is someone good will go on. That's how Dad tries out potential spotlights. If they can win over the open-mic-night crowd, he'll usually offer them a weekend.

There's a girl with a guitar closing tonight, and she's pretty good. I can tell my dad thinks so too, because he's been hanging around the edge of the stage. He'll offer her a weekend, and I'll love watching her face light up. Every single person that plays the Dusty's stage has a dream. Even when they say they don't when they step up there, they've got one by the time they step down.

This girl is a dreamer. She's young, maybe about nineteen or twenty. She's good, too. Even Mason and his friends are listening. I haven't been to their table all night, so I take a deep breath and head over to help clear some of the glasses. I don't want to look like I'm avoiding them.

"Hey, stranger," Mason says, his feet propped up on the edge of the table. He's a little buzzed—I can tell. He's playing with his phone, not really looking at me, but the sloppy smirk on his face shows he's aware I'm here. He's wearing an old pair of Converse, black jeans that fit tight to his legs and gather at his shoes, and a V-neck white T-shirt. Even though he smells mostly of beer, I also pick up his cologne underneath—rich and woodsy. I like it. I like it more than I should.

I also like his haircut. I've noticed it a few times tonight. It's short around his neck, like it used to be. There's still a wave in the top, and it flops a little in his face, but not quite as much as it did before the cut.

He's watching me over his phone. I can see his eyes move to me every so often, and I just smile and continue on with my work. His attention scares the hell out of me, because I know how quickly it can latch on to someone else. But for now, I give myself this little moment. Right now, slightly drunk, Mason Street finds me pretty enough to flirt with, and damn it, I am.

"Do you ever just stop?" Mason asks, pushing his phone back into his pocket and dropping his feet to the ground. He leans forward on his elbows, looking at me across the table. His arms flex slightly, and I can't help but shift my gaze to his bicep and the tattoo.

"What's with the tiger?" I ask, changing the subject entirely.

"He was a makeup tattoo. Covering up something stupid I got when I was drunk once in Vegas. You didn't answer my question." He moves over a seat, so he's closer to me, and I shift my tray to my other hip, just to add a barrier. He notices, and his lip curls up on the side in a devious grin.

"I know. I'm avoiding it," I say back. He's not going to charm me—*this* girl can dish it, and take it.

He sits back in his chair, and folds his arms now, propping a foot back up along the side of the table. He's chewing at the inside of his cheek, and I'm just waiting for him to come back with a second round. I keep loading up my tray, and when it's full, I turn to leave. I'm almost free when Mason catches up to me and walks me to the bar.

"I probably should have asked that differently," he says, pulling the tray from my hands and putting the dirties in the bin before handing it back to me. "I've never met anyone like you, Avery. Not a girl in her twenties, anyways. You just go and go and go. And I was just thinking, you never take time to just stop—and to just *be.*"

I'm sure the face I'm making back at him isn't flattering, but really...that's the stupidest thing I've ever heard. How can I just *be*?

"You know what kind of girl does that?" I say, moving in a little closer just so Mason knows he doesn't intimidate me. "A vapid one, without a kid, and who is planning a beach-house getaway with her girlfriends. That girl is a fairytale, Mason. Make-believe. Us *real women*? We have responsibilities—and we put other people first. Because it's the right thing to do. So no—no, I don't just ever...stop. Too much depends on me going."

I can actually feel my hands shaking I'm so flustered by this conversation. All I want to do is smash my tray in his face and race off to the locker area to lie down and breathe. But I can't.

I can't, because somewhere in the midst of my rant, Mason grabbed my hand with his, and now all I can freaking focus on is the feeling of his thumb lightly grazing my fingers and how much it makes me want to burst into tears.

"One drink, right before close. That's all I'm asking," Mason says, his eyes boring into mine like lasers. "I'm not saying pick up and go backpacking across Europe. I'm just asking you to take a break, for once in your life. Have a beer with the guys and me while Ray closes up. We'll shoot some pool, or throw some darts. Twenty minutes, and then you can go back to living for everyone else."

Mason's hand is still on mine, and my brain is tangled from the many emotions being mixed like a blender inside my chest. Whatever the cause, I nod *yes* slowly, and slide my hand from his.

"So, yeah? After the show tonight—we'll hang out? Just for one drink?" Mason's walking backward, and he's looking at me like he used to in my dreams. This entire week has been surreal, and I'm capping it off with a far-fetched fantasy. My smile is cautious, but it's genuine. I've taken a leap—and there's the possibility that I'll go home to Claire tonight, and cry for an hour. Or, maybe I won't cry. Maybe I won't cry at all, but rather...

And I hate that feeling almost more than any other—I recognize it, it's hope. Goddamned Mason Street has given me hope. He better not crush it.

Mason

I'm not *that* drunk. I'm pretty sure Avery thinks I'm as blitzed as Ben or the other guys. But I'm not even close. I had three or four beers, which for me is nothing. I'm in full control of this. I've watched that girl avoid me all night—and I know she was avoiding me. My mom's not very good at secrets, and she asked me outright why Avery was so bent on her handling *us boys* tonight. I told her that Avery didn't get along with Ben, but I know it's also because she doesn't want to be around me. Not after I watched her cry, and almost kissed away her tears.

The lights are coming on, and the jukebox music is the only thing left in the bar. Josh and Matt are nearly passed out at the table. I'm going to have to call them a cab to take them back to their apartment. Ben's handling his liquor pretty well, but he's busy flirting with the last girl who performed. I told him she didn't look like his kind of girl—she was pretty innocent looking, more of a girlfriend kind of girl—but he didn't care. He never does.

I was glad to see the boys. It's been a couple of weeks since we all split, trying to make sense of the label dumping us. Matt and Josh drove around the country for a few days—they're both originally from Indiana, so they spent some time with their families. Ben had planned on coming home with me, but he got hooked up with some girl in Texas and well....

I can see Avery moving back and forth, from the kitchen to the bar, and back again. She's busying herself, helping out others on purpose, just to avoid spending time with me. I catch Cole's attention while she's in the kitchen.

"Hey, man," I say, nodding toward the door. "She's avoiding me. I just wanna talk. Help a brother out?"

Cole smiles big, and just gives me a nod, letting me know he gets what I'm asking. Cole's a good-looking dude, and I feel okay admitting that. I wondered at first if he and Avery ever had a thing, but it's clear they haven't. And I don't get the sense that there's really any interest either way. When Avery comes back out, Cole stops her before she starts loading up more dishes for the back.

"Ave, if you do all my work, then I won't have a job. So...how about you let me finish this up?" he asks. She turns to look at me immediately, and then back at Cole, biting on the inside of her cheek. She knows I put him up to this, she's just deciding whether or not she wants to play along.

"All right, you sure?" she says, drying her hands on the bar towel.

"I'm sure, Ave. I'm sure," Cole says, almost like he's giving her permission. I see her shoulders rise and fall with her deep breath, and when she turns to me, she looks like she's in line for the world's scariest roller coaster.

"One drink. That's it," I say, walking closer to her and crossing my heart with my right hand.

"Fine, but I get to pick the drink," she says, moving away from me and behind the bar. When she comes back with two Cokes, I just about lose it.

"Ha! Seriously, this is your idea of a big night out. Damn, girl…I've gotta teach you a few things," I say, lifting the straw and inspecting it. "Is that…a bendy straw?"

"It sure is," she says, bending hers and taking a big sip. *Shit, her drink is already a third of the way gone.*

"Alrighty then. Well…how about we shoot some darts," I ask, trying to come up with anything that will slow her ass down.

"Sure. Whatever," she says, brushing me with her shoulder when she passes. She's trying so hard to keep this front up. It's really cute, but it's frustrating as hell.

I follow her to the billiards room and open up one of the cabinets, pulling out the metal darts. Ray never went electronic with anything. He always said it ruined the authenticity, and I tend to agree. These darts are the same ones I learned to throw when I was nine years old. They're still crazy sharp, though. I take a small sip of my Coke and laugh under my breath. I should have known Avery would have found a way around this—a loophole!

"So, what are we playing, first one to zero from three hundred?" I ask, thinking that this game could go on for at least 30 minutes.

"I can't be here that long, Mason. Let's do two hundred," she already looks put out, and it's killing me. I don't know how I'm going to make this girl turn a corner with me, but damn it, something's got to get inside her head.

"Two hundred…okay. But…we're playing to zero exactly," I say, knowing that throwing a little strategy in—and making both of us end our score at exactly zero—might just buy me a few extra minutes.

Avery's eyes are squinted, and she's studying me. I hate that every time we interact she puts our entire exchange through a litmus test. I can see her physically questioning my every motive. It's my fault she's like this with me. And I'm starting to wonder if it's my fault that she's like this with her entire goddamned life.

"Fine, we'll play your way. I'm shooting first. Give me the gold," she's got a little fire in her voice. Suddenly, Avery's got a competitive spirit going on. *This…*I can use!

"You can be gold. But—" I hold the darts back before I give them to her. She flips her hair around and stops her feet right in their tracks.

"No more buts. Just throw the damn darts when I'm done, Mason," she says, and I can't help but laugh at her version of bossy. No doubt, Avery is a strong woman—and I know from experience that she can get her point across when she needs to. But now she's just being difficult to be mean, to get back at me. And while I should pretend it's working, I just can't hold my laughter in.

Her hands are on her hips now, and she's forcing her lips tight. I know she's about to bail on the entire night. I manage to hold my breath long enough to compose myself, and hold my hands up to signify a truce.

"We need to have something to play for. That's all," I say, and she immediately gives me a sideways glance, her suspicion spiking again.

"Fine, if I beat you, you do all my dishes—here and at home—for the next week," she's proud of herself with this one, and the smirk on her face shows me she thinks I'll back off, not wanting to do any hard work. She should know better, though— I've never been afraid of hard work, especially at the bar.

I nod my head in agreement, and step closer to her, reaching out my hand to shake on it. When she slides her soft fingers into mine, it's the most amazing feeling in the world. Other than those few seconds when my fingers were on her face, the only other time Avery touched me was when she slapped me across the cheekbone. I like this touch *a whole lot* more.

She's about to let go of our shake when I hold her grasp firmly, and step in even closer. I've got one shot at this.

"And if I win," I say, my lips unable to contain the shit-eating grin on my face as I move closer to her ear. She's frozen, and I can see her neck speckled with goosebumps, but she's not moving away either. I lick my lips slightly, just to see what that does, and when I hear her breath escape, I know I've got her. "If I win, I get to kiss you. Like I was supposed to a decade ago."

Her face is flushed when I pull away, her lips parted, and her eyes almost afraid—but her hand is still in mine, so I give it one more shake just to seal the deal. I turn away, and I can feel her still standing there, watching me. I wanted to kiss her right then, her neck is so soft and she smells so good. For the last five years, I've done nothing but have one-night stands and flings with girls who smell like smoke and tequila. Avery—she smells like heaven.

"Go on, princess. You wanted to go first," I say, wishing like hell that I kept up with this game. I used to be good—even hustled a few of the locals when I was in high school. But it's been years since I've thrown a dart.

Avery takes a drink of her soda, and I notice her hands are still shaking slightly when she tries to line up her shot. She's nervous, and I hope like hell she throws this game so I can feel how soft her lips are. She shuts her eyes for a brief second, and when she opens them again, her hands are steadier. Her eyes are focused on the board, her elbow bent in front of her, when she releases.

Eighteen. Okay, so this is not going to be a walk in the park. Her next throw is only a four, and her last one is a ten, so I feel like I might have some room to breathe.

"Show me what you've got," she says as she walks by with a little swagger in her step. She's putting up a good act, but I notice the small quiver in her voice when she speaks.

I grab my darts from the table, and take a big gulp of my Coke, wiping my mouth across my sleeve like I would if I were drinking the hard stuff. It makes her laugh, so I got what I wanted.

"All right…let me show you how this is done," I say, holding her gaze long enough for her to blink and look away. I'm smiling while I line up my shot, and I move my arm back just enough to give the dart some sticking power, and then release.

Two.

Avery is laughing so hard she has to actually cover her mouth. It's one of those laugh-so-hard-no-noise-comes-out kind of laughs. Honestly, I love seeing her face like this. I don't think I've seen her smile like this once since I've been back, and it's almost worth losing...*almost.*

As pretty as her lips are when they're smiling, I can't imagine how they look inches away from my own...begging. *Begging.* Like I could ever get Avery to beg me for anything. But just the thought...

I have to shake my head to focus; I'm getting so worked up. Avery's too busy fussing with the feathers on her darts to notice, which is good, because I'm pretty sure what I'm thinking about right now—the way I'm reacting to her—she would *notice!*

After a few deep breaths, I refocus, and line my second shot up. This one's better—seventeen. One more big number, and I'll be in the lead. I've got Avery's attention now, too—and this time, there is no laughter. Instead, her bottom lip is completely tucked under her top teeth, and her knee is bouncing like a damned jackrabbit.

"You look nervous there. Might want to pull out your lip balm...you know, moisten those babies up. Just sayin'," I tease, and she blushes instantly. She stands and turns her back to me, pretending to straighten her shirt and move the stool she was sitting on, but I know she's really just trying to hide her face. I'm getting to her—and I've never wanted to win a round of darts more in my life.

Fourteen.

"That's on the line," she says immediately. She's protesting— it's funny.

"Let's inspect it. Don't you dare touch it until I get there," I say, walking up behind her. It's clearly a fourteen—the dart isn't even touching any of the line. I see it, and Avery sees it. She sees it so well, she's no longer breathing, but just standing there, staring at it, her eyes wide and her hands rolling her own darts in her fingertips.

"Well?" I say, knowing I'm right, but wanting to snap her out of this damn trance she's in.

"Fine. Fourteen," she says, turning around with a huff.

Okay, she actually seems legitimately pissed at me now. She throws three more low numbers, and the look on her face is so stressed, it's actually painful to watch. We go on for five more rounds, and honestly only because I have to hit a *five* to close it out.

When I hit it, I almost want to lie, and say it's on the line, just to give her a chance. I've gone from being willing to cheat—to win the chance to kiss Avery—to wanting to throw the damn match myself. It's not that my feelings are hurt by her reaction to kissing me...well, maybe they're hurt a little. But it's more than that. I feel like I'm taking advantage of her or something, like I'm forcing her to do something she finds disgusting. I know that's not the truth, but it just doesn't *feel* right. There's no delaying it, though, and the regret that spills through my veins when she turns to look at me— her face so fucking disappointed—just about kills me.

I didn't even really get to *talk* to her, which is what I really wanted in the first place.

"Well, you won. Let's get this over with," she says, finishing the last drink from her glass, and slamming it hard on the table before wiping her lips dry with the back of her hand. She's standing there, her arms limp at her sides, and her eyes closed, like she's playing a boring game of hide-and-seek. This...*this*...is nothing like I pictured it.

I walk closer to her, and I hold my breath so she can't sense how close I am. I'm about to call the whole thing off, give her an out, when her bottom lip comes loose, letting out the tiniest of breaths, and I see her shiver. I take note of her hands, which are no longer limp, but balled into tight fists.

I just need to know—just some sign that my hunch is right. I move even closer, and I can see her muscles tighten at my nearness. There are inches between our feet, and one sway of my body, or hers, and we'd be touching. I stare long and hard at her neck—that long, milky neck. Her hair falls over both shoulders. It's long and wavy from the hair tie she was wearing earlier tonight. I reach up gently, and sweep the waves falling over her left shoulder behind her ear, and Avery's eyes close even harder.

She's not telling me to stop. And I know she would if she wanted to—Avery doesn't do anything she doesn't want to do. So I push my luck a little more, and move my lips close to her shoulder first, then her neck. I blow lightly, and every tiny hair on her neck obeys. She sucks in one more short breath, and the sound of it makes me smile.

I spare a glance over her shoulder just to confirm we're alone, and we are. No one is interested in us—we're off in our own universe. Matt and Josh are snoring at the table, and I'm pretty sure Ben left with that girl from earlier.

"So you and I...we made a bet," I whisper in her ear. "You remember the terms?"

Avery nods *yes* slowly, her lips still barely parted, and her breaths becoming quicker, no doubt to match her pulse. What I'm about to do is going to be the hardest thing I've ever done in my entire life. But I *have* to do it.

"We said if you lost, you had to let me kiss you, right?" I say, my thumb slowly stroking the skin along her neck, slipping barely under the collar of her shirt until I touch the strap of her bra. My touch makes her quiver again, and I almost change my mind.

"I won, didn't I, Avery?" I say her name, because I want her to hear me call her by it—not *Birdie*. When she goes home tonight, I want her to think of something entirely new, a new beginning. And I don't want any of those old memories tainting it.

Avery nods lightly, her tongue sweeping over the center of her lips *and driving me fucking mad*! I breathe in slowly, and will myself to go on.

"I'm going to kiss you then," I say, moving both of my hands to either side of her face, cradling it until my fingers are woven deep within her hair, and she's completely under my control. My thumb glides slowly across her lips, stopping at the center, and pausing for just a second, almost begging her to let it inside, to taste it. I move my lips closer now, too, and I turn my head, just enough so she can feel it—anticipate my touch.

I let my nose graze against hers and then along her cheek, while I slowly turn her head to the side so I can press my lips to her ear once again. I inhale her scent, and this time, I memorize it—just in case this was it, my only moment. Then I speak against her ear, my lips touching her just enough to ignite an unbelievable desire to bite her gently.

"But I'm not going to kiss you now," I say, my eyes closed while I hope like hell this is the right move. "I get to kiss you, but I didn't say when. And right now, you're not ready. Don't think this means I don't *want* to kiss you. Because I do—I want to kiss you so goddamned hard that you can barely breathe. And one day—one day really fucking soon—I'm going to. But not tonight. Instead, tonight, I'm just going to thank my lot in life for the fact that I grew up in a bar, learning how to throw darts."

When I let her go, she keeps her eyes closed for another second or two before opening them, and I'm convinced I made the right choice when I see the disappointment on her face. That's what I want—I want her to *want* me to kiss her again. I could kick myself for taking it for granted the first time, and I'll never make that mistake again.

Her eyes are trained on mine the moment she opens them; I just push my hands in my pockets, shrug my shoulders, and give her the sincerest smile I've got. Then, I watch her spin around and walk away, pushing hard against the kitchen door, and vanishing—probably leaving through the back just to avoid me.

And that's okay. Because I know even though she didn't confront me, I'm in her head. I'm *deep* in her head—and she's going to have a hard time shaking this one.

CHAPTER 9: THE NEW KID

Avery

"No, Claire, he *didn't* kiss me; that's what I said," my friend keeps replaying my story to her over and over—hoping that one of these times it ends with Mason kissing me. But it doesn't. It doesn't, because Mason likes to play games, and that's all this is. A distraction.

"Okay, well...are you guys going to go out sometime?" she asks.

"No. That was it—just that stupid game of darts, and an *almost* kiss. That's where the story ends," I say, looking for my orange headband to pull my hair back. I have to get Max to school—*school*. I don't have time to be rehashing *what ifs* and *do I think Mason likes me* with Claire...like we're at a slumber party.

"I don't get it," Claire starts, and I can tell she's going to dive into another round of analyzing, so I stop her.

"I don't get it either, Claire. But I'm done worrying about it. I have to get Max ready. I'll call you later," I pinch the phone between my shoulder and chin so I can slide my headband on while my friend says goodbye.

Max is already downstairs eating his breakfast. He's eating just like we do almost every morning. We're sticking with our routine...only today, unlike the rest, we'll turn left out of the driveway—and go to Cave Creek Public. The teachers are ready, and according to Max's therapists, Max is ready. *I* on the other hand am nowhere in the *realm* of ready.

"So the trick with school is you have to get yourself a good nickname," I hear Mason explaining as I walk down the stairs. I spare a peek, and Max isn't listening to him. I'm actually glad he can shut things like this out because the *last* thing Max needs is a nickname.

"Morning, Avery," Mason says over his shoulder. He heard the stairs. *I hate those stairs.*

"Morning, Mason. Thank you for starting breakfast," I say, realizing my dad is long gone. It's just been the two of them.

"No problem. Was just learning from Max here about his big day," Mason says, leaning back, and sipping on his coffee. It's first thing in the morning, and I can tell he hasn't showered, but damn it if I don't find him appealing. I wonder if I would have found him this alluring before last night? His hair is twisted on the top, thanks to his new haircut, and he's wearing a striped pair of pajama bottoms along with an old Dusty's T-shirt. He hasn't shaved—*I always like it when he doesn't shave*. I stop myself from getting carried away when the smirk on Mason's face registers with me.

"So, you sleep all right last night, Avery?" he grins. *That damn grin*! I'm about to come up with a boring response, when he winks at me, and I just get all flustered, causing him to chuckle. I'm playing right into his hands, and I hate it.

"Max," I turn my full attention to my son instead. "Do you have everything in your backpack?" I pull it from the back of the chair, but Max stops me quickly. I'm making him nervous, changing the order of his things, so I put it back and just smile.

"We need to leave in six minutes, okay?" I set the stove clock. This is one of the tricks Claire taught me, she uses it when she's changing up Max's bedtime routine. He likes order, and when he knows what's coming next, he does better.

I pour myself a bowl of cereal, and reach for the milk, only to find Mason standing right behind me—*close* behind me. "Excuse me, just wanted to get a little milk for the coffee," he says, his breath tickling my neck. I quickly step forward to give myself some safety—some distance. He doesn't *really* want milk. Hell, I don't think I've ever seen him touch milk. He's just trying to get to me, and I'm not going to let him.

I reach in and grab the gallon to pour it over my cereal and then hand it to him, and he purposely puts his hand over mine during our exchange. It makes me flinch, and that makes the corner of his lip raise a hint. *He's winning*.

I pull out my notebook, and review my to-do list—over and over—while I eat my cereal. I have it memorized, but I need something to do for four minutes, and this will work. With a minute to spare, I lay out everything that I'm about to put inside Max's lunch bag to review it with him.

"I have all of your favorites in here. And remember, they're in these bags today, different from the plate, but the food is the same," I say. Max isn't looking at me, so I kneel down next to the table, and repeat myself, only this time I ask him to look me in the eye.

"I understand," he says, his eye contact with me is shorter than he can normally hold it. I know he's anxious. He can't say he's anxious, and he doesn't understand what it means, or what the feeling is, but I know it's inside him. His legs are already bouncing under the chair, so I hold my hand on his knee to stop it.

"Hey, it's going to be all right," Mason says, his hand on my shoulder. This time, I leave it there, and I don't even pretend that it offends me, because it's so very much the opposite. I freeze at his touch, but I slowly let out everything I've been carrying inside. My face is blocked from them both as I stay knelt below the table, and I let a single tear fall down my face. It needed to. I probably need to shed more than that one, but that's all I have time for.

"Thank you," I say, almost a whisper. When I stand, I blot my eyes dry, and take a deep breath before I turn around. Mason isn't teasing anymore—he's sincere. It's surprising...yet, it isn't.

"Okay, Max. It's time," I say, gathering his lunch bag and backpack along with my school things. We're venturing into new. I know it's good, and it's what I've wished for since the diagnosis. But I just can't shake the feeling in my gut—*fear.*

The drive to school was flawless, even the stoplights were on my side. I walked Max to class, and spoke with his teacher, and she assured me she was ready.

Ready.

Seems everyone is ready—but me.

I stayed to watch, observing from the back of the class until the teacher gave me a signal that it would be a good time to "slip out." I didn't want to go, but I knew I had to. I sat in the parking lot for the rest of the day, just watching the minutes tick by, and playing games on my phone.

Picking Max up was almost worse than dropping him off. I had spent so much time conjuring visions of worst-case scenarios, that by the time I actually got out of the car, I had convinced myself they were true. In my head, Max was locked in a closet, kids teasing him, and the teachers frustrated at not knowing how to restrain him. I actually ran to his class and waited outside for the bell to ring. When the other kids came streaming out—many of them running—I started to panic, searching for my son. *Where was he in the mix? Was he in another classroom somewhere? Is this going to work? This isn't going to work.*

He was the last to leave the classroom, walking in a perfectly straight line to the door, just as his teacher had instructed. I wanted to hug him, I was so proud. But I didn't. Instead, I just sat on my knees, forced him to look at me, and asked him how his day was. *Fine* was all I was going to get. But fine was more than enough.

His teacher, Mrs. Bently, gave me a smile and *thumbs up*, so Max and I headed for the car. We haven't talked the entire trip to Dusty's—not because I don't have a million questions, but because our therapist told me to try to keep other things to a normal routine. I'm not working today, but I know my dad is curious, so we'll stop in before heading home with Claire. Max plays on the iPad on the way to Dusty's—it's a reward that he earns for doing well in therapy and for working hard. And today, Max worked very hard.

"Well, how'd it go?" My dad is the first to ask the second I walk in the door. Mason is standing on the other side of the bar, behind him, and as if on instinct...my eyes go to him.

"It went...great," I let the smile crack now in full force, and my eyes water. I've held it together most of the day, but I've got to let some of it out. Max heads to the corner booth—just like every other day. Cole is quick to follow with his chocolate milk, and I watch as Max crawls to the center of the booth, his spot, where he can feel comforted by both sides of the cushions.

Mason is in front of me, hands in his pockets, and the same smile he left me with this morning is still on his face. "Told you it'd be all right," he says, nodding his head in Max's direction.

I don't know why it hits me so hard, but it does, and now I'm sobbing, hands over my face, and my purse and Max's backpack at my feet. Mason is fast, and his arms are around me in seconds, and I let them be. I grip at the back of his shirt, and bury my face deep in his shoulder, the tears pouring out now. I can't stop the shaking, and every time I try to catch my breath and my body shudders, I feel Mason squeeze me harder.

My dad is next to us soon, and I feel his hand rubbing my back. He's offering his shoulder now, too, but I can't leave Mason's—I won't. I need it.

"I'm sorry," I say, my voice muffled by Mason's shoulder. "What's to be sorry about?" Mason says, his voice soft in my ear. "You've been strong...still are. You needed this."

I loosen my grip and let my hands slide down his shirt to his shoulders. It's a nice shirt—it's a plaid button-down, probably something from Abercrombie or something like that. It smells nice, too. Of course, I've just left a giant wet spot on the shoulder, and wrinkled the hell out of it.

I pull it straight as I back away and wipe at the spot I drenched with tears. "Oh," I giggle nervously, "I'm pretty sure you're going to need a new shirt."

Mason looks down and rubs his hand along the wrinkles a few times before sniffing. "Nah, looks fine," he says, his half-smile something I can't help but stare at.

We hold our gaze, and I watch as his smile shifts into something more serious. I want to leave, but something inside me tells me to stay—to see this out. So I do. Mason reaches his hand up once again and slides his thumb gently over my cheek, his eyes trained on his hand. His brow is pinched in thought, and his lips part with a breath, like he's about to say something—something important.

"Yay! First day of school, done!" Claire says behind me, her voice loud and unabashed. Whatever Mason was about to say, he's not going to say it now. He's still standing in front of me, and he's still looking at me with the weight of everything he wants to say just hanging there in the balance. His brown eyes are almost golden they seem so warm.

As soon as Claire is next to me, Mason disappears. What's more surprising is my overwhelming urge to follow him. I don't, though. Instead, I turn to my friend, who is already grilling me with questions about Max's first day. I answer her quickly, and head to the back, my eyes scanning all directions for Mason, wondering where he went.

"Okay, so what was that?" Claire says, changing her Dusty's shirt and completely switching her line of questioning.

"What?" I pretend. This won't last long—it never does. She doesn't even speak, but rather puts one hand on her hip and narrows her eyes on me. I give in to her glare immediately.

"I…I don't know," I say, flopping forward, and putting my palms to my head. "I'm in trouble, Claire."

"Yeah you are," she says, clicking her locker shut and sitting next to me, reaching for Max's backpack. "You sorta like him again…don't you?"

Her tone isn't teasing, which I appreciate. But I don't want to answer her question. I don't want to, because yeah, I *sorta like him* again. In fact, I more than *sorta like him*. And I barely remember what this feeling feels like, but I also *sorta* remember that it hurts.

"Hey, Avery?" Mason's voice calls from the kitchen door. My heart speeds up the second I recognize it, and out of instinct I grip Claire's hand.

"Yeah, just a second," I say, standing and checking my shirt, making sure it's tucked in completely. I brush back the fine hairs, adjust my headband, and get a reassuring smile from Claire that I look somewhat put together.

I try to keep my face normal—not smile too big, not chew my lip with nerves. The closer I get to Mason, though, the more uneasy I get. He's scratching at his neck, and he seems unsure about something.

"Whatcha need?" I say, my stomach now completely twisted on itself.

"You, uh…you have someone here to see you," he says. I don't like the face he's making, and even though I can't read it, I can glean enough to tell that whatever—*whoever*—is waiting for me on the other side of this door is about to change the course of my day.

"Oooookayyyyy…" I say, looking over his shoulder and then back to his face, trying to get one more read. At first, I see nothing but an empty bar. Maybe it's someone from the school, maybe Max had an issue and the principal stopped by—that's okay, I can work with that. I knew there would be bumps along the way.

I scan both ends of the restaurant area. Nothing. For some reason, not seeing someone is making my worry intensify, and I'm starting to feel sick. I start to move to the main door when Barb arrives and opens it wide. She says, "Hello," and I nod at her with a smile. But that smile lasts only a fraction of a second, because behind her, I catch a glimpse of my guest while the door is closing.

Adam. I haven't seen him since the day he left—more than four years ago. I don't know where he's been, and I've told myself for the last couple of years that I don't care. But right now, more than any urge I've ever felt, I want to run to him, slam him hard in the chest, and knock the life from him—just like he did to me.

Mason

I never liked Adam Price. Oh who the hell am I kidding—I never really gave two shits about him. But now...today...I fucking hate the man. He's smug—he looked smug the second he pulled up in that giant black Chevy Tahoe with blinged-out rims. He had on these expensive sunglasses, and when he pulled them off his face, he actually looked around to make sure people were noticing him. Arrogant asshole!

The only thing I can take comfort in right now is those few words I heard Ray whisper under his breath when he pulled up. "I'm gonna kill that son of a bitch," he said. I may have disappointed Ray a time or two, but he's never wanted to kill me.

I feel so goddamned helpless sitting here in the bar. Ray walked in the second Avery walked outside to talk to Adam. I could tell he wanted to stay with his daughter—have her back. But he also didn't want to pry. He's pacing still, moving from the small window by the front door, to the storeroom, and back again, all the while muttering a choice set of words.

Ray saw him first. He sent me in to fetch Avery, and told me he needed to keep Adam outside, away from Max. Before I left, I heard him lay into the man that was once his son-in-law. He didn't touch him, but his fist was raised. Ray may be an old man, but that fist is experienced—before he used to hire bouncers, he used to take care of funny business at Dusty's himself.

"I'm surprised he didn't just shoot him," Claire says, leaning over me to get her own good look in through the window. I planted myself here the second Avery went outside, and I have no intention of leaving.

"People say I'm the asshole," I laugh.

"No one says you're the asshole, Mason," Claire says, reaching into her purse for her keys. She's keeping Max inside, not letting him leave until his dad—who he probably doesn't remember and hasn't seen in years—leaves.

"Oh, they do. I know *that one* does," I say, tilting my head to the window. Claire looks out again and stares at the conversation happening outside for a while before answering.

"I won't lie. Yeah, you've been the *asshole* a few times for that one. But she's got you in a *whole different* place now. Don't screw it up," Claire's bluntness takes me by surprise. She taps her keys on the counter and pulls her bag over her shoulder before heading over to sit with Max at the booth. He's busy on his iPad, oblivious to the domestic minefield threatening to explode all around him. I should go sit with him, too, but I'm stuck on watching over Avery.

Seconds later, the door swings open, and Avery walks in. She holds her hand up to both Claire and me to tell us she's fine, but it's so clear she's not. Her face is red, and her teeth couldn't be clenched any tighter with a vice grip. She walks straight through the bar into the back, and Claire and I follow.

"Seriously guys, I'm fine," she says, her face buried in her locker. She's rummaging through her work apron, and pulling out old Dusty's shirts, but eventually she just stops, and her entire body slumps forward.

"I can't *believe* that guy! What did he have to say for himself?" I let Claire ask the questions, and just lean against the wall, trying to be barely visible. I probably shouldn't even be in here. This is something best left to her family—and Claire is like family. I'm nobody. But God, do I want to be somebody for her.

"He didn't say much. Said he knows he owes me a lot of explanations. Asked how Ray was doing. Asked about you," she says, swinging her arm toward her friend, her voice shaking and growing weaker with every word. "He…he asked how Max was."

That last sentence leaves her breathless. There are tears in her eyes again when she turns around, and I have to force myself to breathe slowly through my nose so I don't smash a hole through the wall, or worse, race out to the parking lot and hunt Adam down.

"What a prick! Did you tell him he'd know if he had any clue what being a father was?" Claire fires back. Avery just shrugs, defeated, her body shaking more now.

"I didn't say much," she says, biting her lip, trying to conceal her disappointment in herself. I can feel Claire's temper—and I love that Avery has a friend who's so ready to battle for her. But right now, I think Avery needs to know she didn't mess up...that it was okay to not have a knockout brawl with her ex in a parking lot. And I think if Claire keeps going, she's just going to have Avery feeling worse. And I can't have that.

"Well..." Claire starts, but I grab her shoulder, stopping her. She looks at my hand first, then her wide eyes flip to mine, and we have a silent conversation. She gets it, and takes a step back.

"He...uh. He wants to have dinner. I said that was fine. It's fine, right? I mean, I should have dinner with him? See what he has to say?" she's trembling the entire time, and her arms are wrapped around her stomach. I take my turn now, knowing that even if I'm not family, I'm needed. Avery needs me—she needs me *right now.*

"Yeah, it's fine," I say, putting my hand on her shoulder, and the second I touch her, her eyes dart to mine with a look so desperate it breaks my heart. She's terrified, and I would give anything to take that away. But I know I can't.

"Right. It's fine," she nods over and over again, and I mimic her slowly.

"It will be fine," I say, knowing that if it's not—that if that fucker does one thing, says *one thing,* to make Avery not fine, I will mess him up beyond recognition.

CHAPTER 10: JUST DINNER

Mason

I went home with Claire and Avery. There was no way I could stay at the bar knowing what Avery was going through at home. I stayed in the kitchen and watched Claire work with Max, walking him through his folder from school, and explaining what homework is. She's amazing with him—the way he responds to her. It's hard to believe she's working in a bar and not doing this—working with kids like Max—fulltime.

Avery keeps coming downstairs, asking us questions about what she should wear. She finally settles on a pink and yellow dress that ties behind her neck. It's beautiful—she's beautiful. And that dickhead Adam doesn't deserve it.

Avery's nervous—first-date kind of nervous. She's sitting at the kitchen table with us, just chewing her nails, and watching the clock. She's meeting Adam somewhere in town, not wanting him to come near the house—near Max—until she knows more.

When the time comes for her to leave, she stands and walks with Claire to the door, away from Max's view, and gives her friend a hug. I stay in my place at the table, but I catch her eyes, and when I do, she keeps them on mine. I nod slowly, letting her know she can do this—she can handle whatever he throws at her. Her eyes are telling me she can't, but I know she can. And I'll be right here, waiting for her to come home.

I help Claire get Max ready for bed, watching her go through the list with him one item at a time—teeth brushing, pajamas, story time. I ask Max if I can read tonight, and he's surprisingly okay with it.

"You have to read all of chapter eleven. That's where we stopped; it was eleven. Make sure you read eleven," he's very insistent, and it makes me smile. I'm tempted to tease and start with chapter twelve instead, but I know Max isn't someone you can do that with.

"Chapter eleven, The Rules of Gravity," I pause for a second to look over the back and front cover of the book. It seems kind of advanced, and I look at Claire who just shakes her head and smiles, so I get comfortable on the floor next to Max's bed and read on. "Gravity is a natural force that gives weight to an object. It is the force that attracts all heavenly objects to one another."

I read three pages of something that feels more like a sixth grade text book, and I notice the few times I look up at Max, that his eyes are closed tightly, but his lips are saying the words along with me. I can't help but smile at my inner thoughts; knowing how easy science is going to be for this kid. He may have so much to overcome socially, but hell…I would have given anything to understand half the crap I just read. And I'm twenty-five!

When I'm done, we shut off the light, and tiptoe the rest of the way out of Max's door. Max isn't asleep yet; I can tell he's not. But Claire says he'll lie there and pretend until he actually falls asleep—because that's what he's supposed to do.

"I'll stick around, wait for her to get back," Claire says, picking up our plates from the table, and cleaning up the kitchen from our small mess.

"You don't have to. I mean…I'm not going anywhere," I say, unable to hide the guilty grin on my face.

"No band tonight?" she says, dusting away the last few crumbs from one of the chairs before pushing it in all the way.

"Nah. I texted Ben, told him we'd hook up tomorrow night and rehearse," I say, pushing my hands in my pockets and holding my breath, almost like I'm waiting for her to change her mind.

Claire studies me for a few extra seconds, her eyes focused and intense, before giving in. "Okay. I'll call it a night then," she says with a shrug. "If you think you'll be okay."

"I'll be okay. If Max wakes up, I'll just follow his lead," I say, and she pauses to look up the stairs before coming back to me.

"He likes you, Mason. She likes you, too," she says with a certain sense of warning to her tone. I don't have a reply for her, and I don't think she wants one—she wants me to know how Avery feels. For some reason, Claire is rooting for me, and I'll take anyone in my corner that I can get.

I walk Claire to the front door, and flip the porch light on so she can see her way to her car, and so Avery can see her way home. "Remember what I said, Mason," Claire hollers over her shoulder while she opens up the passenger door and dumps her stuff inside.

"What's that?" I ask.

"Don't fuck this up," she says, her smile big, and I hold up two fingers, giving her my scout's honor. *Yeah, I'm a real Boy Scout.*

I don't know what I was expecting when Avery came home. For the next two hours, my emotions pretty much run the gamut, and the longer it takes, the more stressed out I get, until I'm full-on pacing from the kitchen to the living room. I actually pick up a book that's sitting on the coffee table, some stupid romance of Avery's, and I even read a few pages—like I've read a book...*for fun...*ever! I feel like the father of a teenage girl—the way I keep flipping up the blinds with every set of spotlights that come down the road, and when it's finally hers, I can't help but open the front door and stand out on the porch.

"You didn't need to wait up," she scoffs, brushing by me quickly, and heading right up the stairs.

Oh no. This is not happening. I may screw things up a lot, but this time, whatever's up her ass, well...that ain't my fault—it's *his*. I follow her to her door, and catch up to her just as she reaches for the handle, and I pull it first, keeping it shut.

"Mason, I'm tired. I just want to go to bed," she's fuming. Whatever that asshole did, his time will come. But she is not making this about *me* tonight. I step in closer, and force her to look into my eyes, and it takes her several seconds to break away.

"Seriously, Mason. I don't want to talk about it," she says, her voice softer, but not by much. Her nostrils are still flaring, and I can tell she's still angry. She's not going to go to sleep. She doesn't have to talk to me, but she's got to let out some of this stress from this...this...crap deck she's been dealt.

"Come with me," I say, grabbing her hand in mine, and pulling her reluctantly behind me. She tugs in resistance a few times, so I wriggle my hand higher on her forearm to show her I'm not backing down, and eventually she gives in and follows me back down the stairs to the front door, but not without stomping her feet.

"Max is sleeping; I can't go anywhere," she sighs.

"I'm not an idiot; just come out front," I say, leaving her standing on the porch while I run out to my car.

"Wait a second, where's Claire? Did she leave you here...*alone?*" She's shouting at me, and I already know where this is going, and I'm stopping it before it starts.

"She left after he went to bed. Like I said, I'm not an idiot. I can handle watching the house while a child is sleeping," I half yell and whisper, waving my hands over my head while I sift through the crap in my trunk. I'm yell-whispering—*what the hell?* I'm so angry and frustrated right now; I want to kick something, but all I can think about is how I owe this damn girl a kiss, and how *more than anything* I want to give it to her—I want to give it to her right now. But to hell if I'm gonna make her associate my lips with whatever pissed-off juju she's got brewing in that head of hers. And if last night wasn't the right time, right now sure as hell isn't.

I find what I'm looking for, and slam the trunk closed.

"Jesus, Mason! Quiet, you'll wake Max up!" she says, and I can't help but stop in my tracks at her absolutely ludicrous statement.

"Really? You think I'm making a raucous? You don't think *all this* is probably enough to wake up half the damned street?" I say, pointing into the fully lit and wide-open house behind her, then circling her and finally pointing all around us in one big-ass motion.

She slips out a small giggle at first, then she covers her mouth, trying to hold it in, but she can't, and pretty soon she's laughing, full-on belly laughing. *Oh my god, she's laughing. It's the greatest sound ever, and all I want to do is kiss her!*

"You..." I point to her, "are going to *ruin* me woman."

Her smile grows when I say that. I'm not even sure where it came from. I've never given anyone an edge like that; never let them know they have anything—any power—over me. But she laughs like that, one more time, her arms wrapped around her body and her green eyes lit up under the moon, and yeah...I'm ruined.

"Now get down here," I say, and she steps cautiously down the steps, still unsure about me.

"Golf clubs? What are we doing, breaking windows? You want me to drive over to his hotel, take a club to his Tahoe, and go all Carrie-Underwood-song on him?" she asks, but takes the club anyway, gripping it tightly, like a baseball bat, to the point where I start to think she might just beat the hell out of *my* car.

"No, nothing like that," I say, pushing the club back down because, hell, she's making me nervous. I hold up one finger so I can run over to the side of the house. I come back with about 15 Coke cans cradled in my shirt, and I drop them on the ground.

"Shhhhhhh!" she says, all serious at first, but soon her smile creeps in. She's playing with me—this is good, this is the right direction.

I stand a can up on a small steppingstone in the middle of her yard and hold my finger up, like I'm calculating the wind. She laughs quietly, and it's raspy, and it's sexy, and I want to make her do it again. I scrunch up my shoulders, and then crack my neck to both sides to focus on my swing. I line it up like I really know what the hell I'm doing, like *this*—hitting a can with a golf club—is a thing people do.

I take a deep breath, and then I hit the shit out of the can, sending it about 30 feet into the street. I set the next can up for her and move the few pebbles I kicked up out of her way.

"I don't know, I think I need a different club," she jokes.

"I only have two. Got 'em at a garage sale," I say, and she squints at me. "What? You never know when you're going to need a driver and a…lemme see that for a sec? Yeah…a seven iron."

"Well, then I want the driver," she says, reaching for my club. I move it back, playing with her. It's probably not the night to flirt—just a second ago she wanted to murder someone. But I can't help it, and I think it's helping her forget.

"I don't know…this isn't just *any* driver," I say, flipping the club handle over in my hand to read the brand. "It's a Big Bertha…*Big Bertha*? Shit, if I knew they made clubs with names like roller-derby broads, I would have taken this game a whole lot more seriously a long time ago."

She's laughing again, so I give her the club, and her eyes linger on mine for a split second longer than they have all night. Everything about what I'm feeling right now is probably wrong, and I won't take advantage of it—this friction we're both feeling—but there's something there. And I know she feels it, too.

Avery lines up her shot, changing her grip, and bending her knees before wiggling her ass for effect. She's doing it for a laugh, so I do—but all I'm thinking about is her unbelievably adorable ass in that pink and yellow dress. She gets more serious when she moves her arms back to swing, and when she drives the club head through the can, sending it almost as far as mine, she's no longer smiling.

"Give me another," she says. It's almost a command, so I line one up for her and stand back to let her swing. She hits this one almost as far, a breathy grunt escaping when she swings.

"Another," she says, so I do it again, and she swings harder this time.

She finishes every can in the stack, and I run to the side of the house to get her a dozen more—every single one of them she sends to the street. By the last one, she's breathing hard, but she pulls the club back behind her head for one last rip anyhow.

"He's getting married," she says, and I can feel every ounce of hurt she's feeling wash over me while she sends the last can to the curb. She holds the club out and stares at the aluminum carnage for a while longer, and I let her.

"She has two kids, and he's adopting them," she turns to look at me with complete emptiness. She is walking devastation—and I know why. "He wants to waive his parental rights...for Max."

I'm speechless. All I can do is stand there in front of her and mirror the same goddamned stunned face she's making. I want to hug her, pick her up in my arms and tell her she's worth so much more, but my feet are buried in a thick cement of fear and regret. I don't know a single thing I can say that will make this—*any of this*—even remotely okay.

"Can he...do that?" I ask, swallowing hard. My question seems so pitiful, so small, but it's the only thing I can think to say.

"Guess so," she says, shrugging, and looking down at her feet where she drops the club. "He doesn't want *her* to know about him."

I've been in exactly five fights in my life, and I was drunk for every single one of them, but what's raging through my veins right now is so much more powerful than the whiskey from the road. I know in that instant that it's not a matter of *if* I see Adam Price again, but *when*. And *when* I do, I'm going to make sure he's got a permanent mark to carry around to let the world know what a grade-A asshole he is.

If I could get in my car and hunt him down right now, I would. But tonight, Avery needs me, and I don't care if I have to be up all night just to get her to sleep. I'll figure out how to get Max to school in the morning if I have to, I'll make lists and call Claire. I'll do whatever it takes to make that pained look on her face go away, if only for a while.

"You wanna drink?" I say, nodding to the porch behind me.

"Yeah, I do," she says, her lip barely curling at the corner. I wait for her to catch up, and when we both take the first step onto the porch, I feel her fingers against mine, and I grip them hard.

Avery

I told Mason to make us rum and Coke, and I can tell he made it super weak. I might as well sip on cough medicine, but I appreciate that he's being so sensitive. We take our drinks up to his room, and shut the door so we don't wake up Max; the second his door closes my heartbeat picks up its rhythm.

Adam shocked me tonight. He shocked me by showing up in the first place. But as strange as it sounds, what he said didn't surprise me at all. Maybe it's because I wrote his parenting rights off in my own mind years ago, or maybe it's because he was always selfish and worried about what people think.

Adam's words hurt—they hurt to hear because they were about Max. But they didn't surprise me. What *did* surprise me were my instincts. Adam was busy doling out fake apologies, talking about how this is all for the best, and how he'll still pay his child support, but that we have to make it seem like a business venture. And all I wanted to do was run home—to Mason.

"You want me to play something?" his voice startles me.

"Huh? Oh…if you want…I guess," I say, my eyes trained on his fingers, and how they grip his guitar.

"Nah, that's okay. I only thought it might distract you," he says. He starts to put the guitar back on the floor, but I grab his forearm to stop him. When I touch his skin, I hear him gulp, and his eyes flicker to my hand.

"I'd like that. Play something...anything," I keep my voice soft, almost like we're sneaking around. It's barely nine at night, but here behind Mason's closed door, it feels like the wee hours of the morning.

"Anything...hmmmm? Okay, well...I was sort of messing around with this; let me know what you think. I thought I'd play it with the band this weekend," he says, tuning lightly and dampening his strings to play quietly. I recognize the song instantly. It's Otis Redding's "I've Been Loving You." My dad played a lot of Otis records when we were kids, and he and Mason used to play those songs together in the garage. But they never sounded anything like this.

I spend the first half of the song just watching his hands—the way they move, the careful selections they make, and the perfectly timed moments. When he hits the chorus, I'm drawn to his face. His eyes are closed; he's feeling this so much. That's how Mason sings—he feels every word, his lips breathing life into each lyric. It's a song I've heard a thousand times, maybe more, yet when Mason sings, it feels entirely different.

He opens his eyes for the last verse, and I look right into them. I know it's an act—when Mason sings, especially on the stage, he has this power of singling you out and making you feel like he's making this poetry, and it's just for you, and you alone. But tonight, I'm the only one in the room. There's nowhere else for his eyes to go, but I think even if there were, they'd still be here, in this place, with me.

When the song is over, the air feels thicker, and I can tell it's making him uncomfortable. I straighten my legs for a stretch, and then bend my knees to stand, but Mason halts me.

"You don't have to go. I mean...unless you want to. We can talk. We can talk about stupid pointless stuff, I mean. Not the heavy shit," he shrugs and flashes a single dimple that has me back on the floor again.

"Okay. What do you want to talk about?" I ask, grabbing an old sweatshirt I find on the floor, and folding it up into a ball behind my neck.

"Come here," Mason says, moving to the far side of his blow-up mattress and laying back with his arm out. I'm weighing this one, everything inside me screaming for me to curl up into his

104

arms, but this tiny voice warning me not to. "Stop trying to find my damn angle, Avery. I feel bad you're lying on the floor is all."

He's right, so I crawl over to the mattress and slide in next to him, my weight making the mattress bounce and shake like a birthday fun house. "Gee, yeah, Mason. This is so much better than the floor. You're a real gentleman," I joke, and he pokes me in the side.

I kick the straps of my sandals loose from my ankles, letting them fall to the floor. Reaching down for his blanket, I pull it over my knees, mostly because I'm still wearing a dress, and the quilt makes me feel less exposed somehow.

"All right, Miss Abbot. Let's see—why don't you tell me about something I don't know. Like…oh, I know! What's with Max and the planet book? Like, seriously—I learned something from that bedtime story tonight," Mason asks. I love that he's asking about Max, and I love the details he notices about him, like how unbelievably smart he is.

"Okay. Well, it's pretty clear he likes science," I start. I turn my head to face him, twisting my body ever-so-slightly to the side when I do, and I feel his fingers curl around my shoulder blade, almost cradling me—like he's hovering. His barely-there touch sends the tiniest chill down my spine, and I find myself wanting him to hold me harder, and I mentally wish for it.

"We went to the planetarium over the summer, and there's a guy there who runs the show. He's like Max," I pause, waiting for him to understand, and when he nods slowly, I continue. "Max really liked the guy. I think he just liked the way he spoke. There wasn't a lot of fluff, just facts—lots and lots of facts. And when the show was done, Max asked to look at the store. He's usually not interested in things like that, so when he picked out a book, I jumped at it and bought it—all fifty-nine dollars of it."

"Damn, that's a rip-off," Mason says. I laugh in response, and I feel his hand get firmer along my back when I do, and the same chill travels down my body.

"Right. Well, joke's on them, because we've read that thing through, cover-to-cover, forty times. Max has it memorized. We're almost to a buck a read," I smile at my joke, and when I look up, Mason's smiling back, his dimples deep. I want to touch them, so I take my right index finger and reach up to his cheek and softly run the tip of my finger over the divot.

"Uh, that's...different," Mason says, his eyes almost crossed while he peers down at my finger on his face. He's unshaven, and I want desperately to cup his chin with the rest of my hand, to feel how rough it is, but I'm embarrassed enough already, so I pull my hand away and turn my face into him so he can't see me.

"You're dimples are cool. Kinda always wanted to touch them," I say. What the hell, I already violated his face—might as well own up to that one. I can feel Mason chuckle deep in his chest, and then his thumb gently slides back and forth on the bare skin of my shoulder. I. Never. Want. It. To. Stop.

"Your turn. Ask me something. Ask me anything," he says, almost eager for me to want to know one of his secrets. I think about it, and then I spare a glance at his face for inspiration. He's looking straight up at the ceiling, his other arm tucked under the back of his neck, completely at ease.

"The tattoo," I start, and I watch as his eyes close tightly, and he slides his hand forward over his face, almost wincing. He tilts his fingers up just to glance at me, and then he shuts them back over his eyes when he sees I'm watching. "What's the story?"

I've hit a nerve, and Mason Street is actually embarrassed, which only causes me to prop my head up with my fist to look him in the eyes. He laughs lightly when I do, and he turns to face me more, but he leaves his arm under my neck. His fingers are playing with my hair now. I wonder if he knows I can feel it? I don't react, though, for fear he'll stop.

"All right, so I'm on the road with the guys...for like...six months. We started out playing some pretty decent venues, but then it turned into some pretty shitty dives," he looks at me when he says this, probably more embarrassed admitting that his tour wasn't a great success than about the tattoo. I just shake my head, urging him to keep going.

"So, we end up in this nasty old casino in the old part of Vegas. I mean, rooms are being rented by the hour, and there's a guy they call the King of Heroine on one of the floors—that kind of a shithole. Anyhow, me and the guys decide to party with some chicks we meet at the casino; they were in town for a bachelorette party. We start drinking at this rundown club, and this one girl,

106

Teresa, is *really* putting herself out there for me. So we drink more, and then we bring it back to the hotel, and we drink more. And—" he pauses, his lips suddenly getting tight; I prod him with my elbow. "I don't know...are you sure you want to hear this story?"

I nod yes, my smile bigger with every piece he tells, probably because it embarrasses him. For some reason though, my wanting to hear makes him get quieter, and he's staring at me hard. "Okay, I'll tell you. But you have to promise me something..."

His words make me a little nervous, but I say, "Okay," anyhow.

"Promise me you'll still see me the way you do right now?"

I nod *yes* slowly, but without hesitation. I'm in—I'm *deep* into this...this...whatever this is that I am feeling for Mason. And who am I to talk—the girl whose ex just told her he basically wants to hide her existence away, like an offshore money account. Mason has a past—I've seen it. And I don't think this is the story that's going to make my heart do a complete U-turn.

"Okay, well...me and Teresa ended up ditching the room party after some pretty crazy, uhm...stuff," he coughs, and I know he means they had sex. And I know it was a roomful of people. And I'm not surprised Mason was in the middle of it. I don't really like *imagining* it, but I'm not shocked or angry. "We sort of ended up at the chapel. And next thing I know, it's the morning, and we're married."

"Ohhhhh," I start laughing now, uncontrollably, because you hear about rash wedding chapel runs in the movies—I never thought they were real.

"Right? But wait, it gets worse," he says, rubbing his hand over his face at the memory. "Turns out Teresa...was the fiancé!"

"Oh shit!" I'm laughing even harder now, covering my mouth with my hand to stifle the noise.

"We got it annulled, of course. But I'm pretty sure she ended up calling off the wedding. Or the dude did. Never saw him, but she told me he found out," Mason says, nodding at the memory.

"So...how does that fit with the tattoo?" I ask, and Mason takes a deep breath, finally pulling his arm out from under me and sitting himself up a little to pull off his shirt. And I now suddenly could not care less about the tattoo—because he's lying back down, his bare skin right there, touching me, and it's bronze, and it's perfect, and there are abs happening and...*oh my*. I force myself to listen to him even though all I want to do is run my fingers up and down his chest.

"If you look carefully, you can still sort of see it," he traces his finger over a few stripes within the delicate tiger wrapped around his bicep. I don't know what he's pointing at, exactly, but I take the opportunity to study his arm. "Look there...it's her name. I tattooed that chick's full fuckin' name...on my arm! I covered it up with the tiger a few weeks later, but the guys kept calling me Mr. Teresa Westerhouse for months."

It might have been a mistake that put the ink on him in the first place, but damn did it turn into something special. I can sort of see a few of the letters, but even knowing the story now as I do, I don't see her name. I'm probably just a little drunk on the high of being in so much contact with Mason's body—but right now, I'm ready to tattoo anything he wants on mine, just to get closer and to touch him more.

"I think it's beautiful," I let the words slip, and my eyes flair when they do, but I just hold my breath, thankful that from this angle, Mason can't see my face.

"Yeah, well I think *you're* beautiful," he says in an instant, and now my heart is officially in my throat. His hand is back to stroking my hair, and he's no longer trying to hide it, instead, his fingertips start at the very edge of my hairline, lacing deep into the strands, softly brushing them out across my bare shoulder.

When I feel his hand run lower down my neck and pull my head in close, I stop breathing, afraid that I'll do something...say something...that will make him stop. In seconds, his lips are on my head, and I can feel him inhale. My body is telling me to look up, to make a move—to take a leap of faith. But then a familiar light floods his entire bedroom, and time actually freezes.

My dad has driven the same damned pickup truck for fourteen years. The lights cast a very distinctive hue, and when I first started dating Adam in high school, I had it down to a science. The second I saw those lights pour in through the front living room windows, Adam was quickly pushed out the back kitchen door.

"Shit, that's my dad!" I say, practically jumping to my feet and cracking open Mason's door. I step one foot into the hallway,

108

just enough to flip the bank of lights off, and then my dad's keys are at the door. I push Mason back into the room and shut his door again behind us, holding my finger up to my mouth. "Shhhhhhhhhh!" I say, giggling uncontrollably.

I lay my ear flat against the wood so I can hear my dad move through the kitchen, get a drink from the fridge, and kick his shoes off by the stairs. The fourth one creaks as he passes it, and I widen my eyes at Mason, warning him that he's coming. Mason leans forward against me, pressing his own ear next to mine, and we both wait. It's hard to tell, but it seems like my dad is standing at the top of the stairs in the middle of the hall for an unusually long time before he makes his way to his own bedroom. I finally hear his door close, and let out the breath I've been holding, sliding my back against the door so I'm facing Mason.

"Avery, you know we're like...in our twenties, right?" Mason says, his dimples back again. I want to touch them. And now we're inches apart, and his bare chest is right here, up against me, pinning me to the door.

"I know, I just..." I start to explain my craziness, but he stops me.

"I get it. It's your dad. He scares the crap outta me, too. He'd kill me, you know?" he says, raising one eyebrow. His body is still right here—with me...against me. And now, it is all I can think about.

"He wouldn't kill you, Mason," I whisper, half trying to be quiet, and half petrified by the feeling in my chest. Almost as if I've lost control over my own body, my fingers slide up Mason's side. I graze the firmness of his stomach with my thumbs, taking my time to trace along the hard lines of his abs and chest until I'm at his collarbone. I hesitate, the reason-side of my brain questioning everything I'm doing, but then Mason's hands find my wrists, and he holds them in place against him, his feet closing the inches now between us until I can feel every breath tickle my ear.

"You sure about that?" he asks, dragging those words out slowly across his lips. The sound of his voice is different now. It's not flirtatious like before. This sound is deeper, hungrier—it's suggestive and luring, and it's breaking down every defense I have left. My eyes are trained on his fingers, his grip strong around my arms. That's the only barrier I have left, and I know the moment I look into his eyes, I will forever be lost.

I consider every angle, avoiding the choice I want to make—the obvious choice—until I no longer can, and I look up at him to find his eyes waiting. His room is dark, and most of his body is cast in a shadow, but the moonlight traces his face, illuminating his eyes. I know my body is shivering, and I know he can feel it, but he's looking at me like I'm strong, like I'm his equal. His long lashes fall slowly as he shuts his eyes, and his forehead moves to rest against mine.

"I'm battling here, Avery," he says, his voice quiet but rough. "I want to kiss you so goddamned bad. But I told you I'd wait until you were ready. And tonight—"

I manage to free one of my hands from his grip, and I press my fingers to his lips, stopping him from making any more excuses. I linger there, feeling his lips open barely, his teeth grazing against my skin, and the sensation forces my eyes closed too. I will never be ready to kiss Mason Street. I won't be ready, because I've spent a decade training myself to *not* want him. And then, when Adam left me, he crushed my spirit, and my taste for passion went away with it.

But I feel like *this* Mason might be my only chance—and I feel like if I don't let down my guard, just a little, he may never try. I've done regret, and I don't like it.

"Mason, what happened earlier…tonight? That had no effect on how I feel…" I swallow hard, willing myself to say the last few words, "about you."

I didn't think it was possible for Mason's muscles to get any tenser, but they do the second I say that sentence. I force myself to live this moment, to accept it, and I open my eyes slowly to find Mason's reflecting everything I'm feeling back at me.

"Avery…" he says, his breath barely able to complete my name. His hands slide up my shoulders and neck slowly, until they cup my face, urging my chin higher until our noses are touching. We're so close…when he licks his lips, I feel the tip of his tongue barely touch my top lip, and my entire body is on fire, tingling with desire, and begging for his touch.

Every instinct within me is telling me to run, but I push that urge down deep—this time, I let my heart have what it wants.

110

When I feel his warm breath against my lips, I close my eyes tightly in anticipation, but his kiss doesn't come—not yet. I feel his fingers slide back into my hair, his right hand moving to the base of my neck while his forehead is still against mine.

A tiny breath escapes me, and I know he hears it, because the second it does, he moves his other hand to my shoulder and slides his fingers slowly under the strap of my dress, lifting it and dragging the knotted strings down the crest of my shoulder. His nose traces the line from my jaw down my neck until his lips find my bare skin, where he leaves his first kiss—soft, and sweet.

He does the same to the other shoulder, until the only thing holding up my dress is the tightness of the fabric around my breasts. I feel his hands begin to move around my body while his lips work their way along my collarbone, and my pulse is racing with nerves, and want, and fear. He can feel me shake, and just as his fingertips find the edge of my zipper, his lips hit my ear.

"I'm going to kiss you, Avery, and it's going to be the best fucking kiss you've ever had," he says, his teeth pulling on the edge of my ear while he breathes. "But I want to feel your body, too. And this dress...as adorable as it is...is just getting in my way."

All I can do is nod *yes*. I know if I try to speak, the words will fail me. I feel a chill along my spine with every inch Mason lowers my zipper, until his hand glides over the bare skin of my back. Seconds later, the dress falls in a pool around my feet. I'm about to step from it and kick it aside, when Mason's hands lift me to him, gripping my thighs, until my legs wrap around him on instinct.

I'm nothing in his strong arms while he turns me slowly, walking back to the mattress on the floor. Along the way, his hands slide around my hips, and up my ribs, my legs squeezing him tighter to hold myself up, and his thumbs rub softly over the thin fabric of my cotton bra until they find the peaks of my nipples. He rests them there for only a few seconds, and I feel his touch run right through the center of me.

Mason kneels down until my back rests on the mattress and his body is hovering over mine, his lips yet to fully take mine in. I know it's coming, and for a second I have a flash of panic that he's going to back away from me and leave me there alone, embarrassed and rejected. But he doesn't. Instead, his forehead rests along mine again as he pulls my leg up high around him, his fingers teasing to go further, but always staying just along the line of my panties.

Just as I feel I may pass out from all of the near touches, Mason lowers his lips to mine, his kiss at first soft, but growing with need every second, until my top lip is trapped between his teeth. His tongue grazes along my bottom lip, and I reciprocate until Mason can no longer handle it, and he kisses me hard.

His tongue explores every bit of my mouth, tasting me and urging me to do the same. As his hands slide up my leg, his fingers wrap around the band of my panties, and in that moment, my mind is actually begging him to rip them away. Instead, he continues to trail his touch along my body, stopping to feel me just long enough and threaten to take our *kiss* a little further. He slides every finger up and over the hardness of my nipple until I let out a small cry of pleasure, and only then does he break away, lifting himself just enough to look down at me…breathless.

"I want you, Avery. I want every bit of you—you're so goddamned sexy and beautiful and amazing," he says, his tongue held between his teeth while his eyes follow the movement of his hands as they push my hair away from my face and behind my ear. "But I only wanted a kiss tonight. And I know you said you were ready…"

"Mason, I want this. I want you…" I start only to have him stop my lips now with his hand.

"God, I want you to want me. And I think a part of you does…and maybe a month ago…hell, a couple weeks ago? Yeah, that would have been fine. I would have taken that sign, and torn the rest of your clothes away to take you completely…not giving a damn about what it meant tomorrow. But here's the thing. I kinda give a shit about what this means tomorrow, Avery. And I know…I know in here," he says, gripping my hand, and holding it to his chest. "I know tonight isn't the night for anything more than kissing. But holy fuck, was that some kiss."

My entire body is pulsing with need, but my mind is washed with relief, because I know Mason is right. And the more it sets in, the more his words sink in. *Tomorrow.* Mason is worried about *tomorrow*—with me. All I can do is smile, softly and genuinely, as I lift my head to kiss his lips one last time, this time gently.

I don't even ask if I can stay, and instead, reach my arms around his body until he's on his back, letting my head rest in the crook of his arm. Mason strokes my hair slowly, tucking it constantly behind my ear—I think in many ways, keeping his hands occupied until he can calm down himself. And I let him, his lips kissing the top of my head every few minutes, reminding me where I am, until I drift to sleep.

Mason

His Tahoe was easy to spot. There's only one decent hotel this far north, so I took a guess this is where he'd be. I was right. I already walked the perimeter of his SUV—no car seats or girly shit lying on the seat. Not that it means he's alone for sure, but I have a pretty good idea he made this trip by himself if he's so concerned about keeping Avery and Max a secret.

I got here at about five in the morning, just as the sun was starting to show over the peaks. Cave Creek is eerily quiet this time of day—most of the drunks from the bars have long passed out and are off the road; the rich assholes up the hill are not yet out for their jogs. I used to like to sit out on Ray's porch at this time. Things were always...*still.*

This would have been easier if Adam's parents still lived in town. I would have just driven over there and drug his pathetic self out into the street the moment I arrived. Instead, I've been sitting here in the hotel parking lot for the last hour, spitting sunflower seeds out my window. I hate sunflower seeds—you have to work too damn hard just to get to anything worth eating. And they don't even taste very good. I chuck the rest of the bag out the window, deciding I'll be long gone and don't really care if Adam looks like a littering asshole.

My adrenaline kicks in fast when I see his door open; I force myself to breathe in slowly to keep my ass planted here in my seat. He's got a small roller-bag trailing behind him. He's leaving town—I knew he would. He took care of what he needed, got that off his conscience, and he'll let some lawyer deal with the rest.

I've flipped on how to play this about a dozen times, but the closer he comes, the more worried I am that I'm going to miss my chance, so I push open the door of the Mazda and just see what comes out first.

"Hey! Adam, right? Adam Price?" I can see a smidge of recognition cast over him as I step closer.

"Do I know you?" he says, standing at the back of his SUV, and fishing in his pocket for his keys. His preppy sunglasses are dangling from his shirt collar, and I immediately regret not being able to knock them off his face.

"Yeah, Mason...Street. We went to..." he gets it now, I don't even have to finish.

"Right, right. Street! Yeah, you're doing that whole *rock star* thing. I heard some song of yours, I think?" he says. *Fucking poser.* He hasn't heard any of my shit because there's nothing to hear unless you come to a show. He thinks I'm on the goddamned radio because someone from high school probably posted something about me on Facebook once. I just let him believe it, whatever...maybe it will give me an edge.

"Yeah, well...so, you moving back to town?" I know the answer to this question, but I just want to watch him lie. I don't know why, but somehow I feel like it will justify being allowed to punch him in the face.

"Ahhh nah. I was just visiting a friend," he says, almost like he believes it. "I'm heading out now, back to Florida. Getting married...you?"

He's got the hatch open, and part of me wants to bring it down on his head, but I don't. I have to be careful, choose my moment. "Just in the Creek for a few weeks, you know...in between gigs, touring."

He closes the hatch again, and he's tossing his keys in his hands, so disinterested in anything other than himself.

"So you're getting married, then. Huh...that's great!" I fake, my insides about to boil over.

"Yep. She's a single mom, kind of a sad story. But I love her kids, you know?" Everything about what he says makes me want to hit him harder, and I don't know what *one* thing is the worst. I'm so mad, I actually start to laugh, and pretty soon, I'm laughing so hard I have to bend forward from my stomach cramping.

"What's funny?" he asks. Dude's so fucking clueless about what's coming at him next.

"Ohhhh, nothin' man. It's just...you. You are such a goddamned fucking phony!" I speak through my laughter, and I'm pretty sure I sound like a crazy man—exactly what I'm going for. The expression on Adam's face melts from someone having a great day—to a total nightmare—in about a tenth of a second, and that's my cue.

I've got him pushed against the back of his SUV in seconds. His eyes are wide as hell, looking from side-to-side for someone to help, and the fact that he's sweating bullets right now, the moisture literally beading up on his forehead in front of my eyes, has me so fucking happy.

"Wanna know what's funny, Adam? I know a single mom, too. And her story? *Oooooph*—it's *really* sad. Strange thing, though, Adam. You know what makes her story so absolutely fucked up?" he shakes his head quickly, and I swear I think I smell pee dripping down his leg. "You, Adam. You make her story sad. You're an embarrassing man—if I can even call you that. I'm sure you remember, but you have a kid. A *great* kid, not that you'd know, because you haven't seen him since you found out that sometimes being a parent's fucking hard work!"

"Who sent you?" he shouts, his paranoia kicking in now.

"Nobody *sent* me Adam. Like I said, I'm just in town…in between gigs. Taking care of some shit. But I know Ray. And I know Avery. And I've…*been around*…*heard* a few things. And I don't like what I'm hearing, Adam," I grit through my teeth, my forearm still pressed into his chest, all of my weight pinning him in place.

"So we're going to make a slight change in plans. Number one, *you* are going to get on that plane and go back to Florida and never show your face here again. Two, you are going to write Avery a letter, and in that letter, you are going to tell her about what a small human being and giant piece of shit you are. You're going to grovel and apologize and tell her you're going to tell your fiancé about Max. And you're going to do that, too. You're going to do that because real men, Adam? We don't lie. We fuck up…we fuck up a lot. But we don't lie."

He's nodding at me, and I ease up a tiny hair when I realize he's gasping to breathe. Then I continue. "You're going to write another letter. This one is going to be for Max. But you're going to send it to Avery, and she gets to decide when…and even *if* your son ever gets to read it."

"And finally, you're going to keep depositing money into Avery's account. Not just because she deserves it—she deserves

116

ten times the amount you give her—but because Max deserves to get something out of you, too. You're Max's dad, and everyone knows it, but you don't get to be his *father*. So you just go do the right thing, tell everyone the truth, and then stay the hell in Florida."

I give him one good shove as I step away and walk back around to the driver's side of my car, but before I get there, I stop. "And Adam?" I turn to look at his face, and I know he's not moving from that spot for a good hour. "You better do what I said, because I'm a crazy motherfucker, and I'll find you. Have a good flight."

When I smile and slip on my own sunglasses, just to mock him, I feel satisfied. I didn't hit him. I wanted to, but once I started laying out all his dirty laundry? Pointing out every failure? I knew I didn't need to. Sometimes, holding up a mirror to someone's face is a lot more effective than kicking their teeth in. Though, just *one* kick might have been nice.

It seemed like an easy enough thing, when the idea popped in my head in the middle of the night, lying there looking at Avery, so peaceful and small and fragile. I'd hunt down Adam, put him in his place, and make sure he never hurt her again. She's a spitfire, yes—that tiny body can muster quite a punch when it needs to. But underneath it all, she's so damned breakable. I know she hates when I call her *Birdie,* but looking at her, asleep on my arm, her tiny lips barely apart, whispering breath...she's like a hummingbird. Like a beautiful, precious hummingbird, and all I want to do is make sure she gets to the next day, and then the next, and then...

I'm falling for her. And it's making my head all fucked up because I'm going to rehearse with the band tonight, and when I came back to the Creek I had only one mission—get this music shit straightened out, get back on the road with the boys, and cut a new record deal. But then Avery happened. And now, I have this *other* mission, and it sort of hopscotched right in front of the music one the second my lips hit hers. But I don't know...I'm not ready to give up on the other things either. And Avery is...*hard.*

It's late morning, and I know she woke up alone. I hate that. I bet she has a million and half horrible thoughts running through her head right now about me, but I had to slip out of there without waking her. She would have stopped me from talking to Adam. And it needed to be done. If not for her, for me—my anger over what he did was consuming me.

The smell of bacon hits my nose the second I open the back kitchen door, and the crackling sounds like distant thunder. Ray's back is to me; he's standing at the stove, frying up a batch, grease bubbling over the edges of the pan with every snap and pop.

"Making a BLT. You want one?" he says, not even turning around.

"Can you make mine a BL, hold the T?" I say, grabbing a beer from the fridge and popping the top off to drop it into the trash.

"You got it. Coming right up," he says, tossing two more pieces of bread in the toaster. I keep pulling out my phone, trying to think of a way I can ask Ray for Avery's number, some reason I would need it, but my heart literally races to the speed of a Ducati every time I try to speak, so I just put it away.

"Here, bacon's still hot, so careful," Ray says, sliding a plate my direction, and sitting down with his own across from me. "I'm heading over to Dusty's after this. You wanna ride?"

"Nah, that's okay. I'm headin' over to Ben's for a while this afternoon. Rehearsing for Friday," I say, talking while I chew.

Ray just nods, taking a second giant bite out of his sandwich. He keeps looking at me, then back at the bacon and bread in his hand. I can tell he's got something on his mind, but I never know if it's going to be a lecture about the guys or just some interesting thing he heard on the news. Ray's really the only father figure I've ever known, and frankly, sometimes the man makes me nervous.

I can't take the stress of his off and on stare, so I cram the last quarter of my sandwich in my mouth, and take my plate over to the sink so I can run upstairs, grab my shit and head to Ben's.

"Hey, Mace...wanna tell me what Avery was doing leaving your room at about six this morning?"

Fuuuuuuuuuck.

I spare a look over my shoulder, and Ray's still nibbling at his food, taking his time. I thought I was out of the woods when Avery was gone when I got back. I knew if Ray saw how we were— *together*—he'd know something was up. I'm still not looking forward to that—that first interaction after you've been incredibly

118

intimate with someone, especially when you have feelings for her, and there's a ton of shit that's still unsaid. But I'd sprint over to Avery's college right now, pull her out of class, and have a long sit-down talk about our feelings and what happened last night if it would get me out of this moment right here in the kitchen with her dad. This moment…feels like it might kill me.

"What's a'matter there, Mason? Cat got your tongue?" he asks, his temper simmering just under the surface. I say one word out of place, I'm pretty sure he's going to slide that chair back into my shin and turn around to knock out my teeth.

"Ray…it's not…it's not," I'm about to say *what you think*. But I don't know *what* Ray thinks. Hell, I don't know what *I* think! I just know that what happened with Avery last night wasn't about me *getting a piece*. And it's not just a one-time thing. And it's all I can think about.

"It was a long night Ray, and she needed someone…to talk to. We *talked*," I am such a goddamned liar.

Ray slides his chair out and walks over to the trashcan where he leisurely slides the crumbs from his plate. He is eerily calm, and I swear I feel like I'm in some horror movie where the dude is going to jump at me with a knife at any second. I'm careful to keep a good distance between us as he walks closer to rinse his dish.

He hasn't responded to me, not even with as much as a nod or a smile. Nothing. I'd guess that he didn't hear me, but I know he did. We're alone, in a quiet kitchen. Part of me thinks he likes watching me squirm like this. Fine—let him make me squirm. Whatever it takes to keep him from knocking me on my ass.

"When was your last long-term relationship, Mason?" he says, still not looking me in the eyes. This is awful, and with every word he says, the more miserable this conversation becomes. But it's inevitable; at least, it is if I ever want to kiss Avery again. And I do. I've never wanted anything more. But this answer I'm about to give isn't going to help.

"I don't know…high school, I guess," I say, knowing that the longest I was with any one girl in high school was about a month—and that was only because she didn't want to break up before we won homecoming king and queen.

"High school," he nods to himself. He chuckles lightly under his breath, shutting his eyes and shaking his head while he dries his hands on the towel. "High school, Mason. You were a kid. And I gotta tell you something—high school doesn't count."

I don't respond, because he's right.

"Mason, Avery was married. And the guy walked out on her. When she needed a man, he turned out to be a boy," his eyes are on mine now, and my stomach feels like it's full of rocks.

"No offense, Ray, but Adam is a douchebag," I say, feeling like I need to stick up for myself. I may be a fuck up, but I'm not Adam Price. I don't run from people when they need me. Of course, no one has ever needed me before.

"You're right, Mason. He is, and you're nothing like him," Ray says, and I feel like I can breathe for the moment. I don't know why that man's opinion of me matters so much, but it does—and now that Avery's in my head, too, it feels like it matters more.

"But here's the thing...I'm not going to live forever. I know, it's a shocker," he jokes, rubbing his hands around his giant belly. "But seriously, Mason. There is going to come a day where my baby girl...she's going to be alone. And what life has put on her plate—well, it's a heavy load. And she needs a partner, someone to help her carry it. But you can't drop things on her when times get tough. And you can't choose something else first, because Avery and Max—they get to be first. They have to be. Because if they're not Avery will fall apart."

I know everything he's saying. It's the debate doing ten rounds in my head right now. I know Avery needs someone, and I know I've only been around a couple of weeks, and everything sputtering in my chest right now is all new and warm and honeymoon shit. But I also know I've never wanted to be anywhere more...not even the road. And I've never wanted to be someone's *someone*. But damn do I want to be her *everything*.

"I get it, Ray. And I won't be reckless. I promise," I say, holding his gaze, which is intimidating the hell out of me, but I suck down that fear and hold it anyway, pushing on. "But just so you know...it's not like Avery is just some girl to me. Your house...it was always more of a home to me than my own home. And Avery—she was a part of that. I might see her differently now, but I've always seen her. She's always been home."

Ray bites at his bottom lip, his eyes lowered and cautious. "Mason, I have always thought of you as a son. I hope you know

120

that. And I'm glad that you feel that way about being here. But Avery has always seen you as more. I'm not naïve; I know when my daughter loves someone. You just make sure that if you decide to open that door—to her *and Max*—that you're ready for everything on the other side."

There's nothing but silence after he speaks, and he doesn't stick around long enough to hear any more of my thoughts. I know he's not really interested. And I know that it would probably make Ray rest a lot easier if I put on the brakes, finished out this little *stint* here at home, and headed back out on the road, without starting something new with his daughter. And maybe my life would be a whole hell of a lot easier, too. But I'm starting to wonder if it would be worth it? Any of it? Without...*her*?

CHAPTER 12: LEARNING HOW TO DO *THIS*

Avery

Everyone is looking at me like they all know. The girl in front of me in class kept turning around and smiling. I think she sensed my mood—I feel ridiculous that I thought last night was anything more than it was.

Before I woke up this morning, alone in Mason's bed, I was dreaming. My subconscious actually went to the place where Mason and I are some happy couple, moving into our first house *together*, picking up Max from school *together*, going to the grocery store *together*. Then I woke up—alone. He didn't even leave a note.

I thought about calling him. I programmed his number from my dad's phone when I left this morning to take Max to school. I thought about calling him all the way to my class. Then I thought about calling him during my drive back to Max's school. I'm still fuming, and the closer we get to Dusty's, the more I want to take one of those golf clubs to his headlights—and then his head.

"Is Mason going to be at Grandpa's?" Max asks from the backseat. His question has me so baffled—I almost drive off the road. Max doesn't look forward to people. He looks forward to earning *things*, like game time or his next chocolate milk. He's never once asked about seeing his grandpa or Claire. Why *Mason*? And of all days to ask, I swear he's intuitive.

"I don't know, Max. I think he has rehearsal with his band," I say, secretly hoping Mason's car is in the lot when we pull in—for Max's sake, of course.

Max doesn't respond, but instead, continues to move his finger around the iPad in the backseat. I've gotten used to the one-sided conversations with Max—once he gets the information he's looking for, he's done. It's something we're working on, closing out conversations and taking an interest in what other people have to say. I tell myself that's why I'm about to ask him the question I'm about to ask.

"Why do you want to see Mason?" I ask, my eyes darting around the parking lot as we pull in. His car isn't here. *Damn.*

Max doesn't answer, which isn't anything unusual, except usually he's *not answering* my question about how he enjoyed class, or therapy, or a visit with one of his doctors. And I should care about those answers more than I do this one—but I don't.

When I park, I take off my seatbelt and turn completely around in my seat so I can face Max. "Did you hear me, Max?" I ask, his eyes moving rapidly around the surface of the iPad, his body language completely tuning me out.

I put my hand on the screen to distract him, and he jerks it away, continuing to play whatever game he's working on. I am walking a fine line right now, and I know I could have kicking and screaming in seconds if I'm not careful; I reach again for the iPad. I don't block it, but I put a small amount of pressure on it with my finger, tilting it just enough to distract Max, and I ask him again.

"Max, you can keep playing this as soon as you answer my question. Why do you want to see Mason?" I ask, my breath held, and my inner voice praying he just answers. I can see his breathing picking up, and I can tell he's frustrated. His finger keeps moving around the iPad, but I know he's having a difficult time seeing the screen at the angle I have it. His frustration is building, and I'm about to give in...

"I need him to teach me something," he says, and I let go of the iPad, and he continues on with his game.

"Okay, well I'm sure he will be around later," I say, getting my things and stepping out of the car. I wait outside his door, not opening it, for a few seconds, just looking at him through the window—watching him live in his own little world. I know he didn't say he wanted to *hang out* with Mason. Mason has something he wants, and that's what Max is focusing on.

But what he said still scratches at me. Max has never asked to learn something from *someone.* He's resourceful—he answers most of his own questions with the help of YouTube. But he used the word *need* just now. He said he needed Mason. I keep playing it over and over in my head, and it both thrills me and terrifies me at the same time.

I don't have a poker face. It's a skill I always wished I possessed, especially with Claire. She doesn't have much of a filter. So basically, I'm an open book for her to analyze without punishment. She's on to me the second I walk in, and I know I only have a few minutes before she's at the lockers with me, swapping shifts.

"What happened? Adam wants you back, doesn't he?" she asks. It's funny how far from the center of my anxiety she is. Under any other circumstances, my dinner with Adam last night would have been enough to wreck me for days. But then I kissed Mason. And slept in his arms. And he left without saying a word this morning. And somehow *that's* the part I don't want to talk about. So I go with her lead. Yeah, let's be angry with Adam for a while.

"He's getting married," I say, knowing that will be enough to set Claire off. I'm right, and she spends the next ten minutes swearing and questioning, getting bits of answers from me at a time until she has the entire story. I let my friend be angry, and I love her for it. I listen to her say all of the things that went through my head—and the entire time, I think about Mason.

"What are you going to do?" she says, and her question jolts me back. I haven't really thought about it, not that there's much to do, so I just shrug.

"I have to think about things," I say, turning to walk back into the bar. Claire follows, and I can hear her muttering behind me. My dad is at the bar, so I head his way to help him dry glasses and get ready for the night crowd. I give Claire a knowing glance, and thankfully she picks up on it. I'm not ready to have the *Adam* conversation with my dad yet, so she quickly changes subjects.

"So, when's Mason coming in," she asks, and for some reason my heart skips, like she hit an open nerve. I stare at the glass in my hands—shining and drying, and hoping like hell my friend doesn't start exploring *this* topic instead.

"He's rehearsing with the guys. Probably won't see him tonight," my dad says, kind of gruffly. He grabs an empty bin, leaving me there to finish the rest of the glasses alone.

"Uh oh, looks like Mason pissed your pop off," Claire teases. I keep my stare on my work and raise my brow a little with a shrug. It's not the best acting, but please let it be enough.

Claire heads to the corner to talk with Max, getting him ready to take home. I finally breathe now that her spotlight is gone. I

124

don't know what I'm doing. I'm letting Mason consume me, and all the while, I have this unbelievably enormous *other worry* that I should be tending to. Adam is getting *married*, and he basically wants to disown Max.

Max never asks about his dad. He doesn't remember him, and I don't bring him up. It's probably not the best parenting. But, I have thought this through a thousand times. Max's therapists don't really see the value in me having a conversation with Max about Adam, and over the years, the topic has just faded into nothingness. I had a worry in the back of my mind that one day Adam would just reappear and want to be a part of Max's life. But now...

"I'm pretty sure that one's dry now," I hear Cole's voice over my shoulder.

"Oh, yeah. Sorry, lost in my thoughts there," I smile, and move on to the next line of glasses.

"So, your dad's pretty much been in a shit mood all morning. Adam bring that on?" Cole asks, tentatively. He's never been very nosey. In fact, it took him months to ask about Max's autism.

"Probably. Dad is possibly the only person who hates Adam more than I do," I laugh. It's true, though; I'm honestly surprised my father didn't sock Adam in the jaw yesterday.

Cole nods at my answer and lifts the last bin of glasses up on his shoulder to carry to the back. "Well, maybe we can make Mason deal with him tonight then," he says. I freeze, unable to follow the line of his sight to the front door where I *know* Mason has just entered.

I'm hyperventilating. I can feel my ears filling up—the few sounds in the bar muffled by the oncoming panic attack. I'm going to pass out if I don't do something, so I crouch down behind the bar and sit with my knees pulled up by my chin, forcing myself to take in deep breaths. I can't believe this is happening—I've survived so many more stressful situations, and this one...*this one...*is the one that's going to take me off my feet? I can hear Ben's laugh—his cackle—and it makes my entire body wash over with a wave of nausea.

I lie down completely now on the slip pad on the floor, my knees bent, and my forearms draped over my head. *This is not happening!* I can barely hear their voices, but I know the entire band is here. I bet they spent the afternoon listening to Mason talk about me, and how *easy* I am.

"Avery? What the hell, you're on the floor!" Claire says, a little louder than I would have liked.

"Shhhhh, just shhhhh!" I say, waving my arm over my head. "I'm fine. Got dizzy. Please, don't draw attention to me."

She comes over to sit next to me on the floor, and puts a towel filled with ice on my head and neck. The coldness shocks me a little, but I'm suddenly hearing again and the room is no longer closing in on me.

"Thanks," I say, wincing at her.

"You should go home. And you shouldn't drive. I can get Max, let me go get him from Mason," she says, and I react by grabbing her arm—my fatal error. Claire's eyes narrow on my grip, and I can see her piece everything together in seconds, and all I have left is my ability to beg.

"Oh. My. God!" she says, again, louder than I'd wish. "You…and Mason!"

"Claire, I'm begging you. Pleeeeeeease!" I whisper roughly, pouring on my best pleading look—hoping she has some line drawn somewhere in her mind that sets off when she's making her best friend uncomfortable.

"I just need the bare minimum," she asks, smirk on her face. She's bribing me—only this time, instead of dirt on someone else or some cute new guy at the bar, she's strong-arming me for embarrassing details about myself.

"We…kissed," I say, keeping it very vague. When her face lights up, I know I've given her enough. But I also know I'll be spilling everything soon.

Claire stands back up and continues to act naturally at the bar, looking down at me every few seconds while I work to sit up and get to my feet.

"Where is he?" I ask, now sitting with my legs crossed and my eyes right at Claire's knees.

"He's still over in the corner, with Max," she says. I take a giant big-girl breath and smooth out the loose strand in my hair. I was banking on the few extra minutes alone to really get my legs back, and to figure out whether or not I want to be angry or coy, but he's already spotted me and is headed my direction.

126

"You're here," he smiles, like nothing's wrong. Of course I'm here; I'm always here. *Jackass.*

"Yep," is all I say. All that time stewing, all of those pretend conversations, giving him a piece of my mind, and that's the best I can do. *Yep.* At least I was short, and I can tell he knows I'm pissed.

"Come with me," he says, grabbing my hand faster than I can pull it away, and walking me around to the front of the bar. I'm expecting him to walk me outside so we can talk about what a *mistake* last night was privately, but instead, he stops in the middle of the restaurant, pulls out a chair, and proceeds to climb on top of it, reluctantly letting go of my fingers. My brain is telling me now would be a good time to run, but my heart is literally drumming in my throat, and dizziness is threatening again.

"Excuse me, everyone! Guys? Hey, can I have everyone's attention?" he's yelling, waving a hand over his head. The bar isn't Friday-night kind of crowded, but there's a good amount of people here—at least thirty or forty—and they're all looking at the unshaven man with the mortified girl standing below him. Just to be sure everyone is watching, Ben stands on a table at the other end of the room and whistles with his fingers.

"I got your back, buddy," Ben winks and holds up a bottle of beer.

"Thanks, man!" Mason says, his smile huge. He's loving this—whatever *this* is. "You all know Avery here, right?"

A couple of whistles have my face absolutely burning with embarrassment, and I cover my face with my hand, staring at my feet.

"She's cute when she's shy, isn't she?" he says, and somehow I know I am now even redder. Oh my god, what is he doing?

"Well, I appreciate y'all indulging me here, but I just wanted to let you know that I like her. I like her...*a lot*! And we haven't really talked this out yet—" he says, then leans down to whisper to me, "I'm sorry I wasn't there this morning. I had something important."

He stands back up to continue, but keeps his eyes on mine, holding our gaze with a serious look before letting his dimples slide in place again. My heart has literally stopped. My eyes are

127

wide, and the words Mason is saying have me wanting desperately to smile—but shock has taken over everything.

"Anyhow, I just wanted to make sure my intentions were clear. I've got some work to do with this one, so I wanted to make sure the story was straight from the get go. I like Avery Abbot, and I'm going to work my ass off to make her like me back. So no hitting on her and messing up my *thing*, got it?"

He points right at his band mates sitting in the corner. They all raise their beers, jokingly crossing their hearts. By the looks on their faces, I can tell what Mason did surprised them, and something deep inside me is waiting for them to start laughing, for the joke to end—the punch line. But it never comes.

Mason jumps down from the chair, his black work boots making a heavy thud on the floor. I manage to find Claire's face in the background over his shoulder. I think she may be cheering, but everything is happening in a blurry slow motion, so I can't really tell. Mason isn't moving away, but instead, he's reaching for my hand, pulling me closer to the tight gray fabric of his T-shirt that is hugging his arms and chest.

In seconds, his hands are cradling both sides of my face, his fingertips pushing into my hairline, and then his lips are on me hard. He's kissing me so wildly, he's moving me backward until he reaches behind my lower back, pulling me close, leaning me with his force. I give in instantly, my body betraying my mind's warning signs, and I grip at his back, holding fists full of his T-shirt in my hands.

His lips are everything they were last night, everything they were in my dream. His kiss is firm, commanding—he is definitely in charge, and I'm following, willingly. He smells of the most unbelievable spices, and with each inhale I'm kissing him harder, suddenly drunk on his scent.

He sucks in my top lip, holding it hostage in his mouth for a few long seconds, his hands holding me close to him, almost like he's afraid something will take me away if he lets go. When he finally releases his hold on my mouth, we're both breathless, our foreheads pressed together while we cling to one another. I'm lost in this moment, content to just stand here, when another whistle forces my eyes open, this one from Claire.

128

"I'm so sorry I wasn't there this morning," he whispers, still holding me close. "I wanted to be, but there was something...something very important...that I had to do. I can't tell you, but I'm asking you to believe me...to trust me. I know I've got to earn everything with you. And I will, Avery. I will. I meant every word of that. I like you...I *more* than like you. So maybe we can start with that?"

My tongue is numb, and my face is still tingling from his touch. I can feel the moisture forming in the corners of my eyes, and I desperately don't want to cry, but I know I'm going to tear up any second now. I just nod *yes* to him, because I like him too. I *more* than like him. But I'm also not ready for him to hear any of that yet. That's...going to take time.

CHAPTER 13: BOXES

Mason

"You dog, you bagged Birdie, didn't you?" Ben says as soon as I get back to the table to join the guys. He's so loud I know Avery heard him. She ducked back into the kitchen as soon as everyone's attention left us, and I saw Claire tail after her. She'll be back there for a while. She looked like she wanted to kill me for my grand display...but she also smiled, so I got what I wanted.

"It's amazing that you don't have a girlfriend," I say, taking a drink of my beer and doing my best to ignore the three sets of eyes staring at me from the other side of the table.

"Fuck you, I have a shit ton of girlfriends," Ben says, punching me in the arm hard enough to make my beer slip from my mouth and dribble down my chin. I punch him back, and he holds up his fists like he wants to go, but he starts laughing right away, then flips me off.

"Dude, you've been home for like, what...two weeks? Who's this Birdie chick?" Josh asks.

"First off, like I said, don't call her *Birdie*. She hates that name, and I lo—really like this girl. So don't be a bunch of assholes to her, okay?" I say, my heart racing with what I *almost* said. Fuck, do I *love* Avery? Josh is right, it's only been a couple of weeks. But I've also known her my entire life, and I kind of feel like maybe I missed out on something a long time ago.

"She's smokin' hot!" Matt pipes in, his attention on me just long enough to add his approval, and then he's quickly distracted by some brunette at the next table.

"Yeah, she's smokin' hot, all right," Ben says, leaning back and folding his arms over his chest while he studies me. "You've known Birdie forever. What's this new...*thing*?"

"I don't know," I shrug him off, pissed that he's still calling her Birdie. I don't really know how to answer him. All I know is something clicked, and I just see her a whole hell of a lot differently now. I know it won't make sense to the guys, but I don't really care.

"Hmmm, a'right then. She's not coming to rehearsals and shit, though," he says, pointing a finger at me like some tough asshole. I just roll my eyes and shake my head at him, not too worried about Avery ever wanting to hole up in the basement while me and the guys pick apart each other's playing.

I nursed two beers and picked at a grilled cheese for about an hour, just killing time until Avery's shift was done. The guys hung around for a while, but eventually, they all headed over to Ben's to watch the game. I could tell Ben was ticked off I didn't go with them, but he'll get over it. How many times has that dickhead blown me off for a girl?

I thought about going home early, hanging out with Max, but once he asked me what three-four time meant in music, he was back in hyper-focus mode on his iPad. So I waited, and then I took off for the house when I heard Avery saying goodnight. I didn't want to look like I was following her, but who am I kidding. I've been dying to get her alone. And I feel like a damned stalker sitting here in the driveway.

The way I see it, I have two choices now—get out of my car as soon as she turns her engine off and scare that crap out of her, or duck, wait for her to get inside, and then crawl into the house later, hoping she doesn't notice. Both are bad ideas, so I kick open my door just as she kills her lights, and wave my hands over her head to try to get her attention.

"What are you, my escort now or something?" she sasses. She's trying to keep that same front up with me, but she's having a hard time now, and I can see the smile creeping into her lips.

"Escort. Stalker. Take your pick," I say, moving closer to her. Surprisingly, she lets me walk up to her until my hands are locked with hers. Ray's not home, won't be home for hours. Claire is here, and it's early, so I know Max is still awake, but we have this little window of time here…outside…before anyone realizes we're home.

"So that was some stunt you pulled today," she smirks, and I move in even closer, pressing my forehead to hers.

"Yeah, you liked it," I tease. She bites at her bottom lip and the smallest giggle slips out. I kiss her in response. Not hard, just a quick peck.

"I did," she says, all breathy and sexy. I don't know who this girl is—she's a far cry from the one who wanted to knee me in the groin a week ago—but my god do I like her. "It's early, and Max is up. I have to get inside."

"I figured. I just wanted to catch you—you know, before your dad beats the shit out of me later?" I wince and put my arm around her to walk inside.

"Oh wow, I didn't really think about that. Yeah, Dad's going to kill you," she laughs. I'm smiling at her, but I know deep down Ray's not real happy about this. And I get it—I understood everything he said this morning. I even thought about killing it all right then and there, just chalking it up to high emotions and an innocent mistake. But the thought of not kissing Avery again—or of seeing her kiss someone else—made my stomach hurt.

I pull my arm away as soon as we get inside, giving a wink to Claire before I head upstairs. "Mason Street, you and I are gonna have words, mister!" she yells at my back. I just wave my hand. I know she just wants to get details, and probably give me her own version of Ray's warning, and she can do that—*tomorrow.*

Max is working at the small desk in Avery's room, his feet kicking wildly underneath. I walk over to the door, but he never looks up.

"Whatcha working on, Max?" I've learned that if I use his name it helps get his attention. Claire taught me that.

"I have to fill in every box for my teacher. I have to turn this in tomorrow," he says, his fingers gripping at the edges of the paper like he wants to crumple it or tear it into pieces. I'm careful, but I move in a little closer so I can see. It's an oversized paper, and there are a few boxes with some sparse color in them.

"Mind if I take a look?" I ask, and he kicks back from the desk, his eyes still on the paper in front of him. I turn it, just enough to read the words. It's a family tree, and it's asking him to draw pictures of his mother, father, and friends. Max has only one small stick figure in each—the same drawing over and over. *Shit!*

He pulls himself in and starts to draw backgrounds and scenes in each box, coloring carefully. They all look kind of the same, just different colors, and I've never felt sadder seeing something than I do right now.

"Can I help...maybe give you some ideas, Max?" I swallow hard. I don't know how this works—I don't know if Max is the kind of kid you can give ideas to. I know he's good at asking questions.

"Claire says I have to make sure everything is colored, and work on this until 7:15 p.m.," he says, continuing to color, his hand moving more quickly now. I just stand behind him, rubbing my hand over my neck, trying to find a way to talk to him, to fill in those goddamned empty boxes.

"Okay, well, what if you fill in one of those boxes with me?" I say, hoping like hell he doesn't just rip the paper in half at my lame suggestion. When he doesn't protest, I keep going. "I mean...you and I...we're friends, right? So, if you draw me next to you, that's one more box done."

He seems to like my idea as he reaches for a blue crayon and adds a tall stick figure next to his. "Why am I blue?" I ask, a little curious.

"You wear jeans a lot," he says, and it makes me laugh. Everything Max says is slow, but he never seems to have any problem talking. And he's funnier than people give him credit for.

"You're right. I do wear jeans a lot. Blue is the perfect color," I say. "Now, how about your mom in that box? What color is she?"

When Max picks up the pink, I don't even question it. It's perfect—fragile, feminine but bold, just like his mother. He's busy working on the mother's box while I'm staring at the father's one—suddenly stuck, and wanting to punch something. I should probably call downstairs for backup, but I feel like this would just hurt Avery, and open up a wound that so far she's been good at ignoring.

Then an idea strikes me. "Everyone in the house has a box except your grandpa. How about we give him that one? He's a dad—he's even a grand dad, so it's like he fits the question in two ways."

I hold my breath the entire time Max finishes coloring Avery's box; when he reaches over for a brown color and starts to draw Ray without even saying anything to me, I almost pass out from the lack of oxygen. The clock says 7:12 p. m., and I've never been so happy to see a deadline approaching.

"Three more minutes, Max, and you're done. I'm going to go do my homework now, okay?" I say, and Max just keeps coloring, silently.

I back out of the room, and turn to head to mine, only to see Avery's back flat against the wall, her fingertips over her lips and a single wet stream down her cheek. I don't know what to say, so I just pull her into my arms and hold her, letting her quiver silently for the next three minutes. When she hears the timer go off on Max's desk, she backs away and mouths, "Thank you," to me. I pull her head forward to my lips to kiss the top before heading into my room and shutting the door behind me.

That was exhausting—a different kind of exhausting. I don't know if I did the right thing, and I don't know how Avery has lived *this*. It's not Max's autism—it's the enormous hole Adam left behind *and* Max's autism. How do you explain to any kid that their parent, one-half of who they are, just couldn't hack it? I know my mom never really explained it to me.

I can hear the water running, and cabinets opening in the hall, so I know Avery's getting Max ready for bed. I'm completely amazed by her. Nothing is easy, everything is so fucking hard—it makes me feel foolish for thinking I have ever deserved anything at all.

When the water stops, I decide to spend a little time on the guitar to clear my head. Maybe part of me is hoping Avery will hear it and follow it into my room. Yeah, that's exactly what I'm hoping.

I don't really like the Beatles. I know everyone says you're supposed to, and I appreciate some of the risks they took, but they just have never really been my *fit*. I'm more of a blues lover, and gritty classic rock like the Stones. But for whatever reason, all my fingers can seem to play tonight is "Blackbird" by the Beatles. That song has always made me think of Avery; it's kind of where I got the nickname *Birdie*. I must play it six or seven times before she finally cracks open my door and slides down to sit against the frame, her knees barely covered by the long T-shirt she has stretched over them.

"You still doing *this*?" I say, nodding my head in her direction, pointing out that she's still in the hall.

"You used to play that all the time. I love that song," she says, and it makes everything inside me feel warm...right. I smile and finish out the last verse, taking my time and improvising a little on the chorus to make it last just a little longer.

"That song always made me think of you," I say, putting my guitar away and purposely not looking at her when I admit it. "That's where Birdie comes from...sorry."

"I wish you told me that. I probably would have liked Birdie then," she says, her smile soft, but still so damned cautious.

"I think we're past you needing to keep the door open," I laugh, hoping like hell she'll come closer so I can touch her. She slides up to her knees and crawls inside, shutting the door behind her, and then sitting with her back against it.

"I'm a terrible mom," she says, her face suddenly full of pain. I hate Adam for doing this to her.

"No you're not," I say, forcing her to look at me, rather than the nothingness she keeps trying to go to.

"I'm not?" she asks, her breathing growing harder. "My son probably thinks his father is dead. Not that I'd know, because I'm such a chicken shit that I've opted to pretend he never existed. I haven't said Adam's name out loud in front of Max once since the day he left."

Her eyes are full of water when she talks, and I would give anything to fix this guilt she's feeling. I don't think she's earned it—any of it.

"My dad left us when I was five," I say the only thing I think might make this better for her. Her eyes shift completely to me when I do, and her breath hitches. I can't take the intensity of her stare along with the weight of the story I'm about to tell her, so I lie back and look up at the ceiling instead.

"I don't remember much. He had a beard...*I think*? I had a baby brother. He died when he was maybe two or three weeks old," I say, and when Avery gasps I stop her. I'm not telling her this to make her feel sad. I'm trying to make her feel less alone.

"It's okay. Your dad knows, but we don't talk about it much. I don't expect people to know about it. I was five when he died. Mom was really sick. I know now she was depressed, but it just looked like the flu to me...you know...from a kid's eyes?" Avery is holding herself tightly, her arms wrapped around her body. "My dad—his name was Mitch—he didn't know how to deal with my mom. He was a truck driver, and he used to be on the road for days. Then one day, he just never came home. Mom doesn't talk about it. And I don't ask. What good would it do?"

"Do you...ever wonder about him?" she asks, her voice cracking.

"I'm not gonna lie. Yeah, Avery. I wonder about him. But I wonder about him less and less every year he's gone. I'd give anything to be able to disconnect from it a little, too—like Max does," I say, and her eyes flash wide for a brief second from my honesty. "You're not a bad mom. You're an amazing mom—an unbelievable mom. Hell, Avery, you're pretty much the best damn human being I've ever met. So please, quit doubting yourself."

I hold her stare for minutes after that. I haven't talked about Mitch for years—and I'm pretty sure I was drunk with Ben the last time I did. I'm pretty sure I was drunk every single time I ever talked about my father. But Avery needed to hear this, and for some reason, I want to tell her things.

The lights flood my room, and I think if they didn't, we'd both be happy to sit here, with ten feet of air between us, just staring into each other's eyes. Avery looks up at the ceiling and takes a deep breath, drawing her legs in close to her body so she can stand. I sit up and walk to where she is at my door, knowing she's going to leave because Ray's home. But before she goes, she pauses and stands on her tiptoes to reach my lips, holding both sides of my face with her cold, tiny hands, and kisses me softly. My body wants to push the door closed behind her and pull her to my bed, but I don't. I let her leave. And I hope like hell she comes back.

Avery

I couldn't wait to show my dad the drawings Max made. I think more than wanting him to be touched by the fact that Max put him in the father box, I wanted him to know that Mason helped Max through something difficult. My father has always been protective, and when Adam left, he stepped right back into his role of guardian.

He was still in a foul mood when he came in the back door, heading right to the fridge and cracking open a beer. My father doesn't drink a lot—part of his creed in running a bar, he says. So when he does, I know he's feeling stress.

"Hey, you're home early," I say, my voice quiet enough so Mason doesn't hear upstairs.

"Uhhh, yeah," my dad grunts, kicking his boots off at the back door, and pulling all of his things from his pockets into one loud pile on the counter. He's doing that thing where he barely makes eye contact with me, like he did the first time he ever caught me kissing a boy.

"I wanted to show you what Max made tonight," I say, hoping this will pull him out of his funk.

"Let's see," he says, breathing deeply. It's Max, and he always takes Max seriously, giving everything about him his full attention.

I open up the folded poster to show him the various pictures; I can see him scratching at his chin, trying to figure everything out. When realization of who everyone is hits him—he breathes hard and heavy.

"He put you in the father's box. I thought that was pretty cool," I say, placing my hand on his shoulder and squeezing. When he puts his hand on mine and holds it hard, I know he's breaking down a little, so I stay still and let him have his moment.

"That…that one's Mason, huh?" my dad says, pointing to the friend box.

"Yeah. Mason, uh…actually helped him with his homework," I say, and my father just nods. "I overheard them. He didn't want Max to be in any boxes alone."

"What did Adam want?" my father asks, not even transitioning. His question jars me—I'm unprepared to answer, so I stammer, which only makes him get anxious. "Did he do something to you Avery? I swear to God, I'll kill that punk."

"No, Dad. No…I just wasn't ready to talk about this with you," I say, all strength completely draining from me. I sit in the chair next to him and look down, ashamed of what I have to tell him. "Adam's getting married. He, uh—"

"That little shit!" my dad's hand comes down hard on the table, and in seconds Mason is behind him at the end of the stairs. I meet his eyes and try to signal to him that this isn't about him, but I think he knows.

"There's more, Dad," I say, keeping my eyes on Mason for strength. He steps down to where my father can see him now, and moves over to join us at the table. When he does, I can see my father instantly tense up. I don't know if this is the best idea, but I want Mason here. I *need* him here. "He wants to sever his parental rights—basically disown Max. He's hiding him from the new girl."

The beer bottle flies across the kitchen fast, crashing into the back door and shattering into hundreds of wet pieces. It scares me, even though I know my father isn't angry with me. He's on his feet fast, tossing the chair to the floor behind him, and going to the counter immediately for his keys.

"That son of a bitch!" he yells, turning and pointing at me. "He can't do this, Avery. He's not going to do that to you…to Max!"

He's out the door, swinging it so hard the deadbolt dents the inside of the wall. I can't help but cry, and I reach to fold up the picture again, wishing I never came down in the first place.

"I got this," Mason says, following my father's footsteps outside. I had almost forgotten he was here for all of that, and I start to protest to stop him, but I think more than me, my dad needs Mason now.

It takes me a while to find the dustpan. We're not one of those families that clean the house often—other than vacuuming and picking up clutter. I spare a peek out the back window and see

Mason talking emphatically with his hands, my father's hands stuffed in his pockets while his feet kick at the ground and his eyes stare at the dirt. I want Mason to get through to my father, to calm him. More than that, I want my father to trust Mason—like I've grown to.

The pain shoots up my arm quickly, and when I look down, there's blood all over my hand. I move to the sink fast to get the cold water running, grabbing for the dishtowel to wrap it around my hand. I was being stupid, not looking at the glass shards on the floor. The cut is deep, and the pain stings; the blood isn't really slowing down, but all I can focus on is the conversation happening on the other side of the window.

I take my eyes off for a few minutes to tend to my hand, wrapping the towel tightly and putting my entire body's pressure on the wound as I lean against the sink.

"Avery! Are you all right?" Mason is next to me within seconds. I didn't see them come in, but now looking at the floor and the amount of blood spread around, I feel rather faint.

"The glass. I was...cleaning," I say, my stomach suddenly feeling sick. "Oh, Mason...I'm going to throw up."

"I got you," he says, sweeping me effortlessly into his arms and marching me upstairs to the hall bathroom.

"I'll clean this. You take care of her," my dad says, his words seeming to cover more than just the broken glass below.

Mason sets me on the toilet and runs a washcloth under the cold water, quickly putting it on my head. Then he starts pulling things out from underneath the sink, sorting through the cleaners and looking desperately for something to use.

"In the back," I say, my throat a little hoarse when I speak. He follows my lead and finds the alcohol and gauze quickly, ripping the box open and coming over to kneel in front of me.

"Let me see," he whispers, taking my hand carefully, unwrapping the kitchen towel now soaked completely in my blood. The cut is still gushing, and seeing it makes my forehead break out into a sweat. I lay forward on the counter, trying to force myself to stay with him. "Shit, Avery. It's deep. I think I can get it to stop though."

He's back under the sink, then moves quickly to the medicine cabinet, tossing everything out on the floor until he finds the jar of Vaseline.

"This is how my mom used to stop my bloody noses. You know, like they do for a boxer. Here," he reaches for my hand again and mushes a giant blob on the cut, slowing the bleeding immediately. He's wrapping the gauze a second later, pulling it tight and ripping with his teeth before tucking the end near my wrist. It looks like a giant snow mitt, and for some reason, seeing it gives me the giggles.

"What kind of fights did you get in to get bloody noses like that? I look like Mickey Mouse," I laugh, half waving my bandaged hand at him, until it stings from the movement. "Ow, shit!"

"Stop moving it, you stubborn woman. Go lay down in my room, I'll be right there," he says, picking up the various packaging and putting everything back in its place. I'm still giggling when he comes in to his room, and he just shakes his head at me, smiling on one side of his mouth.

"Seriously, Mason. This is, like, the worst bandaging I've ever seen!" I'm lying on my side, still a little dizzy, and rolling my near-cast around the air mattress to admire it.

"One, I didn't get into fights. At least not back then. I had really bad allergies, and my nose just bled a lot. But thanks for thinking I was a hoodlum," he says, pulling his shoes from his feet, kicking them to the corner before hitting the lights and motioning me to move over in the bed. "And second, my mom was a bartender, not a nurse. She did the best she could, and so did I."

Well shit, now I feel bad. I stop my laughter and force my lips into a straight line as best as I can. "Thank you. I'm sorry," I say, and he just rolls his eyes at me, which unleashes the laughing again.

"Next time, I let you bleed out," he says, sitting up and pulling his shirt over his head, which now has my laughter completely hushed. I shouldn't be here. Not with my dad downstairs, not with Max in bed down the hall, not for a second night in a row. This is too much, *too fast.*

"I...uh, I should go," I start to get up, but he rolls to his side and lays his arm heavily over my chest.

"Uh uh. Ray's busy downstairs. And you heard him, he said to take care of you. You stay here tonight. I'll set my phone to wake us up before everyone else," he says, his expression not one to argue with.

"I don't know," I start, but he holds up a hand.

"You're staying here. If your father wants to kick my ass over it in the morning, I'll remind him that it's probably not a good idea to throw beer bottles at the wall," he says, and it makes me wince remembering my dad's outburst.

"Okay...and thank you—for taking care of me. I was careless," I start, but he puts his fingers on my lips quickly before rolling closer on his side and kissing me gently on the cheek.

"I think I made it pretty clear today, Ave...I'm in this—both feet," he says, his face serious, the golden lines in his brown eyes lit by the stars outside. I can't help myself, and I reach up and run my fingers through his hair, looking at it curl softly in my hands. He shuts his eyes when I do.

"I like your haircut," I say. He smiles, turning his head just enough so his lips catch my arm, and he kisses it.

"Me too," he says, reaching up and scratching at his hair, before letting his gaze fall open to me again.

"Thanks for talking to my dad—about Adam," my heart starts to speed up remembering my father's reaction. My dad trusted Adam, treated him like his own son when we got married. He used to tell me how happy he was I was marrying a *good man like Adam Price*. I think that's what gets at my dad the most—the guilt. I don't blame him. I was just as enamored. Adam was the valedictorian of our high school, and we both went to college together. My dad didn't even blink when we said we were going to live together—instead, thrilled to see the ring on my finger. It was always his fear—that his little girl wouldn't have anyone to take care of her. And when we got pregnant early, my dad didn't even lecture—he just beamed, over-the-moon to be a grandfather. He was Adam's greatest fan, all the way up until the day Adam walked away. And then...Adam gained the most threatening enemy in the world.

"He wanted to go find him, but I told him he left," Mason says, and I breathe a sigh of relief. Then I realize what Mason said.

"How do you know he left?" I say, scooting away to look at him completely. I know before he says anything—it's written on his face, and it comes out with the heavy breath he exhales. I suppose deep down I maybe knew all along, but it still feels like a surprise.

"That's where I was this morning. I couldn't let him get away with it. I know, it wasn't my place, but I'm sorry, Avery. I just...I couldn't," he says, his eyes falling to mine, pleading with me to understand. He's so afraid I'm going to be angry, but instead, Mason may have just completely crawled inside my heart.

"My hand feels better," I say softly, watching as the line of his mouth inches slowly into a smile.

"Come here," he says, laying his arm flat for me to lie on, his other above his head, waiting to embrace me. I keep my eyes on his as I move my body closer, careful of my hand, and just careful in general.

His skin is warm against my face. I'm lying right along the tiger's tail on his tattoo, and I let my face fall so I can look at it closely, tracing the lines with the tips of my fingers. Mason slides his hand up my arm to my wrist, careful not to squeeze against my bandage, and brings my fingers to his lips, kissing them softly.

"I'm so sorry, Avery," he says, moving his head against mine. "I'm sorry you hurt yourself, and I'm sorry Adam is such a prick. And I'm *sooooo* sorry if I was ever mean to you. I didn't know how much you meant to me," his words literally knock the breath from my body, and I slide myself closer into his arms, pressing my lips to his with all of my might.

"Don't," I say, suddenly not wanting to hear him apologize...ever. For years, all I wanted was to see Mason Street grovel, to feel sorry, and to feel pain. And now all I want to do is love him.

I love him.

CHAPTER 15: FITTING IN

Mason

Claire was on board with my plan. I had a feeling she would be. I was surprised she didn't try to pry for details about Avery and me, but I guess chicks only really do that to each other.

I have almost everything figured out—I thought a Thursday night date would work better for her than a weekend. Max will be covered, and it's easier to get Avery out of work. I haven't talked to Ray again—not since I told him I took care of Adam.

Ben's pissed that I'm late. He keeps texting me, wanting to know when I'll make it to rehearsals. He's like a jealous girlfriend when my time is focused anywhere other than on him.

I figure I'm already on his shit list, so what's a few more minutes. I can see there are kids on the playground at Max's school, and I just feel this pull—like I need to check on him. I cruise by at about five miles per hour, rounding the corner slowly. I'm sure I look like a predator, and I notice at least one of the teachers following my car with her eyes.

I'd speed up and keep driving, except I don't see Max. Maybe it's not his grade or something, but I swear these kids look like Max's age. My chest starts to constrict. My head starts to go to dark places—like Max ran away and nobody noticed, or he's in trouble...or he's being pinned down in a bathroom by some asshole kid. *I was that asshole kid.*

I'm in the parking lot suddenly, like my steering wheel went on autopilot, and seconds later I'm jogging through the lot to the playground gate. *I have to find him, I have to find him.*

"Can I help you?" an older woman says, clearly sent to stop me from entering.

"Hi, I'm sorry. I'm...Max Abbot's uncle," I lie through my teeth. "I just promised his mom I'd swing by to check on him, since I was in the area."

"Oh, well, normally you need to check in with the office to be on school grounds," she says, her hand still blocking my way through the gate. I'm honestly thinking about just shoving her out of my way, but I know that probably wouldn't go over well.

"Right. Right. I really don't need to talk to him or anything, I was just making sure he was doing well at recess, and...look, I sort of panicked when I didn't see him. Can you just tell me where he is?" I ask, and her guard drops a little. She smiles softly and nods. She must understand Max's issues. Either that, or my charm now works on the over-sixty crowd. Whatever it is, she's motioning for me to follow her onto the basketball court, so I do.

"He's in there," she points over to the giant concrete pipe off in the far corner of the playground. I remember that pipe—we used to call it the *tunnel of love* when I was in sixth grade. I kissed Mindy Howard in that tunnel. But something tells me that's not what Max is in there for. I squint; I can see his feet propped up on the sidewall and his hands over his ears; he's sitting perfectly still.

"Does he go in there often?" I ask, my heart sinking.

"He spends every recess in there. His teacher, Mrs. Bailey, will sometimes try to coax him out, but...you know Max. He seems content to just sit in there," she says, staring at the same lonely boy I am.

"Is that Mrs. Bailey?" I ask, pointing to a woman near the tunnel.

"That's her. Come on, I'll introduce you," she urges me to follow, and I do. I'm going to be really late for rehearsal, and Ben is going to shit over it, but I don't care. I have to do something here.

"Mrs. Bailey? This is Max's uncle...I'm sorry, what was your name?" she says, and I reach out my hand to shake Mrs. Bailey's hand.

"Mason. I'm Mason," I say, and she grabs my hand and smiles, clearly on to me. She seems like she's going to play along though, so I ride out the lie.

"Hi, Mason. I didn't know Max had an uncle," she smirks when the older woman walks away.

"He doesn't," I respond with a shrug.

"I didn't think so," she laughs a little. "Are you friends with Avery?"

"Yeah," I sigh, looking at the blue and white shoes now poking out of the end of the tunnel. "He's in there...every day, huh?"

"Uh huh. Every recess. It's still early, and he'll find his way. School is hard, Mason. And for a kid like Max, everything is just a little harder," she looks at me sympathetically.

"Does he have any...friends?" I ask, remembering the homework assignment from last night.

"Like I said, we're working on it...it's early yet. That's one of his goals. He just needs to learn how to *be* with other kids right now," she says, looking back over at Max. Every so often, his feet reposition, but his hands stay cupped on his ears. I think his eyes may even be closed. I just want to run over and give the kid his iPad, something to do, but I know that wouldn't help *this* situation. It would only give him an out, a reason to recluse himself even more.

"Do you think...maybe I could visit your classroom for a few minutes sometime? I'm a musician, and Max has learned some things about music. Maybe, like, a show-and-tell? Just to help him break the ice," I ask, my voice inside warning me I should probably bring Avery into something like this. But I've already made myself a relative, what's crossing one more line?

"I think that might be nice," she says, her smile bigger now.

"Okay, maybe tomorrow?" I say, not wanting to see Max's feet in that tunnel for one more day.

"I'll make some time in the morning, before recess. At nine?" she says, opening up the notebook in her arms and jotting down a reminder.

"I'll be here," I say, making my own mental note to get Avery...and Max...up to speed on my plan. "Thank you."

I shake her hand goodbye and head back to my car, pulling my phone from my pocket to deal with the dozen or so angry texts from Ben.

What the hell? Where are you?

I write Ben back quickly before turning on my engine.

Relax, man. I'm on my way. Be there in 5.

I have to speed a little to get to his house in just under 10 minutes, and he's pacing in the driveway, smoking, when I pull up.

"Fuck, man? Where's your head at?" he says, throwing his cigarette on the ground and stomping it out.

Ben's house is a lot like his life—the paint is chipping off the front door, and there are sheets tacked to the walls over the windows. It's like a cave inside it's so dark. It's a small house on the not-so-nice end of town, and I'd rather move back in with my mom than live here. But he was anxious to get out of his house, and the rent here was cheap, so he jumped on it. He's kept his lease during the tour, though he always talks about how when we hit it big, he's going to buy one of the fancy mountain homes on the other side of the hill.

"My head's right here," I say, not really in the mood to get into it with him. He has some beef with me being with Avery. I don't know what it is, but I know enough to know it's probably petty and stupid.

"Better be," he mutters under his breath. A couple months ago, that would have been enough to send my fist into his face, but I just find it ridiculous now. That's how the last year of touring was. Matt and Josh spent most of the shows so drunk they barely remembered how to play our songs, and Ben got high, drunk, and belligerent. I'm starting to think time apart wasn't such a bad thing.

I pull out my guitar and take my spot on the stool; Josh sits up from the lounger, ready to go. "I was thinking we could start out the hour with some cool covers. You know, like shit we always wanted to try?" I say, looking at Ben, hoping this might just inspire him a little.

"We used to do some Stones," Ben says, taking his spot behind the drums and giving it a little kick. "Oh, and you know what might be cool? What if we did some Johnny Cash?"

My friend actually looks alive, and for the first time in months, I see a hint of *him* again.

Avery's already been at work for a few hours when I roll in. It's funny how nervous I get before seeing her. I actually changed

146

my shirt in the car because my other one reeked of Ben's smoke, and I didn't want her to not want to be close to me.

I pick a spot in the corner, far away from everyone else, because I want to watch her, and when her eyes catch mine the first time as she passes through the kitchen door, my heart actually beats twice as fast. Her lips pull up into the quickest smile, and she keeps looking back to me, to make sure I'm watching her. And I am—I plan on watching her until I follow her home and beg her to sleep in my bed again. Ray hasn't killed me yet!

"Well, if it isn't my only child," my mom says, sliding into the booth next to me and patting my leg. "You and the boys playing this weekend?"

As crazy as my mother makes me, I do love her. She wasn't typical, and she's selfish as hell—but I'd probably beat the shit out of anyone else that talked bad about her. And I still don't believe any of her boyfriends have deserved her.

"We're playin' Friday. You working?" I ask.

"Wouldn't miss it for the world," she winks, leaning into me.

We're quiet at the table together for a few minutes, just watching people walk in and out of the restaurant. There's a certain tension to our silence—an awkwardness that started when I was a teenager, and our relationship changed. I don't know what set it off, but I quit being her little boy, and I think maybe not needing her made her resent me a little. It sounds stupid, even now in my own head, but we both started pulling away from one another at the same time. And I think she's always regretted it. Hell, maybe I have too. I can tell my mother wants to talk now, but she can't seem to speak.

"I uh...I finally kissed Avery," I say, biting my lip and looking at her sideways. My mom is a romantic at heart, so I know telling her this will make her smile—and for some reason, I feel like she needs to smile.

"I heard! Sorry I missed that little speech you made. Claire told me all about it," she smiles, and my mom actually looks proud of me. "You know, I always wanted you to give that girl a chance."

"Sure you did," I say, rolling my eyes. My mom always prided herself on being some great matchmaker—for everyone other than herself.

"Roll your eyes at me all you want, Mason, but I always thought Avery would be good for you. She's grounded," she says, her eyes looking out over the growing crowd, and her face a little more serious than I'm used to. "You've got a lot of me in you. We're dreamers. And that's…that's a good thing. But sometimes you need to remember about the important things here on the ground. Not just all that tempting stuff that's up in the clouds."

The heaviness of my mom's words makes me swallow hard. I don't think she's ever said anything so deep in her entire life, and I don't know how to react to it, so I just nod and smile.

"So, it's your birthday next week," she says, quickly changing the subject, just as uncomfortable as I am. Shit, I forgot. I'll be twenty-six. I wonder when Avery's birthday is? Suddenly there are a ton of things I realize I don't know about Avery—that's definitely going into the *big date* plan. "How about the two of you come over for dinner? I'll make my sauce. You still like pasta, right?"

"That'd be nice, ma. We'll be there," I say, somehow feeling like this dinner is more for my mother than my birthday.

"Good. It's settled then. I'll see you two at six," she says, standing and straightening out her apron and blouse, making sure she looks her best. My mom is always put together—sometimes a little over-the-top, but she's put together. She's always been the biggest tip earner at Dusty's—partly because she flirts with the fat wallets, and partly because, despite her flaws, my mom is a damn hard worker…when she needs to be.

She gives me one last smile, and heads over to greet the newest tables of customers. I don't know why, but the smile on her face when she walks away makes me sad.

I must be frowning, because Avery is looking at me from across the bar, and she mouths, "Are you all right?" I just nod and over exaggerate my smile to compensate. I'm actually better than I've ever been.

The night speeds by. Wednesdays are good dinner crowds—a lot of families come in. I used to like the middle of the week when I came in here with my mom. Ray was never busy, and that's when he'd spend time letting me mess with his guitar. I can tell Ray is still avoiding me a little, which makes me…uneasy. I love that man, but damn, I'm pretty sure I love his daughter too, and if he told me I couldn't be with her, I'm not sure what I would do.

Avery heads to the back and holds up a finger, letting me know she'll only be another minute, so I walk over and sit at the corner of the bar to wait for her. Ray comes out just then with a couple of books to take some inventory; I can tell he stutter steps, not sure if he wants to hang out so close to me.

"Hey, Ray. So we've got a good set ready for Friday night," I say, wanting to break the damned cold ice building up between the two of us. Ray smiles and grunts—he's not sure what to do with me.

I might be taking my life into my own hands, but I stand up at the bar and head over to where Ray's sitting, rubbing the sweat from my palms along my jeans before sticking my hand out for him to shake. It takes him a few seconds to notice, and when he does, he laughs a little under his breath.

"I didn't really do this right, and I'm sorry," I say. He raises one of his graying eyebrows at me, pulling his lip in tightly. "I probably should have asked for your blessing, or something like that. But I really like her, Ray. It's more than *like.* "

He looks at my eyes and then to my hand, chewing at his cheek, considering, before finally gripping my hand, cupping it with his other hand. When he looks back up at me, he's a little teary eyed—it's barely there, but I notice.

When Avery walks out, she sees us shaking hands, and she stops—she doesn't want to interrupt, so instead she waits for my cue. "I'll see you at the house. I'm gonna head out, as soon as Avery's done," I say, and Ray pats my hand once more and stands with his books, nodding. Avery starts to make noise and walks out of the kitchen just then.

"Hey, Dad. I'm heading home. Need anything?" she asks, her eyes locked on mine.

"No, I'm fine baby girl. It's inventory night, so I'll be late. You go on," he says, not quite looking her squarely in the face, probably because he doesn't want her to see how emotional he is.

Ray heads through the kitchen, back to his office, and Avery leans against the bar, looking at me with her lips curled into a faint smirk.

"What's that look for?" I ask, reaching out my hand, which she grabs. It feels so damn good, and natural, like it's how it's always been.

"You're good to my dad. That's all," she says, leaning into me as we head through the front door and out into the empty parking lot. "I like that."

"Yeah, well, I like you," I say, putting my arm completely around her, and drawing her close. I wish like hell I could just take her home in my car—because I'd probably find a reason to pull over somewhere in the desert and put my lips on her body for the next thirty minutes before getting her home. But I know she needs to take Max to school in the morning, so I walk her to her car, then head to mine to follow her the few blocks to her house.

When we enter the kitchen at home, Claire eyes us and gives me a wink—Avery doesn't notice our silent exchange. Honestly, I think Claire is almost as excited about my date night with Avery as I am.

"Max is already asleep, and I think he's actually *sleeping* tonight," Claire says, giving her friend a quick hug and then gathering her things.

"Okay, that's good. I've got a paper to write tonight," Avery says, and I can't help but feel a little disappointment. Claire laughs at me, shaking her head before heading out the back door.

"You need anything to eat?" Avery asks, pulling out the bread and peanut butter. I help her with the jar and slide it back to her. Her hand is better today, but she still has a bandage wrapped over the side.

"Well, I'm a little hungry, but I'm not sure I want to eat a sack lunch for dinner," I joke. She shrugs and continues to make her sandwich.

"Suit yourself," she says, licking the leftover peanut butter off the dull end of the butter knife. I've never wanted to be a knife more in my entire life; seeing her tongue slide up the edge of the metal has my mind flipping through a dozen various inappropriate thoughts.

She takes three large bites, and her sandwich is almost gone. I'm staring at her in awe, watching her pull the milk from the fridge and drink it right from the carton in front of me too. "What?" she says, her mouth muffled from the bite still inside. She raises the carton to hand it over to me. I shake my head and laugh. "It's not like you haven't shared my cooties."

"Ave, believe me, I LOVE sharing your cooties. It's just kind of nice seeing you relax, and honestly, watching you chug milk right from the carton is kinda...well...hot," I say, my eyes almost daring her with the way I'm looking at her.

At first, she makes a tight smile and looks down, a little embarrassed. But then she reaches into the freezer to grab an ice cube, and when she turns her attention back to me, she's making an entirely different face. Her eyes are hooded, and her smile is soft and wicked.

"You mean, hot like this?" She says, holding the ice cube between two fingers and sucking on the end, making sure I can see her tongue run a slow circle around the entire thing. She drags it slowly across her lips, her eyes on mine the entire time. I almost grab her then and replace the ice with my own tongue, but I stop when she slowly trails the cube down her chin and to her neck, drawing a wet line along her collarbone before softly circling it over the rise of her breast.

Fuck me. I'm usually pretty good with signs, but for some reason, this girl has me second-guessing everything. My feet are twitching with the need to charge at her, but my brain is waiting for a clear signal. Avery must sense my hesitation, though, because she steps toward me slowly, reaching for my hand, and placing the melting ice in my palm before pulling the edges of her T-shirt up slowly.

That's enough of a sign for me, and soon I'm helping her pull the shirt entirely over her head, pushing her back against the counter. We're far enough in the corner that we would be able to move to the living room to hide if someone came in.

Unable to take it, I kiss her hard, my tongue diving deep into her mouth, tangling with hers. The feeling of the cold from the ice only makes me want to explore her more, and I suck her bottom lip into my mouth, grazing my teeth against it when I finally let go. As soon as my lips leave hers, she lets out a faint cry, and it drives me absolutely crazy.

My hand starts at her cheek, and then I move it slowly along her neck and shoulders, pulling her bra straps down against her arms. She's arching for me, and I know she wants me to touch her

151

desperately, but I won't—not yet. Instead, I stand in front of her and look at her bare skin, not touching her, until her eyes open to mine, and she's practically begging.

I move closer, and take the ice in my hand, drawing it slowly along her neck and down her breast, right to the edge of her bra line, forcing her to pant. I hold it there, and I stare into her eyes, just watching her breathe—in and out, her rhythm the sexiest thing I've ever seen.

I move my lips to her chest and grip the lace trim of her bra in my teeth, pulling it away from her skin slowly until her nipple is exposed. I blow gently, just long enough for her to think I'm going to pull it into my mouth, and then I move to the next one and do the same.

When I back away again, her eyes are closed, and her breathing is rapid. Seeing her stand there—her breasts barely exposed and being held up by the stretched white lace bra—has me so goddamned hard, I think about speeding this up. But I know these opportunities won't come often, so I'm going to make sure this one lasts.

I move in closer, and once again trail the ice cube over her lips, her pink tongue peeking out just enough to taste it. I move it down her body, along the center of her chest so I can trace my way along the line of the bra to her now hard-as-hell nipple. I stop right before I touch the ice to the tip, waiting; Avery shifts her weight, squeezing her legs once. I'm driving her crazy, and it's such a fucking turn on.

When I move the ice to the very tip of her nipple, she lets her lips fall open with another cry, and this time she says my name, and that only makes me want to torture her more. I hold the ice to the round, red peak, and don't let her move, even though she's squirming to try to get away. Then I move it to the other one, pinching with my fingers to press the ice against her, bringing her other nipple to the same hardness as the first.

"Mason," she whimpers, and I feel her breath fall down my entire body.

Unable to stand it, I have to taste her. I take her frozen nipple into my mouth, sucking hard, and holding it tightly with my teeth until it's warm again. My hand works her other breast, pinching and pulling at the tip until I feel her shift her legs once more. I

152

reach behind her, and unhook her bra to let it fall completely from her body. I wrap my hands around her fucking amazing tits, my thumbs rubbing against the hard tips while she lifts herself up on the counter.

I move my hands to her face, cupping it hard, and bringing her lips to mine. She does the same, her hands starting around my neck and quickly gripping at my T-shirt, pulling it up and over my head. There's no way I'm going to be able to *not* finish this, but I have to make sure Avery's on the same page.

"I'm taking you to my bed," I say, not really asking. When she holds her forehead to mine, and wraps her legs firmly around my waist, I know she's letting me have her completely. I move my hands to her ass and press her body against mine, lifting her from the counter and walking her to the stairs.

I kiss her hard all the way into my bedroom. After I set her down on the mattress, I shut the door behind me, and lock it. Kicking my shoes off, I move closer to her, getting down on my knees since the mattress is so low to the floor. Looping my thumbs into the belt loops of her shorts, I slide her closer to the edge of the bed, staring into her eyes the entire time, hoping like hell I don't read any hesitation. When I don't, I pull off her shoes and socks, then slowly take down her zipper and slide the shorts from her legs, leaving her there in only a small pair of pink lace panties.

I have to rub my hand over my face once just to snap myself back to reality—reminding myself that this isn't a dream, I'm really here for this. Her skin is so unbelievably soft, and she tastes just like she smells—like vanilla.

When I move forward to kiss her, she reaches her hands to the button on my jeans, and I almost lose it right there. "Hang on," I say, holding my forehead to hers and taking a deep breath. "Being with you, Avery. It's…it's hard to take it slow."

"So don't," she says, her eyes boring into mine with desire.

Oh fuck. On her command, I unzip my jeans and kick off the rest of my clothes, leaving the only thing between us the small strip of satin on her panties. I start my lips at her knees, and kiss my way all the way up to the tender spot between her legs. I test it once with my tongue over the silky fabric, and when I do, she writhes beneath me, a soft moan almost doing me in again.

I take the sides of her panties in both of my hands and slide them away from her body, slowly down her legs, watching every new part of her as I reveal it. She's fucking breathtaking, and I've never wanted to be inside a woman more.

"Avery, I really care about you, and this is different than anything I've ever done, or anyone I've ever been with," I say, my eyes unable to leave the small line of hair that points right between her legs. Like a fucking animal, I actually lick my lips, and I hear her breath pause when I do. "I just want you to know that—that you, and *this*—is special. But I'm not going to be able to hold back. I'm going to fuck you, and it's going to be hard and rough and…it's just gonna be that way."

I manage to pull my gaze to her face for just a moment, and in that second, she sits up and reaches her arm around my neck, pulling me down on her. "Okay," she says, her smile so unbelievably seductive I start to wonder if I've ever really known this girl at all.

"I have protection, in my jeans…" I start to say, but she pulls me back to her, shaking her head *no*.

"I'm on the pill; it's okay," she says, her words breathy and *oh my god, I'm going to feel all of her completely.*

Her lips hit mine hard, and she digs her fingers into the muscles of my back, pushing them lower into my sides, begging me to thrust into her. It doesn't take long for me to find her entrance, and when I feel the tip against her soft, warm folds, I can no longer control myself. I push into her fast and hard, and she lets out a small gasp when I do. I look at her, wanting to make sure she's all right, and she grabs my head and pulls me to her once again, kissing me hard.

"Again," she says against my ear. So I thrust into her again, this time a little slower, but much deeper. With my next movement, Avery's legs are wrapped around my body and her hands are clutching at the top edge of the mattress.

"Oh my god, Avery. You feel so fucking good," I whisper roughly in her ear. I'm trying my best to be quiet, but I want to shout her name to the entire fucking world every time I feel her take me in. I know I don't have long left, but I do my best to hold on as long as I can. I grip her leg and bring her thigh up high against me so I can move in and out with even more force.

154

Avery's eyes open to mine, and the look of want and need on her face is so goddamned sexy. When she starts to nod *yes* and bites down on the back of her fist to keep herself from screaming, I completely lose control, hoping like hell I can move hard enough to take her with me. When I feel her shudder against me, I let go of everything and release it all inside of her, collapsing against her with exhaustion.

"Unbelievable. That was...I don't even have a word for that," I say, wishing like hell I wasn't so wiped out so I could lift her up and do it all again. "I didn't hurt you, did I?"

When I look at her, there's a tiny tear forming in the corner of her eye, and my heart literally sinks. I reach up immediately and wipe it away with my thumb gently, kissing her forehead and moving her to my side so I can hold her close. "Oh my god, Ave, did I hurt you? I'm so sorry," I say, suddenly angry with myself for not being in control.

"No, I'm fine. Please, Mason, you didn't hurt me at all. It was amazing," she says, her voice cracking a little.

"You don't sound fine," I say, pulling her face away just enough so I can look into her eyes, trying to read her thoughts. She smiles softly when I do, her hand coming up slowly and caressing my cheek.

"I think the intensity just struck me...I...*oh god*, I'm embarrassed to say this," she says, covering her face with her hand. I grab it to pull it away and kiss her nose.

"Don't be embarrassed. What is it?" I ask, needing to know she's okay, that I didn't just blow the best thing in my life.

"It's sort of like when you imagine something for so long—when you actually dream about it—and then you get to live your dream? I guess...uhhhh, this sounds so stupid, I know, but Mason, I used to dream about being with you like this. I just, I'm afraid it's not real," she says, her eyes starting to tear again.

I pull the blanket up to cover her, then I pull her in closely, wrapping her completely in my arms so she has nowhere to go. "Avery, I'm in over my head here. This whole *feelings* thing, well...it's foreign territory for me. But I can promise you one thing—*this*? This is real. It's the realest fucking thing I've ever known. And I'm a persistent, stubborn bastard, so you better get used to me," I stop short of telling her I love her, but the thought actually runs through my mind. If I weren't such a chicken shit, I would.

She just stares into my eyes for several long minutes, her hand against my face the entire time, like she's trying to memorize me, and I let her. To be honest, I like looking at her eyes. The green against the paleness of her face, and the hint of red to her hair is perfection. If I could paint a portrait of a beautiful woman, this would be it.

"So, we're sort of doing this backward, but...I'd like to take you out tomorrow. You know, on a *real* date," I say, laughing at my earlier thoughts of how I was going to seduce her during our night out. "I already sorted things out with Claire. Oh...and I got your dad's permission."

That last part actually makes her laugh. "You...asked my dad? You asked Ray Abbot if you could take me out?" she says, her giggle making my lungs fill with air.

"Sure did," I say, kind of proud of myself.

She shakes her head and shuts her eyes for a second. When she opens them again, her smile is the brightest I've ever seen. She moves forward and kisses me softly but long. "Thank you," she whispers against my lips.

"You're welcome. But...you should know, we're going cow-tippin', so you might not want to thank me until you see all of the things I've got planned for the date," I joke, and she considers me for a few long seconds before deciding I'm full of shit. "Seriously, it's a surprise. Just some things I kind of want to do...with you."

She blushes then, and I realize exactly everything we *have* done, and I squeeze her against me tightly.

"I mean, clothed activities," I say, rubbing my nose against hers.

I get up to turn off my light, but when I do, I realize Avery is standing behind me, my blanket still clutched to her body. "I feel like such a loser, but...I really *do* have a paper to write," she says, slapping her hand to her face in embarrassment. I forgot all about that—my stomach dropping at the thought of her not spending the night next to me...especially after what just happened.

"Okay, well...I'll wait up," I say, opening the door and looking around the hall and stairs to make sure the coast is clear.

156

"Are you sure? It's going to be a while," she says, chewing at the tips of her fingernails.

"Positive," I say, swatting her on the ass once playfully while she steps into the hall.

"Okay, well…I'll just knock lightly," she says, her finger still dangling from her mouth. I pull it away and kiss her one more time.

"See you soon," I say, and I stand there to watch her walk away, her bare shoulders and back almost as sexy as her front. She smiles one last time before she ducks into her room, and I watch the light flip on from underneath her door.

I think I'm waiting for the panic to set in. This is all new to me…wanting a girl to actually come back? I slip downstairs to pick up our clothes, and I go ahead and indulge in a few gulps from the milk myself. I don't know that I'll ever be able to do that and not think of Avery—and tonight.

When I get back to my room, I pull out the guitar and play for about an hour, hoping she'll be joining me soon. By midnight, I turn the light off and actually pace the small space of my room, opening the door to check on her light every five minutes. It's always on, and I know her studies are important to her, so I take a deep breath each time, and come back to sit on my bed. I wish like hell I read. I actually read a few news blogs on my phone, but I'm just roaming over the words. I'm not paying attention to anything.

By two in the morning, I give up and let my eyes fall shut. I'm so fucking tired, and as badly as I want to wait for her, I just can't.

I don't know when she came in, but when my eyes blink open, the faint sound of Avery's phone alarm is chirping next to me, and her hair is draped across my chest. She blinks her eyes open slowly and the cutest yawn on earth leaves her lips, followed by what has now become my favorite smile.

"You made it," I say, smoothing her hair back and tucking it behind her ear.

"I came in an hour ago. It was a tough paper, but I promised. And I missed you," she says, literally stealing every last piece of me with her words. She promised—the heaviness of that single word burning in my chest, and locking up my soul. And even though I haven't said it yet, I know I love her. And I know I can't lose her or let anything happen to her or even see her cry without it absolutely wrecking me.

CHAPTER 16: POPULAR

Avery

I'm pretty sure I've formed a habit. I almost didn't go back to Mason's room because it was so late by the time I had my paper done. But...I promised. And I wanted to be there. I wonder if I could ever get to the point where Max would understand me sleeping in Mason's room instead of ours? I wonder if I could ever get to the place where I'm not living with my dad? I wonder if I would ever live with Mason?

When I make my way downstairs, breakfast is at the table, and everything seems just like normal. Max is breaking off pieces of his pastry, taking small bites and chewing them longer than necessary. Mason is picking at a piece of bacon, and my father is loading up his own plate.

"Good morning," I say, trying to force the redness from my face.

"Breakfast is ready," my dad says, sliding a full plate my way. Breakfast is important to my dad—it's his *thing.* He's always made it for me, ever since I was a little girl, and having him do that still, even knowing that I'm *with* Mason, fills me with a sense of relief that some things never change.

I sit down next to Mason, but I leave enough space between us to keep it friendly, not make my dad uncomfortable. I guess I'm also hiding things from Max on some level, too.

I notice the table is shaking a little, and on instinct, I move my hand to reach for Max's leg, but I stop short when I realize it's not his that's bouncing up and down—it's Mason's.

"You getting ready for a sprint race?" I say, nodding my head toward his leg. He looks down at it and smiles tightly, shifting his feet to cross them at the ankles.

"I...I uh, gotta talk to you," he says, keeping his voice low and leaning over closely to me. What he says has my mind racing a million miles a minute, backtracking on last night, and already diving into the deep end of heartbreak.

"Okay," I say, forcing my voice to be strong rather than break out in tears. I step outside and Mason follows; I fight against my instinct to turn around and slap him immediately.

"I wanted to talk to you about this last night, but well, we didn't really *talk*," he says, his mouth pulled up into a half smile, throwing me a little.

"Mason, what is this about?" I can't help the way that comes out, and I can tell he hears the suspicion in my voice.

"Oh god, Avery. No," he laughs a little, coming over to reach for my hand. I give it to him, reluctantly. "I need to talk about Max."

In one moment, I'm relieved, but in the next, I'm full of worry. "What about Max? What happened?" I say, my body moving to head back inside to my son.

"He's fine. No...no, he's fine," Mason says, laughing lightly and pulling me back to him. "It's just...I did something. And I probably should have talked to you first, but I was there, at his school, and it all just came out sort of fast, and I had to do something."

I'm sure the face I'm making still reads panic, because Mason takes a deep breath and apologizes again. "Let me start over," he smiles. "I drove by the school, and I saw Max, sort of hiding out alone. It hit me, and I know it's not my place, but I stopped in and talked to his teacher during the recess. She said he's having a hard time making friends, which I know...is part of his challenges. But, I just wanted to help. So, I'm coming in today, to be his sort of, I don't know...show and tell?"

Listening to this has me grinning so hard it's actually hurting my jaw. I am so overwhelmed by Mason's love for Max it has me wanting to cry. This moment, on top of the hour of sleep I got, has me incredibly emotional. "That's...amazing, Mason," I say, just hugging him to let him know I approve.

"You're sure? I mean...I didn't mean to overstep my bounds. I know Max isn't expecting it, so...I'm not sure what I do here," he lets his shoulders slump with a deep breath. Max does like order, but things like this can be managed, and while I may not be able to help Max make friends instantly, I can help him be okay with bringing one to school for the day.

160

"I got this part," I say, smiling at him. "What time are you coming in?"

"His teacher said nine," he says, his hands in his pockets of his baggy jeans.

"Okay, let me take the lead on this," I say, tugging at his arm, and urging him to follow me back inside. Max is just finishing breakfast, and my dad seems to have covered mine with a napkin. He pulls it off when I come back inside, never once taking his eyes off his newspaper.

"It was getting cold," he says, clearly annoyed that Mason and I are messing around with his routine. Like Max, my dad likes things a certain way, too—but I think that's just because he likes to be the boss.

"Hey, Max? I need to talk to you about something. Can you look at me for just a few seconds?" I say, taking one small bite of my bacon, and wiping my hand on the napkin. Max looks in my direction, but not in my eyes—close enough. "Your teacher called last night while you were sleeping. She wanted to let you know that there was a change for today. You're supposed to bring a guest to school, just for a little bit, and she asked if it could be Mason. He's going to come in at nine."

Max twists his lips and looks away, not comfortable with something being different. "Why are we having a change? Thursdays are for centers. I get to do the planet center," he says, his legs swinging a little in his seat.

"Yes, and that will all be the same. This is just one small thing she's adding to the day," I say, and his legs slow just a little. I look at Mason, and urge him to join the conversation.

"Max, the teacher wanted me to talk about music. But, she also wanted you to show the program you've been working on," Mason says, looking at me for approval. I nod for him to keep going. "I won't be there long, but I'm going to need your help."

Max doesn't look at Mason while he's talking, but the second he's done, he stands and walks to my purse, reaching in to pull out the iPad. "I'm going to take this to school," he says, putting it in his backpack.

"Okay, but just for today," I say, not really sure what Mason has planned, but hoping this works out.

Mason

I promised Avery I would text her the second I left Max's class. She wanted to come, but she had to turn in her paper. I feel pretty good in Mrs. Bailey's hands—I like Max's teacher, and I think she's on board with my crazy idea.

I'm standing in the hallway with my guitar at 8:55 a. m., and I can hear the sounds of chairs and desks scooting along the floor. I knock at her door, and hold my breath, hoping she hasn't forgotten. When she opens it and smiles at me, I feel relieved. "Glad you could make it," she says.

"Wouldn't miss it," I say, holding up the guitar and moving the strap over my neck and shoulder.

"Class, we have a special guest today. This is Max's..." she looks at me quickly, squinting, and questioning what to call me. She knows I'm not his uncle.

"Friend," I say. "I'm Max's friend."

The guitar always gets attention—women and kids fall for it every time, and it has Max's entire class quiet and staring at me for what happens next. "Hi," I say, my voice a little higher than normal from my nerves. I perform in front of people all the time, but for some reason, having a couple dozen five-year-olds bake me with attention has my pulse ticking up a notch.

"Does anyone in here play an instrument?" I ask, sitting on the edge of Mrs. Bailey's desk, resting the guitar on my knee. A few kids raise their hands, and I ask them what instruments they play. Some say piano, and others make up instruments or don't really answer with an instrument at all.

"Okay, does anyone in here *write* music," I ask, knowing one kid will surely raise his hand. He has to. Max's eyes are looking forward, and when I ask that question, I can actually see his pupils flex, and his hand shoots up instantly.

"Max, you write music?" Mrs. Bailey asks, herself a little surprised.

"Yes," he says, his hand back down, and his attention once again somewhere not quite at me.

"That's right. Max does write music. And actually, he has been writing a song on this really cool program on the iPad. I was

162

hoping he could show everyone, because I'm not very good at it," I say, looking at Mrs. Bailey for reinforcement.

"Max, do you have your iPad with you?" Mrs. Bailey asks. Max doesn't say anything, but instead goes to his backpack along the wall and pulls out the iPad, bringing it to his desk. He flips it open, and starts working on the program at his desk, not really understanding that he should show it to the rest of the class. I've got to help him out here.

"Max, I don't think the others in the class can see, and they're new to that program like I am. Can you stand up front and show it once?" I ask, hoping I'm not pushing for too much. Max moves to the front of the class, and flips the iPad around holding it in front of him for a few brief seconds before turning it back so only he can see it. It makes me laugh inside, but I keep it to a smile.

"Can we show them how it works? I'd like to play something, and then maybe you can write it on the program?" I ask, waiting for Max to acknowledge me. He doesn't, but he's standing still, waiting with his finger in place, so I think he's with me on this. I play a little bit of the song I've been working on, and I can see Max shake his head, probably because he already knows this song. He taps out a series of notes really quickly, and when he hits play on his iPad, the music I just played replays to perfection.

This is where Max suddenly leapfrogs over me and my cool guitar in the eyes of his classmates. A few kids actually say "Whoa," and some near the front are standing, trying to get closer to see what Max is doing. Mrs. Bailey motions to them to stay in their seats, and she smiles at me, urging me to do it again.

"Okay, but you've heard that one before Max. Let's try something different," I say, and I can see his eyes immediately move to my hands, just like the first time he watched me play. I play a different song this time—one of my earlier ones that I used to play with Ray, and I let it go on for about thirty seconds, just to challenge him.

Max's hand is fast at work when I am done. He puts all of the notes in place and sets the iPad to play as a piano, then sets it to begin. Not a single note is off—it's amazing. I didn't really do anything complex, but I know that if I had to write these songs on paper, it would take me several minutes, maybe even an hour, to get down what Max does in seconds.

We repeat our demonstration a few more times, and each time, the kids react and look at Max—a little differently. When my time is up, Mrs. Bailey announces that it's time to get ready for recess and then centers. I watch Max put his iPad back in his bag and take his seat, anxious to get to the planet center.

Before I leave, I pull Mrs. Bailey aside and ask her to keep an eye on Max's bag and his iPad, and she assures me she will.

I can hear the kids running to the playground behind me while I walk out to the parking lot, their feet trampling the pavement fast to get to the monkey bars and ball basket. I spare a look when I'm putting my guitar back in my trunk, and I search for Max. Just like yesterday, I'm having a hard time finding him in the sea of five and six year olds running in all directions. My heart sinks a little when I finally spot his feet sticking out of the tunnel, and I feel stupid for even trying. But then a girl with long brown braids walks over and bends forward, saying something in the tunnel; I see Max's feet shift, his body scooting closer to the end of the tunnel, then she climbs in the other side, and puts her feet up just like his.

They don't talk, and I can barely make them out from the fence, but she's staring at him. And she's staying by his side, while the rest of the playground goes on like normal. My eyes are actually tearing up, and if anyone ever caught me crying, I'd deny the hell out of it, but seeing Max *not* be alone is maybe the best thing I've ever seen—other than his mother's smile.

I text Avery the second I'm in my car.

Max did great. There's a girl sitting with him. One down, the rest of kindergarten to go!

I wait for her to respond, and I know she will. I know she's probably been staring at her phone ever since the time hit nine o'clock. Her reply comes seconds later.

I'm so happy!!!

Me, too.

164

CHAPTER 17: JITTERS

Avery

"Why the hell are you so nervous," Claire asks over the phone, while I toss every piece of clothing I own on the floor, looking for something—*anything*—that will make me feel like a pretty girl on her first date.

Max is staying with Claire at Dusty's until the crowd lets up, and Cole is taking over her shift. I'd give anything for those two to hook up, but I know neither one would make the first move. Claire talks a big game, but she's really quite the wallflower when push comes to shove.

"Claire, do you know how long it's been since I've been on a date?" I say, not really thinking about it until she fires her answer back at me.

"Yeah, about half as long as it's been for me," she says. *Ouch.*

"Sorry," I say, sitting down on my bed and hoping something will jump out at me. "Claire?"

"What, pumpkin?" she asks, the sass back in her tone. I'm about to make her day.

"I...slept with him," I swallow hard, waiting for her reaction.

"What! Oh my god, oh my god, oh my god! Avery Abbot, you better tell me everything this time—no glossing over the details. I want Cinemax porn kind of details, you hear me? It's not every day that your bestie gets to see the hottest man to ever be spawned in your hometown without his clothes on!" Her tirade has me laughing, and I promise her I will give her every last juicy drop. It will embarrass the hell out of me, but she'll harass me until I tell her, so it's best to just get it over with.

"I'll fill you in tomorrow, while the band's playing. But look, I've gotta go now. He's going to be here any minute, and I'm still wearing sweatpants," I sigh.

"Who cares, he's just going to rip them off of you," Claire teases.

"Not helping!" I giggle.

"Just go with simple and comfortable. I'd wear jeans," she says, hinting that she might know a thing or two about my date.

"Jeans, hmmmm?" I ask, kicking out a few piles on my floor to unveil my favorite pair.

"Yep. Now have a good time, and don't worry about anything. We've got you covered," she says, hanging up before I can grill her for any details.

Jeans—I can do jeans. I slip on my favorite comfortable pair with the small jewels on the back pockets and pair it with a black tank top—this look never really goes wrong. I put my low black boots on just in case I need to do any walking—*what if we really are tipping cows?* I brush out my hair, and tip the ends with an iron so the waves look even, and then splash a little bit of my body spray on my neck just in time for there to be a soft knock at my door.

Deep breath. I barely get a glimpse of him before his lips are crashing into mine and he's dipping me backward, holding me close to his body so I don't fall. I start to laugh when I feel like his grip is slipping, and he teases me, pretending to let go only to catch me and pull me back to my feet.

"First off, you look amazing," he says, and I smack at his arm.

"You didn't even look at me!" I protest.

"I did, in that split second when I almost dropped you. I looked at you and your hotness," he smiles, the freaking dimples doing their job. "And two, I had to get that out of the way or else it's all I'd be thinking about doing. I should be good for the next hour then."

"Hour?" I protest, knowing full well I can't go that long without kissing him again. Especially with him smelling like that, and wearing those light blue jeans that sit low enough on his hips that when he raises his arms I can see those two muscles leading into his boxers, which peak out right above the waistline.

"Okay, maybe ten minutes," he winks, holding out his hand. I grab it and am immediately soothed by the sensation of his fingers intertwined with mine. It's such a simple touch, holding hands. But having Mason's wrapped around mine feels so natural, and for the first time in years, I don't feel alone.

Mason leads me to his car, and I look around for clues while he walks to his side. He catches me, and starts laughing. "You're not going to find a map in here," he says, looking over his shoulder while he backs out onto the road.

"Can you give me any clues?" I ask, and he just slips on his sunglasses and smiles.

"I can tell you that you'll be out all night. Good thing tomorrow's Friday," he says, his eyebrows raised just above the rims of his glasses.

I huff, but it's really only for pretend. Truth is, Mason could be driving me to a grocery store where he plans to walk the aisles for hours, and I'd happily join him. These last few weeks have been a dream, and I never want to wake up.

We pull up next to a barn about thirty minutes north of Cave Creek, and Mason jumps out quickly, rushing over to my side to get my door. "I can let myself out of a car ya know," I say, though I secretly like that he's going full-gentleman tonight.

"Just preserving your energy," he says, tipping his glasses down to give me a look that has my body tingling and wishing we were alone. He holds my eyes for a few long seconds and then shakes his head. "Damn."

"Damn, what?" I ask.

"Just...damn," he smirks, and I blush.

Mason leads me to the other end of the barn where there's an older man saddling up a few horses. "Hey there. Are you Jeff?" he asks, and the man dusts his hands against his jeans, sending puffs of dirt in the air, before turning around to shake Mason's hand.

"That's me. You must be Mason?" he says, his mustache groomed into this perfect handlebar. We have a lot of cowboys in town, but the further away you get from the big city, the more authentic they are. Jeff here looks like he's probably the real deal.

"I've got 'em saddled for ya. You'll want to follow the green trail on the map. Dinner's at eight," he says, handing the reigns over to Mason. When I realize Jeff is leaving us alone, with two ginormous horses, I start to laugh nervously.

"Do you even know what you're doing?" I say, taking the reigns of the smaller horse from Mason. I pet my horse along his nose, and he dips his head down to sniff me. I've been around horses a lot. I'm not a great rider, but I'm comfortable with them.

When I look back to Mason, he's already swinging his leg over and getting ready. I don't know why I'm surprised to see him

167

so relaxed on a horse, but I can't hide my shock. "You are full of surprises, Mason Street," I smile, lifting myself up and climbing onto my horse.

"Her name's Dixie. This is Red. I had to sell them when the contract fell through," he says, running his hand down his horse's neck and back up again. When he looks at me, his smile is forced and flat, and I feel heartbroken for him.

"I had no idea. I'm sorry, Mason," I say, my brain entertaining silly thoughts like running away with him and his horses right now.

"It's okay. It was just one of those things; I always wanted horses. You know, like some people always want a racecar or…whatever. I didn't get to see them much, and it didn't really make sense to own them anyhow. It was the first thing I did with the money we got, and it was probably a stupid financial decision. Jeff works for the ranch I sold them to. They let people ride. I haven't been up since I've been home, but it felt like a good time to come…with you," he says, and the way he's looking at me feels like he's been looking at me for forever.

We ride Dixie and Red for about an hour, winding through a trail along a riverbed and through a few small hills deeper into the desert. By the time we reach a small group of people, the sun is starting to set.

"Here," Mason says, dismounting and reaching to hold Dixie for me while I climb down myself. We never rode fast or hard, but my thighs still hurt anyhow. I know I'll pay for this tomorrow, but I'd ride for hours in pain just to end up here with Mason.

There's a large campfire going, and a few older men sitting with guitars and playing. I notice three or four other couples walking over to a small table to pick up food, and I smile up at Mason.

"Are we having a cookout?" I ask, watching him pull a rolled up blanket from the back part of the saddle.

"I figured I could take you to a fancy restaurant anytime," he says, reaching for me. I fold right against his body, his arm tucking me in tightly.

The fall weather is starting to settle in and the desert air is chilly at night, so Mason lays out our blanket close to the fire, and makes me comfortable while he goes to make our plates. The three men playing and singing on the other side of the fire are singing

168

old country tunes, and they remind me of my mother. She loved Willie Nelson and Waylon Jennings.

Mason comes back with two plates piled high with more food than I could ever eat, and we both sit close together on our blanket, devouring barbecued chicken legs, cornbread, and beans. I'm barely though half of my plate and I have to stop.

"Are you giving up?" Mason asks, his mouth busy working a bite while he talks.

"Uhhhhg, I'm so full," I say, lying back on the blanket and pushing my plate toward him. He just looks at me and grins, then grabs my cornbread muffin and eats it whole. "You are like a bottomless pit!"

He stands up and brushes the crumbs from his shirt, then picks up our plates. "Bottomless pit of *lovin'*," he says in his most ridiculous fake sexy voice. I roll my eyes at him, and slap at the back of his leg as he steps over me. "You know you love me."

I can't help but smirk when he walks away because he's right—I know I do.

After dinner, we snuggle close, and Mason pulls the bottom edge of the blanket up over my legs to keep me warm. The old men tell a few stories, but we're not really listening. We're whispering to one another, like young campers up late at night.

"When did you know you wanted to play music?" I ask him, situating myself along his arm so I can watch his eyes animate while he talks.

"I used to watch your dad play with some of his friends, and I liked the way everyone looked at him. So one day I asked him to show me how to do a chord, and he did. The next day, I asked him to show me another. And we just sort of kept on going like that for months until he finally just gave me a guitar of my own," Mason says. I love the way he loves my dad.

"I'm glad he taught you. You're better than him, though, you know?" I say, leaning my weight into him, just needing to be closer.

"Yeah, I know," he says, his face serious at first but quickly falling into a grin.

"How about you. Why are you studying English?" he asks.

I have to think about it for a few seconds, because my answer has changed since I took my first classes years ago. "I've always loved reading," I start, but then I pause. "It's more than that, though. It's like I really understand books, and the story underneath the story. And, I had this fantasy of getting my PhD. I wanted to teach at some fancy college back East. But now…I think I just want to finish something."

Mason's stare at me seems thoughtful, and he leans forward to brush a hair away from my face and kiss my forehead lightly. "You're amazing, you know that?" he says, still looking at me with the same intensity.

"I guess," I say, looking down at my lap, uncomfortable with his compliment. There's nothing very amazing about me at all.

"No, you are. Look at what you've done, on your own. If you want to teach at a college, Avery, you should," he says, lifting my chin to look at him. "You should."

The way he's looking at me forms a lump in my throat. I'm not used to anyone challenging my decision to give up. My father supports me, and I know he'd cheer me on in whatever I do. But Mason—he's doing more than that. He seems to actually believe in me.

"Why don't you talk to your mom much?" I ask, wanting to divert the focus away from me for a while.

Mason lies back when I ask this, taking in a deep breath and folding his arms under his neck. His shirt lifts up just enough to show off his bare skin, and I want to touch it, so I lie back against him and run my hand under his shirt just to feel his warmth. I feel his body react when I do, so I don't linger there long.

"My mom did the best she could," he starts, but then chews at his cheek for a few seconds, his brow bunched, until he turns his body to face me. "No, that's not true. She probably could have done better. She was always pawning me off on people, your dad more than most, so she could go on long weekends with guys she'd meet at the bar. She was always looking for that *quick fix* in life— marry rich and live easy. When I got old enough to realize what she was doing, I'd confront her about it. We had some serious fights when I was a teenager."

"That's when you stayed at our house a lot," I whisper, connecting Mason's story, which I already knew, but for some reason hearing it from him made me feel differently about it all. I felt sad, for him and for Barb.

170

"Yeah, Ray said it was better for me and my mom to have space, rather than ending up hating each other," he says, his eyes coming to mine while he talks, and his lips tighten into a soft smile. "He was right. And I don't hate her. I thought I did for a while, but I realize that she and I aren't very different. We're both selfish in our own way. And I know my mom loves me...she loves me the best she can."

For some reason his words make me want to hold him tightly, so I cling to his side and squeeze his entire body to mine. When I do, he pulls me up to his face and kisses my lips softly. Then, he just stares at my eyes for minutes, the sounds of everything else behind us fading away. The longer he looks at me, the faster my heart races, but I can't tear my eyes away. I won't.

"I love you, Avery Abbot," he says, and my stomach leaps up into my chest, my ribs constricting with every second that passes since he said it. I can't help the tear that forms in my left eye, and I don't dare stop it from sliding from my cheek onto his arm. It's the happiest tear I've ever shed, and I'll never forget it, or this moment.

"I loved you first," I say, my lips actually shaking with my nerves as I speak.

Mason chuckles lightly at me, smoothing my hair from my face and turning completely on his side so we're both lying under the stars staring at one another—alone among a dozen strangers. "Okay, but I get to love you more," he says, cupping my face in both of his hands and pulling my lips to his, his eyes intent on our barely touching lips before flicking back up to look into mine. Then he closes them completely, and kisses me for the rest of the night.

CHAPTER 18: RIGHT AT HOME

Mason

"Ben, you can drink until you vomit after the show. But for now, for the love of god, man...can you just stick with beer?" I plead. I'm tuning my guitar on the side of the stage, playing through a few riffs on some of the songs we're going to do.

"Come on, loosen up, princess. It's just one shot," he says, carrying a tray over to me and the guys. I know Ben; one shot turns into twelve out of nowhere. But it's our first gig together since we all split and headed different directions a couple of months ago, and I'm actually excited about some of the songs we're playing tonight. We're even playing the one I've been working on. It's going to be a little rough, but I don't care.

I give in to Ben's pressure and tip my glass back fast, the tequila burning on its way down. "Wooooooo!" Ben yells, smacking his hand hard on the table. "Okay, just one more..."

I look at him instantly, and he slaps my back. "Just kidding!" he laughs, his breath foul as fuck in my face.

Avery is next to me seconds later, and I can't help but smile at the sneer she gives Ben. "You want some, Birdie?" he says, breathing out in her face.

"Knock that shit off," I say, shoving him away from her. I don't care if it ruins our show for the night; I'm not letting Ben treat her like that.

"Damn, lighten up, Mace. I was just messin' with her," Ben says, his balance a little wobbly when he walks over to the stage steps. He's had more than just one shot, and if I had my guess, he tipped a bottle of Vodka right before we downed that tequila.

"It's okay. I'm used to Ben. He's an asshole," Avery says, her breath against my neck, lulling me back to a happier place.

"It's not okay, and I'm sorry you're used to it. He won't do that again, I promise," I say, kissing her lightly, and squeezing her hand.

"I'm covering the back, so I can sit with Max for a while. My dad's going to hang back there with him, too. But I'll come up front sometimes so I can get a good look at that sexy lead singer," she winks and actually reaches around to grab my ass.

"That's all I am to you, just some piece of meat, huh?" I tease. Honestly, I don't care what Avery wants me for, as long as she wants me.

She smiles while she backs away, and when she spins on her heels to go back to Cole and turn in her orders, I watch every step her long, sexy legs take. "I gotta hand it to you, man. If I knew Birdie was going to grow up and turn into *that*, I would have made a play for that piece a long time ago," Ben says over my shoulder, the words coming out a little rough.

"Yes, I'm sure she would have found you completely irresistible," I poke back at him. He's trying to get under my skin; it's his new thing. But tonight is about starting over, so I'm not going to let Ben push my buttons.

"You ready, kid?" Ray asks, his hand flat on my back. For some reason, every nerve in my body is firing, and for a brief moment, I fear my fingers are so jittery that I won't be able to pick out a note on my guitar. I shut my eyes, take a deep breath, and look at Ray.

"Ready," I say, turning around to get with the guys while Ray announces us to the crowd. Dusty's is full beyond capacity tonight. It's not just me, but the whole band. And as much as I've felt like a failure the last few years, it seems that the people around here think just the opposite. There are people waiting out in the parking lot, just hoping to be able to hear enough or find a way in.

"Okay, guys. Look, I'm not gonna lie. The last few times we've played, we sucked. We hit bottom, and we fucking wallowed in it. We're better than that. Let's find it again, right now. You ready?" I say, looking into their eager faces, Ben probably more eager than he should be.

"Fuck yeah, man!" Ben shouts. I just laugh and shake my head, shouting along with him. Matt and Josh grab their guitars and climb the steps to take their spots; Ben gets comfortable behind the drums, tapping out a few rhythms that make the crowd go absolutely nuts. As soon as Ray is done introducing us, I take the mic, and I look out at hundreds of faces, a few of them familiar.

"So I brought my band this time," I smile, and the girls eat it up. I'll never get used to this reaction, and it makes me blush. I rub my hand over my mouth and chin, hiding my red face until I finally spot Avery in the back. I wink at her, and the group of college girls hanging at the front of the stage goes crazy, screaming my name and telling me exactly what they want to do to me. A month ago, that would have had me ready to fly through the show just to get them up to a hotel room or the trailer after. But I'm so far from interested now, and I actually find them comical.

"We thought we'd play some oldies, cuz...y'all know Ray, right?" I say, drawing everyone's attention to Avery's dad, sitting in his usual spot at the edge of the stage. He stands up and gives a cursory wave; he hates it when I do this.

"Well, Ray...he's *reeeeeallllly* old," I joke, and Ray's wave turns into him giving me the finger in a flash of a second, which only makes me laugh even harder. "But I love this man. He gave me my break, taught me everything I know. So tonight, Ray? This is for you."

We launch into three Johnny Cash songs with a little bit of a modern rock twist, and everyone in Dusty's is on their feet, moving and yelling for more. I look at Ben and nod during the last Cash song, "Folsom Prison." He nods and smiles back. These songs were his idea, and he was dead right—we've never sounded better.

We play five more covers straight, ending with my version of "Wild Horses," this time the band coming in to join me for the last half, and people are actually dancing in the middle of Dusty's, finding space in the crowd. Avery makes her way up front for this one, and I sing the entire thing to her, my eyes not leaving her face once.

I know I'll lose her back to the crowd soon, so I lean over and whisper to Matt that I want to play my tune next, a little out of order. He steps back and tells Ben, who just shrugs and mouths "Whatever." Once we're all on the same page, I take the mic again and get Avery's attention before she can step away.

"So, we've been working on some new stuff. If you guys are up for it, we'd like to play a few for you tonight. What do ya say?" I ask, holding the mic up over the crowd in front of us, amplifying

174

the screams. Tonight is good for our ego, I just hope it doesn't go to Ben's head.

"All right, well...this first one... I've been working on it for, fuck man...oh, shit, sorry Ray," I wince, and everyone laughs. I always give Ray a hard time about his beef with my swearing. It's funny to watch him get angry, at least it is when he's not *really* angry. "Anyhow, I've been working on this one for months. I couldn't seem to quite get it right. Then this girl...well, she sort of helped me see where all the pieces fit. It's called "Perfect," and it's about her."

The hush in the audience is palpable, and every girl up front is turning her head, looking around, trying to figure out exactly who *she* is—every girl but the one I'm staring at. Avery crosses her legs nervously, perched atop one of the stools at the end of the bar. I see Claire come over behind her and poke her arm, teasing her a little, and I see a few of the girls up front notice and cover their mouths to giggle.

The song starts with the melody I played for Max—just me playing soft and slow, and I close my eyes to really take it in, make sure I get every note right. When I look back at Avery, she's chewing on her fingernails again, but her smile spreads the entire span of her face. God that smile—I'd do anything for it. I lean forward so my lips brush the mic, and I start to sing.

Maybe I've been too daft to notice. Maybe I was just too young.

Whatever it was that kept us from us. Whatever that was, it's done.

I hate that I missed...
Every moment...
That you needed someone by your side...
But I won't falter now.

The band kicks in on the break, and the crowd starts literally swaying with us—like those crazy things you see when Springsteen sings one of his classics. *Un-fucking-real!*

I look back at Avery, and she has both hands over her lips, her eyes soft and watering. I love that everyone is getting to hear this song, and I can't believe how people are reacting to it, but truly—

this girl is the one that matters. And seeing her face look like that has my heart pounding out of my chest.

What if I could go back? What if you changed your mind?
Would you still want me so bad, if I wasn't so damned blind.
I hate that I wasted...
So many kisses...
Before my lips knew yours...
Perfect. All you are is perfect.

Time won't let us go back to the place we used to know,
but I won't stop till you let me love you completely.
My heart, breaking in two, that's what you'd do, if you didn't let me...
Oh girl just let me, love you...completely.

I can't help myself when the band breaks into their solo, and I walk to the side of the stage, down the steps and right to where Avery is sitting. I push my hand into the hair that falls down the side of her face, and pull her to me for the deepest kiss of my life. When I back away and smile, her eyes are drenched in tears, but I know they're the good kind, and I mouth "I love you," and head back up to the stage to finish the song out with the guys.

The crowd absolutely loses it after that, and we make it through six more songs before wrapping it up for the night. All anyone wants to talk about is the kiss, and my song. I hear Ben working his angle with some girl, telling her how everything we do is collaboration. I don't really care, whatever helps him with his game. All I want to do is get to Avery.

My mom finds me before anyone else, and she squeezes me in her arms like I'm still a little boy. "Mason, you were so good. I'm so proud of you," she gushes. My mom always gushed when I played, so I sort of take her compliments at half value.

"Thanks, mom. Hey, you see Avery?" I ask, trying to lift my head up high enough to find her in the crowd.

"I think she had to get Max home, hon. She was here for most of the show, though. I think she maybe missed the last song," she says, and for some reason, I'm filled with worry that she left. I pull my phone from my pocket and dial, but she doesn't answer. I try again, but still no answer.

"That…was the shit!" Josh says, his arm draped over my shoulders while he downs what's left of his beer. "Dude, if you can write more crap like that, we're totally going to get picked up again."

"Thanks, man. Seriously, you guys killed it," I say, pounding knuckles with Matt and nodding to Ben. "Even you, you drunken asshole."

"You love me," Ben slurs, his hand already on the ass of the girl he's marked for tonight. The sight of it actually makes me laugh, because not so long ago, my hand would have been on some stranger's ass too. But all I want now is Avery…*Avery!*

I text her quickly, taking a minute before the next barrage of people come up to us to talk.

Are you okay? My mom said you had to get Max home. Is he okay?

I keep my phone in my hand so I can feel it buzz with her return, and I continue talking with people who all want to tell us how much they liked the show. The more people collapse on me, the more overwhelmed I am with the need to climb right through their asses and race to Ray's to make sure Avery and Max are okay. I finally see Ray standing behind a group of girls all waiting to get my attention, and I start to move through them. One actually grabs the front of my jeans when I walk by—*holy shit!*

I smile at her politely because, well face it, I'm still human, but I keep my focus on Ray and let her fingers slip over my body while I move forward.

"That was some gig, kid," Ray's smiles. He's relaxed—this is good.

"Is Avery all right?" I half interrupt before he can say anything else. His reaction to my worry isn't quite what I'd expect. He just folds his arms over his chest and furrows his brow.

"She's…fine Mason. Max was having a hard time with the crowd, so she took him home," he says, watching me basically freak out in front of him.

I breathe deeply when he tells me everything is fine—for some reason Ray's confirmation holding a lot more stock than my mother's, and he starts to smirk at me.

"Sorry," I say, blowing out a big breath and cracking my knuckles behind my neck, when I look back at Ray, I see he's still chuckling. "What, joke's on me?"

"No. Nothing like that," he says, patting me on my back. "You worried about Avery. I like that."

Hell, if I knew that would be all it took, I would have told him about how that's all I've done since the day she smacked me hard across my face.

"Hey, pansy. You comin' out to celebrate with us or what? We're hitting Spanks," Ben says, now somehow holding hands with an entirely different girl. That man's charisma never ceases to amaze me. Ben's a heavier guy, decent looking I guess, but a big guy. But he always bagged the best looking chicks. Of course, second best now.

"I uh…" I look down at my phone just in time to see Avery's text.

Sorry. I was going to text as soon as I got Max to bed. I'm good. Too many people. Started to upset him. I'll wait up! XXOO

"I sorta promised Avery I'd come home. Next time, though, okay?" I say, and I can tell Ben is more than disappointed.

"Whatever," he says, flipping me off and putting his arm around the new blonde he's with, following Matt and Josh out the door. I feel a tight pang in my stomach from watching them leave, and for a split second, I think about saying "Screw it," and catching back up to them. But that thought passes quickly, and it's replaced by wanting to be with Avery as soon as possible.

There are a few people left hanging around the stage while I pack up my guitar and store the guys' stuff; I nod at them as I walk by, but before I get too far, one of them stops me. "You're Mason Street, yeah?" he says, holding out his hand for me to shake. I look at it for a good hard second, and decide he seems decent enough, so I shake it.

"That's me. You enjoy the show?" I ask, pulling my case up to rest it on the table.

The guy laughs a little under his breath and looks at both of his friends who seem equally amused. "Mason, I'm Kevin Quill," he starts, and I don't even think I hear the rest of what he has to say. Kevin Quill has launched the careers of about a dozen singer-songwriter types like me—as in multi-million-dollar kind of launched their careers. I'm looking at his card and reading his name over and over when I realize he's still talking.

"I'm sorry, huh?" I say, my eyes coming up to meet his finally.

"I said I was wondering if you and I could sit down and talk sometime, maybe see if there might be an opportunity for me to work with the Mason Street Band," he says, his perfect white teeth shining right back at me, almost putting me in a trance.

"Uh, sure. I mean, *yes*. That'd be great," I shake his hand again.

"Good, give me a call tomorrow. We'll talk," he says, throwing a couple hundreds down on the table to cover the bill, and leaving with his friends. I look around the bar, and no one is left to bear witness. The only person who would even understand why my jaw is hanging open is Ray, and I can't find him anywhere, so I just throw the guitar in my trunk and head straight to Avery.

CHAPTER 19: PROMISES

Avery

There was no way Mason was falling asleep when he came home. He sounded like one of those state fair auctioneers the way he rattled off everything that happened after I took Max home. I didn't really know who Kevin Quill was when he said his name, but I played along to make him feel good. I could tell that he must be someone important.

I probably fell asleep hours before Mason, so I'm careful getting out of bed. I sneak into my room to grab my clothes from my drawer, and I notice Max's eyes are wide open and looking *almost* at me.

"Good morning. I didn't want to wake you. We have a session with Jenny, and then I'll let you pick your favorite thing to do today," I say—while inside, my mind is racing to get two steps ahead of wherever Max is going to take seeing me slip into the room, not out of it.

"There is a meteor shower tonight. I would like to set up Grandpa's telescope," he says, laying flat on his back and blinking at the ceiling.

"That sounds like a good idea," I say, clinging to my clean shirt, and slowly sliding backward to the door.

"Can I sleep in Mason's room sometime, too?" he asks, and my eyes grow wide. This is where Max is different—he's caught me, completely, but he doesn't really question the whys. All he cares about is figuring out how he can have the same privilege I do.

"You'll have to ask Mason," I say, swallowing hard, knowing that Max is going to ask. I'm going to have to prep Mason for this one.

"All right, I'll ask him tonight, after he watches the meteors with me," he says, sitting up quickly and moving his feet toward the floor. Max rubs his eyes as he stands and walks to the bathroom, shutting and locking the door, completely cutting me in line.

Max is slow in the bathroom. He gets distracted, and usually forgets his purpose. I know I have a good fifteen minutes of alone time, and I use it—sneaking back into Mason's room and running my fingers along his arm to wake him just long enough to warn him about the barrage of expectations that will be waiting on him when he finally wakes up.

"Hey," he says, his voice groggy, and his breath smelling of stale beer and smoke. I pull my cover to my nose, and he covers his mouth when he realizes. "Oh, sorry. Hang on, I'll brush my teeth."

I tug on his shirt and force him back in his bed. "You can't. Max is in there right now," I say, biting at my lip in anticipation of the next part. "He…he caught me."

Mason's eyes are fully open at that, and he turns his head quickly to me, mouthing, "Oh, shit!"

"I handled it…sort of," I say, slipping out of his bed, out of his reach. "So, he's going to ask to have a sleepover sometime. Like, oh, probably tonight. Yeah, uh…and good luck with that!"

I race through his door and slam it shut behind me, tossing my clean clothes to the corner of the hallway, and sprinting down the stairs. I only make it about halfway before his arm is hugging around my midsection and my feet are no longer on the floor. "You threw me under the bus!" he says at my neck, tingles shooting down my entire body from the tickle of his scruffy chin.

"I did no such thing," I say, and he pulls me close again, lifting me, and backing me up the stairs and to his room.

"I call bullshit," he says, a huge grin on his face. "You're the one who's going to end up suffering anyhow. What are you going to do when Max and I are in here having fun all night, and you're stuck over there all by yourself?"

It's hard to concentrate when he has me pinned to the door, his tongue working its way up the crook of my neck and his nose tickling the lobe of my ear. "I'll just read. Maybe even two books," I say, and in a way that thought sounds like a gift from heaven. "Besides, it's lights out at eight o'clock. So, I'm not so sure who's getting the short end."

He starts to tickle at my sides and I giggle uncontrollably. "Oh, I'll show you lights out," he says, his fingers working their way up my sides and coming closer to the tips of my breasts, when

181

I hear a loud knock on the other side of the door, and push his hands away quickly.

"It's Max. Be nice!" I whisper, and Mason opens the door to my son, who's now changed into a bright green outfit. He only likes certain kinds of shirts, and sometimes for him picking out an outfit that he finds comfortable requires a little flexibility in the matching category. His shorts are kelly green today, and the shirt is almost florescent. At least I won't lose him at the store.

"Tonight is the meteor shower. Do you want to watch it with me through Grandpa's telescope?" he asks, turning to look at the door handle while he speaks. This must be really important to Max, because usually we have to bribe him to ask people to interact with him. I kick at Mason's foot so he understands how important this is.

"I'd love to, Max. What time does it start?" he asks, looking at me with a devilish grin. He's found a loophole to my bedtime rule.

"The best time to start is nine thirty. Mom, I am going to have to sit up later," Max says, not really asking.

"Okay," I say. I let it go this time because I can't believe how far he's getting.

"Got it. Okay, I'll be there," Mason says, holding his breath that Max won't push for the next part, and when Max starts to walk away, I think he might have just dodged it.

"I'll bring my blanket and pillow over later to set up my bed," Max says, no longer really engaged with us and now just assuming that the rest of his plan is already enacted. In a way, Max is the ultimate closer—he never even gets remotely close to hearing *no*.

All I can do is raise my eyebrows at Mason and shrug, and while I finish getting ready for the day in the shower, I start to feel bad. I also know Mason can't handle Max completely on his own. There are too many nuances, and I wouldn't send him into that unprepared. When I finally meet them both downstairs for breakfast, I lean over to Mason while Max is eating.

"I'm coming too. Looks like the spare room is going to be awfully full tonight," I smile, and he visibly sighs with relief.

Mason

At first I wanted to take the meeting with Kevin alone—having Ben involved in any type of business discussion is usually non-productive. But playing together last night, the way the four of us were on stage—that felt more *right* than any other performance we'd ever had. I feel like something good is beginning, and I don't want to fuck it up by being shady and doing things behind the guys' backs, so I called them this morning to break the news and set the meeting with Kevin for this afternoon.

Ben's legs are hopping up and down so much that the whole damn table is shaking, and I'm just waiting for Kevin to call the meeting off for fear that our drummer is a coke head. To be honest, I'm not so sure he isn't.

"Let me get to the point, gentleman," Kevin says, pulling the black-rimmed glasses from his face and folding them on the table in front of us. "Your sound is perfect for what we're putting together right now. That whole rockabilly, folk-rock kind of thing is hot, and we're scheduling some big tours. What I'd like to do is have you slated to open for most of the shows in the Southwest."

I cough when I swallow my water because what he is saying is the last thing I expected. I thought maybe we'd get another deal like the last—tour some small venues, build a base and maybe record an album if we were lucky.

"We're in," Ben says, shaking Kevin's hand before the rest of us really have time to process.

"Wait, I have a few questions," I pipe in, and I can feel the guys staring at me, just wanting to punch me in the face for even having a hint of a reservation. "Sorry, but we've sorta been down a road before, and I want to know where this one is leading. When you say *open for a few shows*, what kind of numbers are you talking about?"

"Off the top of my head, probably about twenty or so—primarily Arizona, Nevada, Utah, Denver, Southern Cal, maybe a couple in Texas," he says, pulling up his briefcase to the table to pull out a set of papers that look like contracts. "You'd be opening for some of our up-and-coming bands, venues that hold about twenty."

"Twenty people?" Ben asks, and I want to kick him. Kevin just laughs it off.

"Twenty...thousand," Kevin says.

"Fuuuuuuck me. Where do I sign," Ben asks, perching himself up on his elbows like an anxious child.

"What about recording? Will there be any possibility of that?" I ask, not sure how much Kevin really believes in us.

"Absolutely. Let's see how the shows go. They'll run through the end of the year, and if the response is good, we'll know by late November if we need to schedule some recording time."

The guys are already reading over the various points of the contract, and my paper is sitting in front of me, my pen on top, just waiting for my signature. I know how big this break is. But something has my hand trapped, and I can't seem to get myself to commit.

"Look, Mason. I understand your reservations. I know your story—I don't come into deals like this without doing my homework. I'm going to be really honest, what I'm offering you is the best deal you're going to get—and it might be the last," he says, holding out his hand, just waiting for me to shake it.

My mind is racing a million miles a second, trying to line up every last piece of my life into a neat and tidy row. But it's impossible. The only thing I know for sure is that my dream is hanging on by a thread, and Kevin is holding the other end, and that seems to be enough to get me to shake his hand tonight. I sign my name on that small black line, handing over my life, and then I wonder what the hell I'm going to tell Avery.

"Hells yeah, man!" Ben says, raising his half-empty glass of whiskey to the rest of us for a toast. "To second chances!"

"To second chances!" everyone cheers. I'm not sure which chance I'm referring to, though, and I'm not sure if I'm welcoming one or saying goodbye.

"Okay, you pussy-whipped son-of-a-bitch. No excuses, we're going to celebrate this, and you're coming with us *right now*. You better have dollars in that wallet of yours because we're going to Spanks!

I roll my eyes, but I know I can't really get out of this one, not if I want to survive the next two months on the road with Ben and the guys.

184

"Fine, but not all night okay?" I say, guzzling down the rest of my beer. I reach into my wallet to settle up the tab, but Kevin pushes my hands away.

"This one's on me. I have a good feeling about you guys, and if I'm right, then buying you a beer is the least I can do," he says, and I let out a big breath, taking in his compliment.

Spanks always goes the same. I don't know why I thought this time would be any different. Beers turn to shots, and then the next thing I know every naked girl in the place is hanging around our table while Ben hands out everyone else's money because the fucker never has his own.

"Mason, dude, come on. Just give me one more twenty. I swear this is the last. I *need* to have a little one-on-one sesh with MaryAnne. Come on, buddy," Ben says, leaning heavy into my arm. I know if I moved too quickly he'd fall flat on his face, and I'm tempted. But it's more tempting to give him the twenty so he'll leave.

Matt and Ben are practically making out with two of the girls. There's always been a loose 'hands off' rule at Spanks—that's why we've always come here. It started when we were seventeen, and Ben found a guy to make us fake IDs. Usually, after a few hours of lap dances, I've picked out a girl and taken her to the bathroom for a little *bonus*, but everyone in here looks different to me tonight—it all seems sad and pathetic.

"How about you, baby? You want some of this?" one girl says, running her hands up her body and squeezing her tits together just to jiggle them in front of my face. I'm pretty fuckin' buzzed, but I haven't drank enough to make me want that. All I want is Avery.

"No thanks...but I tell ya what. I'll give you this twenty, and how about you make that guy's day over there and hang out with him *and* your friend," I say, tucking my last bill in the side string of her panties and pointing over to Ben and...what was her name? MaryAnne?

The girl pulls the twenty from her hip and stashes it in a small pouch tied to her wrist, then she rolls her body against mine just once before she leaves, just to show me what I'm missing. I can feel my pants get a little tighter on instinct, but my head is still on

185

straight, despite how drunk I truly am, and I keep my hands to myself and watch her walk away.

I have half a beer left, and I finish that off along with one last shot and then I find Matt to let him know I'm leaving. "I got things, man. But hey, let's hook up tomorrow, okay? You keep an eye on that one, make sure he doesn't land his ass in jail," I say, throwing my head backward to where Ben is now in heaven with two strippers at once.

When I stumble from Spanks, I'm struck by how cold it is outside. When we came to the bar, it was maybe five or so in the afternoon. Still in only a T-shirt and my jeans, I beep open the back of my car and look for a jacket. I find a nasty old gray sweatshirt, so I put that on just to stay warm and then walk over to the edge of the parking lot to pick up a cab. That's always been my line—I don't drive drunk, and neither do any of the guys. I drove us here, so someone will give me a lift back to my car tomorrow.

"Hey, I need to get to…" I pause for a second, suddenly not able to remember Avery's address. "Ah hell man, you know where Dusty's is in Cave Creek? Get me there and then I'll walk you through the rest."

The driver just nods at me, and I settle back into the corner of the cab, my head resting against the window. The closer we get to Cave Creek, the less lights there are along the road until finally the sky is pitch black. I don't know what made me look up, or why I even decided to sit like this for the ride home, but in that very second I see a white light streak across the sky and my heart falls into my feet.

Max!

I pull my phone from my pocket, and when I realize it's 10:45, I go into a full-on panic attack. "I'm sorry, I just realized I'm late for something. Can you drive a little faster? I swear man, I'll pay for your ticket," I clutch the seat in front of me, half considering diving from the car and just sprinting the rest of the way home.

I feel the car move a little faster, but it's never fast enough. The driver gets me to Dusty's, and I still see Ray's truck in the lot, which for some reason makes me feel a little better. At least he doesn't know what a huge, fucking asshole I am. I give the driver directions for the last few blocks and hand him my credit card the second he pulls up in front of Avery's house. I'm waiting at his

186

window for him to hand it back to me, and when he does I literally bolt inside.

The house is dark—completely dark. I try to control my breathing so I can listen to see if I hear anyone, but there's nothing. I race up the stairs, slipping on the middle few and banging my shin hard against the steps, gashing open the front of my leg. "Shit!" I say.

I push open my door and fling on the light, but no one is there. The bed is empty, and Max's pillow and sheets are gone. For some reason, this makes me worry even more, so I race to the other end of the hall and stop at his and Avery's door, holding my hand to my forehead and closing my lips tightly, trying not to make any noise even though I'm panting and my stomach is churning with the want to throw up. I don't hear anything, but I'm not sure that I would. I turn the handle on his door slowly and push it open gently, careful not to let it squeal, and when I see his body laying stiff in his bed, arms straight out next to him and his eyes shut tightly, I collapse to my knees. He's sleeping—and I watch him for a good two minutes to make sure he's *really* sleeping, not just *pretend* sleeping.

I manage to get the door closed, and I slowly walk back to the steps. My body is drenched in sweat now, so I pull the sweatshirt over my head and throw it at my door before climbing back down the stairs to the kitchen. The lights are all off downstairs, but I can see a hint of light coming from the back yard, so I take a deep breath and push the back door open, following the sound of sweeping.

Avery's back is to me, and she's sweeping thousands of tiny pieces of glass into a pile in front of the trashcan. I can hear her sniffle every few seconds, and it breaks my fucking heart. I can't believe I did this—I can't believe I forgot, that I missed something so important.

"Let me get it," I say, grabbing the end of the broom. She lets it go from her hands instantly, and her body just goes still. I don't know what to say, so I just start sweeping.

Ray's telescope is lying on its side, and I can tell from the crystals I'm piling up that his lens is what broke. That's the first thing I'm buying with any money I make from the tour, a new one of these. I'll just get the best one I can.

Avery walks over to the small patio table to get the dustpan, and then comes over to my pile to start scooping it into the trash. I bend down with her and grab her wrist when she does, hoping like hell she doesn't jerk away. Instead, she starts crying.

"I totally blew it. I'm so sorry. I was out with the guys, we signed a deal, and…fuck, there's no excuse. I'm so sorry Avery," I say, the words coming out sloppily, though seeing all of this has me sobering up some.

"I know," she whispers, standing back to her feet and sliding away from me a little. Her movement rips right through me, and I hate that she's running away from me.

"Honest to God, Avery. I had no idea how late it was, and I completely forgot," I keep saying words, like somehow one of these times I'm going to say something that's going to make it better.

"He was pretty good at first. We were just going to watch the meteor shower without you. I told him you were stuck in traffic. But then he found this," she says, holding out a folded piece of yellow notebook paper. I unravel it, and walk closer to the porch light so I can read what it says.

Dear Max,

I am sorry that I was not a better father to you. What you have isn't something I can fix or make better, so I left. I know it wasn't the right thing to do, but I just don't know how to be your dad.

When you are older, please let me know if there is anything I can do for you. I owe you that.

Sincerely,
Your father,
Adam

That fucking douchebag! I threaten him, and I swear I plan on following through with that threat, regardless if it lands my ass in prison, and this is the letter he writes? I'm pacing now I'm so mad, and I'm about to unleash one hell of a rant when Avery's soft voice absolutely wrecks me.

"I'd let you read the one he wrote to me, but I burned it. He said you made him send the letters, and that's the only reason he

188

did. What the hell were you thinking, Mason?" she says through the downpour of tears that are streaming from her eyes.

"Avery, this is *not* what I meant," I say, reaching for her. She shirks away from me though, and it feels worse than being slapped.

"God, don't even, Mason! You smell like a fucking casino!" she yells, pulling her sweater across her body tightly. "Max can read. Not well, but he can read. I didn't see his letter tucked inside mine, and when it fell out from the envelope, he found it. Here's the thing though—Max doesn't know how to *understand* that letter. He's black and white. And that letter? It's gray. It's all kinds of gray! He asked me who Adam was, and then he argued with me, saying over and over that his dad is dead. I didn't know what to say, so I just tried to get him to come back outside. But then it was getting late, and he didn't see any shooting stars, so he threw the telescope to the ground, screaming that I made him miss the meteor shower."

She sits down and holds her face in her hands, her body shaking with each sob. I stand there and look at her—at this mess I made. "Avery, I was only trying to help," I say, pleading.

"He screamed for an hour and fifteen minutes, Mason. The neighbors called the cops. I know the guy who showed up, and that's the only reason it didn't get worse. He walked to the backyard and saw me, holding him…fucking rocking back and forth and waiting for it to stop. You can't just *do* things like that, Mason. You have to live up to *Max's expectations*. Forget about mine," she says, standing to her feet and brushing by me. "Can you just finish cleaning this up? I'm tired. I'm going to bed."

She doesn't turn back around to look at me again, and I'm glad, because I think if I saw the disappointment on her face it would kill me. I spend the next hour cleaning every last piece of glass from the patio and fixing what I can on the telescope. By the time Ray gets home, I've completely survived being drunk, and have gone straight to hungover.

I fill him in over an entire pot of coffee, and he does his best to console me, but I can tell I've let him down, too. By the time I shower and lay in my bed, it's four in the morning. My eyes are fighting to stay awake, but I'm losing the battle, and quickly. The only thing left running in my mind is my biggest fear—that I might

189

not be the kind of man who can do this either. That maybe I'm just as weak as Adam Price.

And maybe Avery deserves something better.

CHAPTER 20: PAPERWEIGHT

Avery

I don't want to go downstairs. Max is already at the table with my dad. I can hear them going about business as usual. For Max, last night isn't even a memory. He's already on his checklist of what today brings. It's Sunday, and usually we do something fun. I don't even remember what we had planned now. Maybe it was the zoo.

Mason's door is open, so I know he's left his room. I can't hear his voice downstairs though. And I don't think I can handle seeing him.

When he didn't show up at the house after his meeting, I was nervous. When the night grew longer, and he didn't respond to any of my texts, I started to feel dread. And then nine thirty came and went, and Max noticed, growing more and more agitated each minute. I didn't know how to set up the telescope. It's old, and my dad has repaired it more times than I can count. I didn't have it mounted steadily, and I know that's why it tipped over so easily when Max pushed on it.

I know my dad won't care. The broken lens isn't a big deal. The thing that keeps eating away at me though is that damn letter from Adam. I know Mason meant well, but I don't think he realized exactly how self-absorbed Adam was. Maybe it's my fault; I didn't portray an accurate picture after my dinner with him that night. My feelings—Max's feelings—are of no consequence to Adam, and Mason must have put the fear of God into him for him to have even written the letters in the first place.

Adam actually blamed me for Max's autism. He pointed to some article he read that said the "mother's genes are the main contributing factor." I know that's bullshit, but that's because I've done nothing but live, eat, and breathe research about Max's diagnosis since the day his first doctor wrote it down on a file.

That's Adam, though. When I look back at our relationship, I can see those pivotal moments—warning signs that he was not a good person. He wasn't really a gentleman in high school, demanding we go *dutch* to prom, always calling the shots in our relationship. He was more interested in making sure my father loved him and approved of his plans for me, than involving me in the decisions and planning our future together. Adam picked where we went to school. He dictated whether I took morning classes or evening classes. And our pregnancy was because he insisted on not using protection.

I'm not saying I was completely complacent, but our lives definitely happened according to Adam's will. His leaving forced me to be strong, and in some small way, I'm thankful for that. I need to be strong—Max needs me to be strong. And I have to be strong now.

Mason is sitting with his back to me at the table when I finally walk down the stairs. I know he hears me come down, and I can visibly see his shoulders tense.

"Out of bacon. Do you want some eggs?" my dad asks, his face telling me he's in on everything that happened.

"I'm not very hungry," I say, and Max picks up on his opening.

"I'm not hungry sometimes, but you make me eat," he says, taking a bite of his pastry. He's hungry this morning, so I'm not even sure why he's being contrary.

"You're right Max. But it's because your body is still growing, so we need to make sure we take care of it," I say, sparing a small glance at Mason. He hasn't lifted his head from his plate once, and from the look of his breakfast, he isn't very hungry either.

"What's on our schedule for today?" I say, going to the small whiteboard on the fridge. It's the zoo—sort of the last place I want to be today, but I will go.

"Zoo, and you said this time I can feed the giraffe," Max says, standing and carrying the crumbs from his shirt over to the trash. Max doesn't really like to be messy, so he's always meticulous about cleaning up after a meal.

"I'd like to come," Mason says, completely knocking the wind out of me.

"We won't be there all day. I have homework, so we're only staying through lunch, and it's kind of expensive to get in without the pass," I say, trying to deter him.

"That's fine. Five minutes—five hours, I'll take what I can get," he says, and the pained look on his face makes me start to soften my resolve. But then I remind myself that I can't just swoon because my heart and body wants Mason Street—I have to use my head.

"Here, you can use my pass. Just hold your thumb over the part that says senior," my dad says, flicking the card from his wallet onto the counter. I grimace at my father when he does this, and he just pulls up one side of his mouth and shrugs.

"Fine, we're leaving in fifteen minutes," I say, and Max cleans the rest of his table space and heads up the stairs to change and get ready.

"Well, I'll be home early tonight. I'd like to hear about that deal you made, Mason. Maybe you and I can chat about it later?" my dad says, purposely asking in front of me. I was pretty sure Mason's meeting was a success. I vaguely recall him saying something about a *deal* last night, but I didn't really have the mental space to ask him about it. That…wasn't really my focus. And that was the problem. I'd lost my focus. It was time I got it back.

"That'd be great, Ray. I've got some questions about it," he says, his eyes on me the entire time.

I can't look at him squarely, and whenever my eyes hit his, my heart actually stings. My dad packs his small cooler and gathers up his books before heading out the door, and the second it shuts behind him, it feels like the room gets a million times smaller—the air completely gone.

"Ave, we *have* to talk," Mason says, his voice desperate.

"Well, I guess we have all day," I say, banging about the kitchen. I get more and more forceful with everything I touch, first slamming the cabinet when I reach for a coffee mug, and then tossing dishes in the sink rather than setting them down. I finally snap one of the plates in two, and it forces me to come to my senses.

Mason doesn't interrupt me, and he doesn't chastise me for acting out. He just sits there and watches, never once judging. He's making this so unbelievably hard.

Max is downstairs seconds later with his usual zoo-ready backpack. He likes to use the binoculars, and he has a book on all of the animals. He'll read us the paragraph about each one, and he likes to see them all, so I know that I'm in for at least two hours of walking.

The drive is silent—and I'm grateful Max is in the car. It gives me time to prepare my thoughts, to play out every possible alternative Mason might throw my way. Of course, when he's sitting right next to me, it's hard to stick to my plan. His smell has permeated my car, and I'm pretty sure I'll never be able to get it out completely. He's wearing a long-sleeved black T-shirt and black jeans, and it's probably my absolute favorite look on him, so I keep my eyes plastered to the road.

We get to the entrance, and the man scanning passes at the gate does a bit of a double take when he runs Mason's card under the machine. I can tell he's thinking about questioning it, but then he looks at Max, already wearing his binoculars and anxious to get to the first animal, and he waves Mason through.

It only takes us minutes to get to the first section—the lizards and snakes. Max will be busy here for several minutes, so I stand back with Mason while Max moves from window box to window box.

"Avery, what can I do?" he asks, and I wish like hell I had an answer for this one. I planned for this question, so I give him the only response I can.

"Nothing, Mason. Nothing," I say, my stomach twisting at the actuality of what's about to play out.

"It can't be *nothing*. I'm so sorry—truly, deeply, unbearably sorry. For everything," he says, and I know he is. And I forgive him. But it still doesn't change the fact that he and I aren't a good idea.

"I know you are, Mason," I say, forcing myself to be brave and look at him. When I do, the stabbing sensation is back, and talking becomes even harder. "I'm not angry at you. Don't get me wrong, I was. And I wish like hell you let me handle Adam, but I know your heart was in the right place—with everything. And I know you didn't mean to miss our date with Max. It was a mistake. A simple mistake—one that anyone in the world could have made."

"But..." he says, knowing there is one.

"But I can't make mistakes with Max," I say, my breath shallow, and not reaching the depths of my lungs. "And as much as I want to be with you, Mason, I'm not the only one with something at stake. And I have a feeling your life is about to get a whole lot more complicated."

He doesn't respond, and I know it's because I'm right. He just stands there, his eyes burning a hole through mine, his hands linked behind his neck while his arms flex. Finally, he tilts his head up and breathes out hard, letting his arms collapse to his sides before walking over to look at one of the reptiles. I give him a few minutes alone, and then I follow.

"He's signing us to a Southwest tour," he says, not looking at me while he speaks. I knew it was coming, but my stomach still hurts hearing it anyhow.

"That's amazing, Mason," I say.

"Is it?" he asks, turning to me, his hands shoved in his pockets, and his lips shut tightly.

"Yes, it is. This is your dream, Mason. And you *have* to see," I say, knowing he does.

"What if I don't go?" he asks, and the way he's biting at the edge of his lip, I can tell he's serious.

"You have to go. You'll regret it," I say, my insides kicking myself. But I also know a thing or two about regrets. Not that I regret a minute of my life with Max. But Adam—I regret him.

"But, would it make a difference?" he asks, this time reaching forward and holding my chin lightly with his thumb and forefinger. My lips tingle just wanting to kiss him, but I can't.

"Probably not," I lie. As soon as I speak, his hand drops from my face and his eyes close.

"Because of Adam and the letters?" he asks, looking at Max with his face pushed close to the glass of an exhibit.

"Because of a lot of things," I say, promising myself I won't cry now in front of him.

We follow Max through the entire dark room back out into the sun, and start the large loop that winds throughout the zoo. The desert animals are next, and I know he will spend a lot of time on these, so we walk slowly until Max is satisfied. Mason is quiet, and it starts to feel like we're angry with one another the longer the silence goes on. By the time we reach the elephants, I'm frustrated with him, and I'm about to ask him why he even bothered to come, when I feel his fingers push through mine.

The touch of his hand startles me, and I let out the smallest cry, which only makes him squeeze me tighter. Neither of us looks at one another, but we keep our hands locked for the small walk that is left. I let Max sift through a few things in the gift shop, and he zeroes in on a resin paperweight with a scorpion sealed inside. We take it to the register, and before I can hand over my card, Mason gives a ten to the cashier.

"I used to have one of those when I was your age," he says to Max, who isn't really listening to him, but just looking at his new treasure, wondering how someone got the scorpion sealed inside.

Mason looks at me next, and smiles softly. I mouth "Thank you," for giving Max the gift.

The ride home feels heavier. Mason reaches for the radio at one point, turning the music up a tick, looking at Max in the mirror to make sure it isn't too loud. Max is busy with his scorpion though, completely lost in that world.

"My birthday is tomorrow. My mom is making dinner, and she wanted *us* to come," he says, his head flat against the passenger window.

"I'd love to have dinner with you and your mom," I say.

"Max, too," he says.

"We'll both be there," I say, my words lingering with everything else I want to ask. We're only a few miles from home, so I force myself to stay here, in this moment. "When do you leave?"

"Tuesday morning," he says, and I can hear him swallow hard. "Avery, I don't know what I'm supposed to do."

I reach over and put my hand on his knee, and he covers it with his hand, his eyes low, looking at our touch. I squeeze once to get his attention, and he turns to me. "You're doing it. You have this tremendous opportunity. And we...we probably rushed into things a little."

"I'd do it all again. Just the same," he says, his face serious as he looks at me. All I can do is suck in my bottom lip and force a smile in return, because I know if I say anything else, I'm going to fall to pieces and run us off the road.

When I pull into the driveway and park, Mason gets out and walks right to his car. "I've gotta meet the guys. If your dad calls, tell him I'll stop by Dusty's," he says, his words barely ending before his car door shuts and his engine is on. His eyes are intent on the gravel drive in front of him—and nothing else—as he pulls away. I gasp for air, forcing myself not to cry until I get Max inside, and I can hide in the bathroom.

Mason

The partying for the guys never really stopped. The three of them were passed out still when I got to Ben's. He never locks his door, and I just walked into the house, greeted by a coffee table filled with half-eaten take-out boxes and a few flies.

I managed to wake everyone up, but they weren't really good for much, and anything we talked about right now would only be remembered by one of us. I think they soaked in enough to know we had to catch the bus in Phoenix while the tour we were joining was passing through on the way to Vegas. I told Ben I'd just spend the night at his house Monday so we could leave early together in the morning. I didn't want to have to leave Avery more than once.

When I pull up, the Dusty's sign is flicking off and on again. If I come back here after our tour, I'm going to fix that for Ray. The last thing that man needs to do is climb a ladder, and it's probably just a short in one of the bulbs. Ray has a local country band booked for tonight, so the parking lot is full of mostly pickups and girls with big hair and bigger hats. I recognize the song when I walk through the bar, and it hits me that this is the same band that was playing when I first rolled into town weeks ago.

I sit down on one of the stools and give them a good listen, I guess hoping it might help me remember everything just a little more vividly.

"Hey, man. I heard about the tour. Congrats," Cole says, pulling the cap from a Heineken and sliding it over to me, and then popping one for himself—we both take a drink, a sort of silent *salute*. "Ray's waiting on you. Said to send you on back when you showed up."

"Thanks, man. Hey, in case I don't see you—take care of these guys...a'right?" I say, and Cole shrinks his eyes a little when he looks at my hand before finally shaking it. He doesn't say anything else, just gives me an understanding nod and smiles before getting back to the growing line of ladies waiting for him at the bar.

Ray is busy in his office, filling out a few order forms and checking them against the inventory books. I used to help him with this when I was a kid. I was good at counting crates. "You know, the business is out there, old man," I say, and Ray laughs lightly and pulls the reading glasses off his face.

"I can't concentrate worth shit out there when someone's playing," he says, kicking back in his chair, and motioning for me to sit down. "So, tell me...how's this thing working? When do you leave?"

"We hit the road Tuesday, early. We'll be gone at least six weeks, maybe eight," I say, watching him chew on the end of his pen and study me. I can read the thoughts he's not saying out loud, what he really wants to know. What does this mean for Avery and me? It's the same question I had, and the same one she answered *for* me. And it's probably going to be the theme of whatever album my ass is lucky enough to write.

"You coming back after that?" he says, his own way of getting to the point.

"I guess that depends...on a lot of things," I say, rubbing my hand over my face, trying to find feeling somewhere.

"Well, I've got something...sort of a good luck thing I wanna give ya," Ray says, grunting as he gets to his feet and moves into the back storage area. I can hear a few boxes sliding around, followed by more grunting.

"You want me to come lift whatever it is? You sound like a walking hernia," I joke, and Ray's face reads *smart-ass* when he comes back into his office. He moves closer to his desk and sets a dusty guitar case on top, flicking open the buckles on the lid.

"I had her fixed up," he says, reaching in and lifting his old guitar—a classic Les Paul. The color was always my favorite, tan in the middle, and burnt black around the edges. Ray taught me everything I know on this guitar, and I secretly wanted it for most of my life.

"Ray, I...I don't know what to say," I say, my hands shaking as I take the guitar from him and hold it close to my body.

"I don't really play much anymore, and it just seemed like a waste. I got her out when you first came to see me, sent her over to Pitch Fork's for tuning up. Just turned out I had an occasion to give it to you," he smiles, and I know he's proud of me. I also know he knows how conflicted I am about leaving, but he's a good enough man not to make it worse with a lecture about the promises I made.

I strum a chord, and it sounds like it did the first time I heard it, my mind flooded with memories—from the first time I drank chocolate milk on the stool out front to the first time Ray pushed me up on that stage. I want to race home and test it out, plug it in and see how it sounds...but then I'd also have to show it to Avery, and we'd have to talk about it, talk about me leaving, about me disappointing her, and letting down Max. And she'd have to remind me that there's nothing I can do to make her change her mind...again.

"I know I should probably say it's too much and I can't accept it, but...I'm not going to lie, I want it," I smile, and he laughs at my honesty. I play a few more chords and then hand it back over for him to tuck safely in its case.

"The handle's shot, so be careful when you lug it around. You might want to invest in a better case," he says, handing it over to me completely.

I can't get over looking at it in my hands. The depth of his gift isn't lost on me, and it has my eyes tearing a little, so I set the guitar down on my chair and walk around the desk to give him a hug.

"I'm proud of you, Mace. Real proud...no matter what happens, huh?" he says, pulling me square with him, his hands on my shoulders. "Ave's real proud of you too. She'll come around; she's just careful. She has to be. You get it, right?"

"I do," I say, my heart absolutely sick knowing that after tomorrow night's dinner, there's a chance I may never see Avery Abbot again.

CHAPTER 21: DINNER FOR FOUR

Avery

Early this morning, I told Max about having dinner with Barb. I told him, because I knew if I made solid plans with him, I couldn't back out. And I want to back out—I want to desperately. But I'd hate myself for it.

I sent Mason a text, and told him we'd meet him at his mother's apartment. He was gone early this morning, and I noticed everything was cleared out of his room. My dad said he was spending the night with the guys because of their early start on Tuesday, but I know Mason is just avoiding me.

I'm not angry with him. Honestly, I've blown it with Max millions of times. And the more distance I get from the letters coming from Adam, the more I appreciate Mason making him write them. The result might not have been very good, but the intention was heartfelt. It doesn't change the fact that me being in a relationship with Mason is a bad idea. I need to have one hundred percent of my focus on Max and his success, and anyone else in my life needs to have those same priorities. Mason doesn't—and that's okay.

I brought Max's dinner. I know Barb will understand. I have it clutched in both of my hands in a small Tupperware container while we wait at the front door. Max is fidgety today. He had some additional homework to finish after school, which of course wasn't part of his plan. I bribed him with a few extra candies, and I'm sure he won't want his dinner. I'm also sure he remembers how I skipped breakfast the other day, so this evening might end up getting cut short.

Mason opens the door, and he's dressed nicer than I expected. His shirt is a white button down, tailored to his chest, and the ends aren't tucked in to his black dress pants. He's wearing black dress shoes, and his sleeves are rolled up, revealing a piece of the tiger's tail and a really nice silver watch. He waves us in; when I pass, he pulls me in for a hug, and kisses the top of my head. He smells like a dream.

"Sorry, we're a little underdressed," I say, looking down at my flip-flops and long maxi skirt. I pulled my hair into a ponytail before we left, so at least I look like I gave some thought to how I looked. Max is wearing purple shorts and a yellow shirt, and he looks a little like an Easter egg.

"You look beautiful," he says, his eyes hovering over my face for a few long seconds. "I dressed up for my mom. I got the sense this was a big deal to her."

Not sure what to do, I hand Max's dish to Mason. "It's for Max. He won't eat other food, so I brought his normal dinner," I say, suddenly feeling awkward and out of place.

"Right, good idea. I'll let my mom know. Come on in, we're in the kitchen. Dinner's almost ready," he says, walking to the back of his mother's apartment. I follow him, taking note of all of the pictures of Mason on her walls. It's like reliving my own youth seeing him grow in school portraits. I stop at one—a family collage holding several photos in the same frame.

"My mom likes pictures," he says, his breath tickling my shoulder and causing goosebumps to rise on my arms. I know he notices, but he doesn't draw attention to it or embarrass me. "Every photo I take or get, she hangs it up."

It's completely the opposite of what I expected to see in his mother's home. I never visited their house when I was a kid— Mason was always at ours. And his mom moved so many times later in life, there was just never really an opportunity. "She seems proud of you," I say, dialing in on one photo in particular, a young Mason with his mom bending down in a garden to smell flowers.

"Yeah, I guess..." he says, his gaze somewhat lost and his mood melancholy as he takes in the full line of photos on the wall. "They just don't seem real. I mean, I'm smiling in these pictures, but...I don't remember having these memories."

Mason's memories are wrapped up in my home, with my dad, and while I'm glad he has those, I'm sad he doesn't have them with Barb.

"Ehhhh, I'm just being crazy. Ignore me," he shrugs, shaking his head and forcing a renewed smile on his face. He's putting on a good act—for his mother *and* me.

Barb is busy putting the final touches on the table when we walk into the kitchen, and I smile when I see the small sheet cake she made. It's almost like she's trying to make up for a dozen missed birthdays with this one dinner.

"Avery, oh honey, thanks for coming!" she says, giving me a hug. Barb has always been nice to me. When I first started waitressing at Dusty's, she would handle the rough customers for me, sometimes throwing them out all on her own.

"Thanks for having us," I say, pulling the lid from Max's dinner of fruits, veggies and crackers. "I hope you don't mind, but he's sort of picky."

"Of course not," she says, pulling out a plate for me to set up for Max.

We all get situated around the table, and Barb scoops large heaps of pasta into each of our bowls. Her sauce, on the potholder on the table, is still bubbling; when I put my spoon in to pour some on my plate, the sauce snaps, and a drop burns my arm. Without a word, Mason dips the corner of his napkin in his ice water and presses it to my arm.

"Better?" he whispers, and I just nod.

"So, Avery...did Mason tell you the news?" Barb says, her face beaming. She should be proud—Mason deserves this. In fact, he should be headlining, not just opening for bands. But his time will come; I know it will.

"He did. It's very exciting," I say, and I notice that Max is swinging his legs under the table while I talk. I reach next to me and stop them with my hand. "Max, Mason is going to perform some concerts in some other states. Isn't that neat?"

Max takes a big bite of one of his crackers, chewing with his mouth open, not quite finishing his bite when he finally speaks. "I think he should just stay at Grandpa's," he says, and I hear the air escape Mason's nose in one swift exhale.

"I know, we all are going to miss him, but we want other people to get to hear his songs, too," I say, knowing that for Max, missing Mason is partly about not wanting to see something he's grown comfortable with change. But I also think that somewhere, in the midst of things, Mason has become his friend.

"You should play our song for people," he says, going right back to his crackers.

Mason laughs a little under his breath at first. "I will, Max. I'll make sure they know who my writer is," he says, his eyes meeting

202

mine and holding on. Every look twists my stomach a little tighter, just as does every minute passing—every second closer to the time when he'll be gone.

Mason ends up telling us stories about his first tour, about places they played and how much smaller they are from the places they're about to go. He does most of the talking; I can tell he's trying to fill the silence because his mom doesn't really have much to say.

We all manage to save room for a small piece of cake, and, after some teasing, Mason gets away with not having to blow out any candles. I help Barb clear the table when we're done, and Max takes care of putting his container away. I know he's going to get antsy soon, so I pull the iPad from my bag, and set him up on the sofa with it for a few minutes, so I can help with dishes. Barb is packing up a few to-go boxes for me to take some leftovers home to Ray when an old Otis Redding song comes on the radio.

Mason smiles when he hears it, and walks to the corner of the kitchen to turn it up. "May I?" he says, reaching for his mother's hands.

She doesn't answer, wiping the small tear in the corner of her eye with the neckline of her blouse, and smiles at him, her lips tight, holding in her emotions. I watch as she gives her son her hand, and he moves her the few steps to the middle of the kitchen floor and pulls her in for a dance. I almost feel like I'm intruding, but I'm so grateful to bear witness to this moment. Mason is giving his mother a gift, for nothing in return, just because he wants to. I pull my phone out when they aren't looking and snap a photo, then message it to him instantly—Mason will finally have a memory attached to one of those images of him with his mom.

We listen to a few more songs while Barb brews a pot of coffee, but Max's patience starts to wear. He's no longer staying in his seat very long, instead pacing around the room on his toes while playing his game on the iPad. We usually go to the store in the afternoons on Mondays, and I know Max will want to make sure we have everything we need for his lunch bag next week.

Maybe I'm inventing a reason to leave, or maybe Max is about to have a meltdown. Either way, the longer I hesitate, the more my body fills with anxiety, until I can't handle it anymore.

"We have to go," I blurt out, stopping Barb and Mason mid-conversation. I can tell Mason's taken off guard, and I can actually see his mind working on ways to convince me to stay. "I need to get some things for Max, and he has school tomorrow. I didn't get much done yesterday, and I need to take advantage of Claire filling in for me tonight."

"Right," Mason says, his face down at his feet.

"Well here, take this home for your dad," Barb says, tying the top of a plastic bag tight around a few containers of food and handing it to me.

"I'll walk you out," Mason says, his hand resting on my back, and his fingers barely grazing my skin, like he's unsure if his hand belongs there. We get to the car, and Max is quick to settle in, shutting his door and buckling up. I can see the iPad light up his face in the back seat, and I know Mason and I will have a few minutes out here alone before Max will insist I get in the car.

"So, you leave tomorrow?" I ask, setting my small bag of food on the rooftop of the car and turning to face Mason, pulling my arms tightly around my body to warm myself from the breeze.

"I do. Early," he says, his lips partially open, like more words are just hanging on his tongue, waiting to be said. He reaches his hand up, running the back of it down the side of my face, watching his fingers caress my cheek slowly, tracing every centimeter of my profile. He sweeps a few loose strands of hair behind my ear and holds his hand there, just staring at me.

"I should go," I say, taking in a deep breath, and holding it like it's my last.

"I'll be back," he says, his eyes giving away the uncertainty I know he really feels.

"I hope so," I say, my teeth tugging at my lip while I hedge on saying the rest. "But I understand if you can't. Max isn't expecting you, and I'll be okay."

I won't be okay, and as I stand here and pretend I'm strong, I know I'm crumbling inside. But Mason has this life—he has this *gift*—and it just doesn't match with anything in my world. And I know that forcing it won't make it so.

I stretch on the tips of my toes, reach my hand around Mason's neck, and press my lips to his lightly, and I whisper, "Good luck," but what I'm really saying is...*goodbye*. I grab the

204

pasta from the roof of my car and open my door to get in, my body almost anticipating him to protest— to grab me, and pull me back to him, to refuse to let me go. But I shut the door, and the sounds of outside go completely silent.

It's Max and me, just like it always is—and Mason is on the outside, looking in. He holds up his hand and stretches his fingers, and I can hear him say, "Goodbye," through the window. I hold my fingers to my lips, and then press them flat to the window; he touches the other side, his touch sliding along the glass as I slowly drive away.

I cry silently for the short drive home, and I force my breath to regulate by the time I pull into our driveway so I can get Max upstairs, help him with his bath, and put him to bed. I don't have the strength for groceries tonight, so I'll make do with what we have. But the distraction of my routine is welcomed, and the next hour goes by rote as I work my way through the nightly checklist. I'm usually at work for this part, so I look forward to reading the planet book with Max. I offer to read extra tonight, mostly because I don't want to go back to the thoughts in my head, but Max tells me he's done. I put the book away, and I pull his heavy blanket over his body. My body itches to hug him, and so I ask him if I can hug him goodnight since I don't get to do this part often. He lets me, but his body is rigid when I do, and I can tell he doesn't want me to touch him for long.

"I'm going to work on some homework downstairs and wait for Grandpa," I say, pausing for Max to respond, but he only shuts his eyes, squeezing them tightly, readying himself for me to shut the lights off. He'll pretend to sleep for a while, and eventually he'll fall into it for real.

I spread my notecards out across the kitchen table, and add a few more to my mix. I have one final paper to complete, and I have a lot of time, but I need to keep myself busy until my eyes grow tired. I slide the cards around the table a few times before giving up, and pulling them back together with my rubber band and deciding to focus on reading. I'm only slightly more productive doing this, making my way through one entire page in the hour it takes before my father finally comes through the door.

"Hey, you wait up for your old man?" he smiles, clearing out his pockets, and piling his usual work stuff on the counter.

"I did. Barb sent me home with leftovers. You want some? It's really good," I say, going to the fridge and pulling out the bag.

"That would be great. Thanks," my dad says, slipping his shoes from his feet and falling into his chair, rubbing his hand over his eyes. "I'm beat today."

"Well, Barb's carbs should put you right to sleep then," I joke, and my dad nods in agreement.

I heat his food up and put it on a plate for him, sliding it over and getting us both a glass of milk. I used to love waiting up to watch my father eat dinner. My mom would always have leftovers ready for him, and she'd let me sit up extra late on the weekends so I could keep him company. I was always closest with my dad, and I think it's because of our late night talks, which grew more and more complicated the older I got.

"So, Mason's leaving tomorrow," I say, starting our most difficult talk yet.

"He is," my dad says, chewing, but keeping his eyes on me, waiting to dissect my reaction. I don't have one though—I almost feel emotionless. "You okay with this?"

"I am," I say, my stomach fluttering with my own doubt. "It's better this way. I have to focus on school and Max."

"Hmmm," my dad says, sitting back and wiping at the corners of his mouth with his napkin. He folds his arms and sucks in his top lip—that's his tell, and I know he doesn't believe me. "You know, it's okay to mess up baby girl."

I'm not sure what he means, and my natural instinct is to be defensive. I hold my breath and bunch my brow. I'm unsure what to say, so I just shake my head, and my dad chuckles softly.

"I'm not talking about Mason. I'm talking about you. You have yourself locked into this pattern—and if everything doesn't fall into place every second of every day exactly how you have your blueprint set—you take it out on yourself," he says, pausing to let me catch up. I nod to let him know I'm listening.

"I have to," I say, my eyes tearing up from the pressure building in my chest. I don't do failure well, and even talking about missteps fills me with anxiety.

"Bullshit," my dad says, slapping his hand on the table, causing me to jump. "Life is full of things that don't go according to plan, Avery. And Max needs to learn how to make adjustments for those things. I'm sorry, but you not letting the spontaneous things in life happen isn't good for Max. And baby girl, it's going to kill you!"

"But what if he hurts himself? What if someone hurts him when he's angry or frustrated? What if I can't be there to calm him down?" I'm crying hard tears now, my body shaking; my dad reaches across the table, clutching my hands in his, forcing me to look him in the eyes.

"That's life, Avery. And you *can't* always be there. That's why he needs to learn about life's peaks and valleys now, while you're here to guide him," my dad says, shaking my hands against the table, literally trying to shake reason into my body. "You love Mason, and Avery, he's a good man. He's real, and he's going to drop the ball sometimes, and he might make you have to make some hard choices, make some changes in your life. But don't give up on your own happiness just because you're afraid it's too damn hard to have. Because Ave, you only get to have *right now* once in your life—there are no re-dos, there is no going back and doing *right now* again. You get this once, and you can take a chance on it, or live regretting you didn't. I can tell you what, though...the Avery that takes a chance on her own happiness is going to be a hell of a lot stronger for Max than the one that gives up."

I'm too terrified to cry, but my insides are holding on, just waiting for the sobs to come pouring out. "I don't know if I can do this," I say, my voice cracking with my own fear.

"Go," my dad says, his lips tight, and his face daring me. My legs are wobbly as I try to stand, and my hands shake as I reach for my purse and pull out my keys. "Girl, I can't drive you, so you're going to have to pull yourself together. Just breathe—and go tell that boy you love him, and you'll see him soon."

I nod *yes* and race through the door, dropping my purse open on the porch, spilling the contents everywhere. I shove everything back inside, and toss it in the passenger seat of my car, firing up my engine and actually peeling out of the driveway when I leave. My heart is thumping in my chest, and it races faster and faster the harder I press my foot on the pedal. The streets are quiet, and the main drag is dead on a weekday night, so I don't even bother to stop at the four-way stop between my neighborhood and Barb's. I circle through her apartment complex, but I don't see Mason's car, and panic fills me.

"Ben's!" I think, slamming the car in reverse, and pulling back out on the main road through town. Ben is closer to the city, in a rougher part of town, so I slow down as I get closer, careful to watch for any other drivers. I recognize Ben's car out front, so I know which small house belongs to him, but I don't see Mason's car anywhere. I keep the engine off and I wait, like I'm stalking him in the dark. Minutes pass, and not a single car drives down Ben's road—nothing to even give me hope. I'm about to give up when a light flicks on at the side of the house, and the side gate swings open. I get out of the car without even thinking, just hoping it's him.

"Mason?" I say, my voice a loud whisper.

"Oh shit! Damn, Birdie. You scared me," Ben says, and my heart literally explodes with disappointment.

"Is Mason here?" I ask, my mouth watering with the need to be sick.

"Nah, he took off an hour or two ago with Matt and Josh. They had some things to take care of, and I think they were going out for a while, meeting Kevin and one of the bands we're leaving with tomorrow. You need something?" he asks, and I don't know what to say. I *need* Mason. I just stare at my phone, considering calling him, but I can't help but note the shakiness of my fingers as I slide them back and forth over the phone screen. My whole body is shaking, so badly that I have to hold myself up against Ben's car.

"Are you...all right?" Ben asks, his face bunched at the sight of me. I feel really ill, and my body is covered with beads of sweat.

"Yeah, I uh...I suddenly don't feel very well. God, I'm sorry," I say, shuffling my feet backward closer to my car, suddenly questioning everything I'm doing.

"You want me to just tell him you stopped by?" Ben asks. I stop and look at his feet, scratching at the side of my face, and tugging at my lip while I think about his question. I could call Mason right now. I could sit here at Ben's house, or in his driveway, and just wait. Or I could have Ben tell him to call me. But the end is always the same—I'm always...waiting. I'll be waiting for Mason, just to tell him I'll keep waiting. And that's the

208

change I would have to make in my life—to decide to wait on Mason for the rest of my life. Because in my heart, I know that the second he gets on that bus in the morning, his career is going to take off—he's *that good.* And I have to decide if I want to wait for those moments he can fit me in between everything else. And I don't know if my heart can take all of the doubt and worry that comes along with Mason's success.

"You know what, it's nothing," I say, and my pulse slows down as soon as I give in. "I'll just…I'll just call him later this week. Really, it's not important."

Ben just nods and shrugs his shoulders. "A'right then. Well, see ya when I see ya! Hey, maybe the next time we play Dusty's we'll be fucking millionaires!" he says, tossing the small bag of trash in the can outside and heading back through his gate. All I can do is smile and hold up my hand, a total farce to the self-loathing now kicking off inside. I get back in my car, and I drive home. My dad has gone to bed, and I'm thankful—I don't think I can handle having him talk me into risk ever again. I'm starting to think regret is just easier, and I resolve myself to learning how to swallow it.

CHAPTER 22: THE ROAD

Mason

The shows are good. That's what's getting me through. That and the way the crowd reacts every time we play some of our new songs. People seem to love "Perfect." It's probably because out of everything, that's the one song I play with everything I can. We did a cool thing during the last show—I talked the guys into letting me play it solo on the piano. My piano playing isn't the best, but the melody is simple enough. I had chicks in tears by the time I was done.

I think about her every time I play it. We've been on the road for a month now. Kevin started us out with this folk rock band called the Tenenbaum Revival. They have a lot of radio hits right now, and I really dig their sound. They're from Denver, and the lead singer is married to the bass player. I envy their lives, the way they get to be together. It's easy when your paths are the same, I guess.

I called Avery the night before our first show. She didn't answer, but I figured she was busy with her shift. But she never called back. I sent a few texts, and at first she'd respond—simple things like smiley faces and "happy for you" notes. But I quit sending things a couple weeks ago. Maybe this time apart has made her start to think that everything was a huge mistake. If she wants to forget me, maybe I should let her.

I miss Max. I found a book at this little trading post in Utah. It was all about rocks from other planets. He'd love it—probably memorize it. I bought it with the intention of sending it to him, but every night I just flip through the pages and think about him and Avery, wondering if she's working or getting to tuck him in. I wonder if that girl in the playground ever became Max's friend.

"Mace, we need to do sound check in thirty. You know where Ben is?" Matt asks, popping his head in the green room.

"Probably giving his paycheck to a hooker," I say, causing Matt to chuckle. "I'll go look for him in a few."

210

We're in Reno tonight. Probably the smallest show we've played. Kevin wasn't lying, this tour is different, and I really believe there is a recording deal waiting for us at the end of this. We have a couple weeks left before Kevin decides if he wants to tack us on to some more shows.

Ben has behaved, for the most part. Only once or twice did I have to drag his ass to the bus out of some nightclub or bar. He's had a few flings, probably five or six different girls, but so far he's kept them out of the bus. I think if we weren't bunking with the other band, it would be a different story.

I walk out to the lot, and notice a few groupies hanging out over on the other side of a fence where the busses are all lined up. During our first few shows, the women were always hanging around to see Ryan, the lead singer in the Tenenbaums. But they've started screaming for me when I walk out, too. It feels pretty surreal, and there have been some pretty tempting offers, not gonna lie. But I keep waiting for that hint of reddish blonde hair in the crowd. I keep waiting to *feel* something—a pull, I don't know, *something*.

The girls scream as I climb into the bus, and I wave once just to show them I appreciate them—and I do. I hope they want more of our songs, want to buy our albums, and come see our shows over and over. But I don't want to sleep with them. I guess maybe after a while I'll get over that, and then maybe I'll want that, too.

"Ben, get your ass up! We tune in twenty!" I say, kicking at the bathroom door, hearing him sniffle and move around inside.

"Hang on," he says, and I hear the sink for a few seconds before the door finally pops open. Ben's eyes are wild, and he keeps rubbing his arm along his nose; I know the second I see him he's fucked up. He's been like this before. It's been a while, and he's never completely fallen into full-on addict, but he's dabbled—usually when some stripper hooks him up, or he shacks up with the wrong girl. I'm sure that's the case tonight.

"Fuuuuuck, dude? What did you do!" I say going into the bathroom to search for what I know is there. There's a small bit of powder left on the sink counter, so I grab a handful of toilet paper, wet it and wipe everything clean.

"I'm fine man, really. Just a little hit," he says, his arms twitchy and his whole fucking body keeps jumping around. He sits

211

on one of the benches in the living room area and looks at me, his whole foot bouncing up and down. "I might have overdone it, maybe a little."

"You think so?" I yell, leaning back against the other bench seat, pulling my hands to my temples and rubbing. "You think you can play through this?"

"Yeah, I'll be good," he says, edgy as shit. I shake my head, and pull the blind back to look out the window; just making sure we're really alone. The last thing I need is someone walking in on this. My phone buzzes once, and I know it's Matt or Josh wondering where the hell we are.

"Look, I'll just tell them you're not ready yet for tune. We can do that without you. But fucking get it together," I say, watching him stand and look around the bus, like he's searching for something.

"I just need my wallet. Shit, I think that bitch took my wallet," he says, heading to the back of the bus to check the bed area. My phone buzzes again, so I pull it out to let Matt and Josh know what's up. When I see an unknown number, I shove it back into my pocket, but the second I do, it buzzes again.

I swipe the string of messages open, half expecting to see spam or crazy fan messages from some chick who probably found my number.

It's Claire. Mason, you need to call me. Now!

Mason, R U there?

Mason, 911 – it's an emergency!!!

Claire—the only reason Claire would have my number is Avery, and now I'm just as twitchy as Ben. My fingers can hardly dial, but I manage to hit the return call button. I'm pacing as I wait through the rings, and Ben is storming around me, tossing cushions over and opening and shutting drawers. I shove my finger in my ear so I can listen to the other end of the line.

"Mason, oh thank god!" she says, and I feel my heart sink to my feet, knowing that whatever she's going to say, it's going to be the worst news of my life.

212

"What's wrong, Claire. Is it Avery? Is she all right?" I say, forgetting where I am, and stepping off the bus. The screaming starts the second I come outside, but I can't handle Ben's jumpiness in the bus, so I walk around to the other side to muffle the sound as best as I can.

"It's not Avery, Mason. It's Ray. He...Ray passed away, Mason," she says, and just like that, everything around me turns bright white and my body loses all feeling. I sit down on the pavement, and push my head between my knees, my hand cupping the back of my head, and I'm rocking—like I'm trying to rock away everything she just said.

"Mason, are you there?" her voice sounds like she's talking through a tin can, so far away.

"I..." I can't catch my breath, and I start to sob hard, my chest convulsing and my mouth gasping, just trying to take in air. Claire senses my break down, and she talks softly.

"Mason, I'm so sorry. I'm so sorry I had to call you and tell you, and that it had to be me, and it had to be now. I know you're probably in the middle of stuff. But it's Max," she says, and I don't know that I can handle it—handle more. My eyes are wide and staring at the pattern of parking lines that stretch hundreds of feet in front of me, drifting in and out of focus until the white and black bleed together into a giant block of gray.

"Max is missing. He overheard Avery talking to one of her aunts, and she hadn't had a chance to explain things to him yet. When she went up to his room, he was gone. She's looking everywhere, Mason. Your mom is looking, too. We shut Dusty's down for the day. Your mom said I should call you," she says, and then I listen for several seconds to the silence that follows. Somehow, I get back to my feet, push down the vomit that is threatening to come, and start pacing again.

"Where have you looked?" I ask, closing my eyes and flashing through a million visions—Ray's face, the first time he put me on stage, the way he looked when he gave me the guitar, Max, Avery. In the last two months I've built this file of memories, and it's all wrapped up in the Abbot family—they're *my* family.

"We've looked everywhere, Mason. We went to his booth at Dusty's, tore apart the kitchen, searched every nook of the damned house," she says, and something triggers me.

"School. You have to go to his school, Claire!" I yell, walking back into the bus now. Ben seems to have found his wallet, and he's sitting on the edge of a sofa watching some show play loudly on the TV. I walk up to it and flip the switch to turn it off. He starts to protest, and I shove him back into his seat.

"There's a tunnel, in the playground. It's Max's safe place. He has to be there, Claire. He has to be," I say, making a stern face at Ben when he starts to argue with me again.

"Okay, I'll go look right now. I'll call you back," she says, hanging up. I stare at my phone and manage to bring enough sense to my head to save her number as a contact. I shove the phone in my pocket and sit back on the sofa to think.

"What the fuck, man?" Ben says. I'm not even remotely close to being in the mood to deal with him, so I just point at him to stay put and walk out of the bus. It doesn't work though, and he's quick to follow me.

"Who was that? Fuckin' Birdie? What, she want you to blow off the tour? Come back and be her bitch boy?" he can barely finish his last sentence before my fist lands at his jaw. As much crazy crap that I've done, I haven't really been in a ton of fights, and the crunch of his bone against my knuckles stings; I have to shake my hand just to get feeling back in it. But Ben is so goddamned high, he's right back in my face, shoving me until my feet lose their balance and I stumble into the side of the bus.

I shove him back, adrenaline fueling my entire body; I keep pushing at his chest until he trips onto the ground again. "You say one more word about her, and I swear I will end you," I say, my knee weighing into his chest. He spits to the side, and it's bloody.

"She's just being selfish," he says, and I can't help but laugh at how absolutely wrong he is. I walk away from him, back to the bus, and climb inside, slamming the door behind me. Seconds later, it swings open, and I clench my fist, ready to go another round, but I soften when I realize its Matt.

"Josh is outside, cleaning him up," he says, his opinion of Ben obvious in the face he's making. Of the three of us, Matt is the one who has always had the least amount of tolerance for Ben. "What'd he do to earn that?"

"Just Ben being Ben," I say, chewing at my tongue, forcing myself not to say anything more that I might regret. I sit back

214

down and lower my head into my hands. I have to think—process everything. I'm trying to figure out my next move, when my phone rings and I answer quickly.

"Yeah," I say, and I can already hear familiar voices in the background.

"It's Claire. You were right, Mason. We found him. Oh my god," she's crying now, hard. "How did you know?"

"I just knew," I say, my heart finally beating for the first time since I heard Claire's news. "What...I mean, how...I..."

I don't even know what to ask her next or how to move forward. All I know is that I'm no longer where I need to be, and I'm looking at Matt, square in the eyes, and I know he knows too.

"It was fast, Mason. With Ray? It was fast, in his sleep. He didn't feel a thing," she says, I know trying to sooth the burn of the guilt that is absolutely choking me now. "It was a heart attack. He ate like shit, and he drank a lot—probably more than he should."

"It's not fair," is all I can say, and I'm crying again. I push the palm of my hand deep into my eyes, trying to force myself to get a grip; I take a deep breath and look at Matt. "He was a good man, and I wasn't there. And it's not fucking fair, Claire!"

"I know it's not, Mason. But there's nothing you can do...nothing you could have done," she says, and I don't know that that's the case, but I appreciate her saying it anyhow.

"When...I mean, is there...a service?" I ask, not even sure how these things work.

"It just happened—this morning. I don't know any details yet. Avery's...she's working through it. Probably something this weekend. We'll make sure you know, though—I'll call you, or your mom will," she says, and I can't help but notice that it's not Avery, which only makes my tears come faster.

"Thanks, Claire. Hey, call me if there's anything..." I start, but I know there's nothing I can do. I'm four hundred miles away, and my foundation is crumbling.

"I will," she says, and then she's gone. I just sit there and stare into Matt's eyes, talking without really talking, for minutes.

"There will be other bands," he says finally. I don't know what to say back to him, so I just blink and breathe through my nose slowly, trying to make sense of everything. "You need to go. And I'm fine with that. And Josh will be fine with that. And Ben—

whatever. There will be other bands. And there are other drummers. And *this* isn't *everything*."

My body is tingling everywhere, and I swear if anyone walked into this situation right now, they would think that I'm the one who's high as a kite.

"If I leave, they'll drop us—drop everything," I say, my insides squeezing at the fork in my road. Both paths are hard—there's nothing easy left, not that *this* was ever easy.

"Like I said, there will be other bands," he repeats, and I look down, finally understanding what he's trying to say. Matt always knew that we'd never be able to stick to this together for long. I think we all knew Ben would probably ruin us first—the label can only handle so much. We'd replace him, or they'd decide to take me solo—put me with a band they're used to, that they use for lots of singers. And I know that's probably closest to the truth. The songs are all mine—but I feel beholden to Josh and Matt...and for some reason to Ben.

"There will be other bands," I repeat, nodding up and down, convincing myself.

"Yep," he says, smiling softly to show me he understands.

There will be other bands.

CHAPTER 23: A GOOD LIFE

Avery

"My father had very few regrets," I say to the rows of familiar faces looking back at me. It's an unusually warm day, and hundreds showed up for Ray's service, so all I see are waving programs and note cards as people fan their faces.

"You all knew him, and most of you knew him well, because that's who my father was. He loved fiercely, he embraced friends easily, and once Ray Abbot was on your side—it was hard to lose him. Some did...but those people were few and far between.

"He never stopped parenting. He was giving me advice up until the very end. I didn't always follow his advice, and per usual, my father was right—I regret not taking those things to heart. But his lessons will always stick with me, and in his absence, I'm vowing to take his place in this world—at least as best as I can. I'm going to enjoy this earth and the people on it every chance I get, and I'm going to appreciate every single one of you."

I'm struck when I glance over the dozens of smiles looking back at me. No one is crying, and they shouldn't. Ray Abbot spread joy in the world—it's why he loved music so much, and why he tried to encourage people who had that talent to share it with the world—people like Mason.

"I know many of you are worried about what will happen to Dusty's. It's been around a long time. My father opened it years ago, and I don't intend on closing it. Please, bear with me though—I'm not my father, and I don't really know the ins and outs of the bar business. I plan on getting some help...*eventually.* But these next few months might be a little bumpy. We'll open back up in two weeks—an open mic night, in true Ray Abbot style. In the meantime, spend your weeknights with your loved ones. I'm asking you to do this for me. Squeeze in those moments, and make time. These moments are precious, and...as my father said to me not so long ago, 'you only get to do *now* once in your life. Do it right.'"

I manage to hold it together until I leave the stage and edge back up into Claire's side. I lose it again the moment her hand slips in mine. We aren't a particularly religious family—we've been to church a few times, but when it came time to settle on services for my dad, I just went with the same *everything* that he did for my mom. This stuff mattered more to her.

The minister directs everyone to the burial, and I walk along with Claire. Max stayed at the house with Jenny, his therapist. She's been so helpful on guiding me through this with Max. My dad's death isn't like Adam leaving—Max has memories, even if they're really more like habits for him, and my dad played an intricate role in his life. He filled a box—and now that box is empty.

The line of cars to the interment is long, though only about half of the guests come for this part—it's mostly family and close friends. Claire guides me to the site. We picked a simple stone for the marker—right next to my mom's. I can't watch this part, so I clasp Claire's hand and lay my head on her shoulder while others walk up to say their farewells. This part isn't for me—my goodbye happens in my head, with my memories. I don't want to taint those visions, the picture I have of him, with anything else.

I recognize the broadness of Mason's back immediately. He's not looking either—he wants to remember my dad just the way I do. Claire said he would come, but I didn't want to count on it. Somewhere in the back of my mind, though, I hoped for it. When he turns to face me, something pulls us together, until our eyes meet. I don't look away, and neither does he. We stare into each other, my head on my best friend's shoulder, for the rest of the ceremony.

Claire hugs me tighter to get my attention when people begin to leave. Everyone wants to say *something* to me, and I know they have to—I would have to too. But when you're on this side, you don't really want to hear it. This part takes almost an hour, and by the time it's only Claire and me, I'm faint and thirsty.

"There's one person left," she says into my shoulder. And I know exactly who it is.

"I'm okay, you go on to the house. I'll go with him," I say, squeezing her arm to let her know I'm sincere. She kisses the side of my head and gives me one last look, trying to fill me with strength. I don't have much left.

"Thanks for coming, Mason," Claire says over my shoulder, and my insides twist just hearing him breathe.

I watch her walk away and make it all the way to her car before I turn to face him completely. "Thank you so much for coming, Mason," I say as Claire drives away, and I finally take him in. He's wearing a black suit with a gray shirt underneath. I can tell by the creases on the pants and sleeves that it's new. He wanted to look nice for my father, and it warms my heart to know that—to see him here looking like this, all for him.

"I hope you know I wouldn't have missed this," he says, his eyes just as sad as I feel inside. "It wouldn't have mattered where I was or what I was doing. I would have come."

"I know," I say, forcing my lips into a tight, closed smile, fighting the urge to cry. "You were a son to him, in every single way."

Mason reaches for my hand and threads his fingers through mine, holding it in front of him loosely. "I'm sorry I wasn't here," he says, and he turns his head to the side when his eyes start to water. "I should have been here."

"No, you were right where you were supposed to be, Mason. You made my dad so proud. You were right where he always wanted to see you," I say, wrapping my hands around his wrist and hugging his arm.

"We left the tour," he says, and my breath completely stops. This is *too much*—too much for *right now*. I want Mason here, and I want him to stay here and never ever leave—but I don't want it to be because of guilt or grief or both.

"Mason, you can't...you have to see that out—it's your dream. He would have wanted that," I say, my hands moving to the collar of his shirt, my fingertips running on his neck, willing him to look at me.

"Kevin understood. It just...it didn't feel right. None of it did, and it's not where I wanted to be," he says, his eyes back to mine, still red with emotion.

"I hope you didn't do this just for me," I say, immediately sorry how harsh my words came out. "I don't mean it like that. I just…I don't want you to do anything rash—not when everything is so raw. Just, promise me you'll think about everything."

"I promise," he says, his eyes not leaving mine, and his face still serious. "Can I take you home? My mom brought a lot of food over to your house before the funeral. I told her I'd come over to help."

"Thanks. And thank your mom for me. Mason, she's been amazing—I don't know what I would have done without her," I say, taking his arm while we walk along the blacktop to where his car is parked.

"I'm glad my mom was here, too," he says, opening my door and slipping the edges of my long black skirt inside before shutting it.

We don't talk for the entire drive back to my father's—I guess *my*—house. But Mason leaves his hand in mine the entire time, holding onto me tightly. And when we get to the house, he runs around the front of the car to help me out, grabbing my hand again. He keeps it in his for the next two hours, only leaving my side for minutes at a time to help his mom serve a few guests and to run upstairs once or twice to visit with Max.

When the house finally empties again, Mason and his mother are the last to go. I wonder if, perhaps, Barb wasn't with him, if he'd try to stay—if he'd say something…*more*. But she's loading up the back of his car with her empty trays, and Mason and I are standing at his car, the last light from the sun rapidly disappearing.

Claire has been staying at our house, sleeping in Mason's old room. I know Mason saw her things in the room, and I overheard him thank her for not leaving me alone.

"Promise me you'll call me, if you need *anything*," he says, his finger lifting my chin, tilting my head to look up at him.

"I promise. But we'll be okay, Mason," I say, forcing my mind to shut off the floodgates of everything I now have to figure out.

"Promise me anyway," he says, and I just smile and nod. He brings me into his arms then, holding me close, and I reach around him, my hands hard against the warmth of his back. He feels like home, and I never want to leave, but I also don't want to hide in him. I want to deal with everything that's in front of me, and I want him to too—if we both end up in the same place when we're done, then it's meant to be.

220

After he and Barb leave, I sit in the hallway waiting while Max finishes taking his bath. He asked me for privacy the other day, so our compromise was letting one of us sit in the hallway. I can't help but remember the last time I sat here now though, and I look at the doorway, Mason's old doorway, and pretend that the light on inside is there for him. When Claire opens the door, my illusion shatters, and I turn my attention back to the half-open bathroom door in front of me.

I feel Claire's body slide down the wall to sit next to me, and I'm enormously grateful for her company. But it's still not the same as if Mason were here. Nothing is. And I'm convinced nothing ever will be.

Mason

I've gone to visit Ray every day since the funeral. It's been three weeks, and I'm pretty sure I've formed a lifelong habit—I no longer think I would know how to begin my day without waking up at the sunrise and bringing my coffee to his gravesite to have it with him.

I talk when I'm there. I talk a lot. And I swear he answers. Maybe he just taught me well, and I know everything he would say. Whatever it is, my mind is clearer out there with him.

Matt and Josh both stopped by to visit yesterday. They've decided to stay in Arizona, and we'll probably play together every now and then. Nothing formal, just gigs for fun. Ben handled the news about as well as we all thought he would, swearing me off for good and leaving without ever looking back. The more distance I get from him, the better I feel about my decision to end the tour early. His house still sits vacant, and I hope like hell he never comes back. I think Ben was going down a very dark road, and I think his poison could have taken us all down with him.

Kevin was just as understanding as I told Avery he was, but he didn't make me any false promises either. He told me they could cover the last stretch of the tour, but that they probably wouldn't look our way for gigs again. It was a tradeoff I was willing to make, and for once, I've never felt more resolved about a decision.

"Let's see…what do I have on tap to talk about today," I say, sitting down in the soft grass next to Ray's stone. I pull a coffee from Jill's Donuts out, and place the cup above his name. I always get one for him, too—though I usually end up drinking both.

"Avery's doing well. She's opening the place back up tonight. She took the semester off school, and they let her drop her grades until she can pick back up again. I fuckin' hate that she had to do that. Sorry, I know you don't like swearing," I say, unable to stop my smile while I sip at my hot coffee.

"I've been careful with her. You know, like we talked about? But I gotta tell you Ray, I'm afraid we're falling into a pattern. I visit her, but I don't stay long. I help out with small things, say hi to Max, maybe play him a song or two to practice on his music program. I feel like I'm just an appointment on her calendar, and I don't know how to break that cycle. It's like a giant game of double dutch, and I don't know when to jump into the ropes. Hell, girls were always better at that game."

I break off a piece of the donut and toss it in the grass for a couple birds that have gotten used to me. I think they actually wait for me to show up every morning now, too.

"I'm playing tonight. Josh and Matt might join me. There's a bunch of us—people who you've helped over the years. Avery doesn't know, actually. She thinks it's just open mic night, but we all signed up for the slots under different names. I guess it's sort of a tribute thing. Everyone I called wanted in, and then people called more people, and then it just became a thing."

I lie back and put my hands under my neck, looking up in the branches of Ray's tree at the birds I just fed. They're fighting over my crumb, and it makes me feel bad, so I throw them the rest of my donut.

"I'm thinking about doing something crazy," I say, and I hold silent now for a while, almost like I'm expecting to really hear his voice. The longer I lay there, the less crazy my idea sounds, and I get a funny thought in my head. "I know you know what I'm thinking. You were always two steps ahead of me, so maybe you can just let me know if I'm being stupid on top of crazy. Anything—a sign, or whatever the hell people call it. Just let me know old man."

I smile in anticipation, and I prop myself up on my elbows, scanning the empty cemetery around me, just waiting for something to happen. The birds continue to pick at my donut, but that's about the only activity that happens for the next ten minutes, so I decide to give up on my little experiment. I pick up my empty cups and bag, brushing the grass from the back of my jeans when I stand.

"Okay, maybe you're right—crazy and stupid," I say, shaking my head with a little laugh. "I guess I'll see ya tomorrow."

Once back inside my car, I pull out my phone to check for any messages from Claire or Avery. Seems my handyman services aren't needed today, and I feel a little sad about it. I drive by

Dusty's to see if anyone's there yet, but the lot is still empty. I see the *Open Mic Night* announcement written on the marquee though. I changed the bulbs out last week, one of those nagging things I wished I had done when Ray was still alive.

I keep driving, and as badly as I want my car to take me to Avery's, I don't go—I only go when she wants me—at least for now. I make the turn down my mom's street, and I'm dreading the empty day ahead of me. But just as I'm about to turn the engine off, I hear it—it's Ray's sign. Maybe I just want it to be there, but it seems so rare for this to be happening now.

My car radio is tuned to one of the popular stations, the ones that play nothing but the top hits. But for some reason, right now, they're playing Otis. It's "Tenderness," and the words could not possibly be any more exact about Avery. I'm stunned silent; I sit there and listen to every last plea that man makes when he sings—begging me to listen to him, to try what he says, just like Ray would. Before the song is over, I'm actually laughing, and I back out of the driveway to head into the city for the day.

"You sneaky old man, you. You want me to go ahead and try crazy," I say, my hands playing drums on my steering wheel. "All right, but if this blows up in my face, and I come out looking like an idiot—that's all on you."

Avery

"Ave, I can't find a spot anywhere in the damn lot," Claire says over the phone.

"Hang on, I'll meet you out back. I'll move something so you can get in," I say, holding the phone on my shoulder while I push a crate in front of the door to hold it open. I see her pulling in, Max in the back seat; I wave and hang up.

I slide two of the trash bins as far forward as I can, and it leaves her just enough room for her car.

"Thanks! I swear, there must be a thousand people here!" she says, holding the back door open for Max. Claire picked him up from school for me today and went through homework at home, knowing how much I had on my plate for tonight's opening. I'm doing my best to juggle, but it's still a lot to keep up with. I'm not sure I'll be able to fit school in the mix.

224

The dining room is already packed, and there's a wait, several people deep, just to get a chance to be inside. It looks like I'll be flipping on the outside speakers for tonight's gigs.

It's all hands on deck tonight. Max learned how to work the video editor on my phone, and he said he was going to record the reopening. I've been keeping my eyes peeled for Mason—he said he would try to come. He's been helping out at the bar over the last two weeks, getting things ready, and sorting through the inventory. He always understood that side of the business better than me—he spent a lot of time here with my dad.

Barb's running the front door, making the list of acts for the night as people sign up. I told her to cap it at twenty or else we'd never make it home, but I can already tell she's blown that—the lists looks to be about two pages long. I guess it's a big night though, so what's one all-nighter to kick Dusty's off with a bang?

"We should probably get things started," she says, yelling above the crowd of thirsty college coeds in between us. Cole brought in a friend to help work the bar, and I'm starting to wish he brought two when some of the customers start to push their way up front and pound on the bar.

"Hey!" Claire whistles down at the far end, standing up on one of the stools and holding a bottle over her head. "All right folks, listen up. This is Avery's first night, and we're all figuring this out, so cut us some slack, okay? We'll get to you, and you're in for some great music tonight, so just take it down a notch and relax."

A few of the men start to applaud her, mostly because they like the view of her black Dusty's shorts from where they're standing, but they're the right men to have on her side—big, tattooed, and ready to step in if the college guys get out of hand. Things seem to settle into place after that, and Cole and his friend Derrick get the drinks flowing fast.

I take the mic from Barb and flip it to *on*, tapping once or twice until I hear the pop of the sound. I've always been behind the stage—in the dark, listening to Mason or my dad—or off to the side while my father did the announcing. My next task has my arms sweating, and my hands shaking uncontrollably; when I step up on the stage and see nothing but a sea of ball caps, cowboy hats, big hair, and hundreds of faces, I almost fall off the stage.

I take a deep breath and close my eyes, remembering how simple my dad always kept things, and I go for it. "Hey there everyone. Welcome to Dusty's!" I say, and the entire place busts out in applause. It chokes me up to see how much people love Dusty's, because I know it's really a reflection of how much they love my dad, and I have to pause for a few seconds and hold my hand over my mouth until I can regain my composure.

"Whooooo, sorry. I'm probably going to do that a few times tonight. Thanks for bearing with me," I say, getting a little laughter from the crowd. "So are we all ready for some music?"

This time, there's thunderous applause, and I hear Claire's whistle in the back again, too, which helps me to smile.

"All right, well, my dad—Ray Abbot—ran this open mic night for thirty years, and he always kept it simple. You get up here, do your thing, and if we like you, we'll have you back. So, how about we all give a big welcome to..." I look down at the clipboard Barb handed me for the first name. "Sam...I am?"

I'm starting to think Barb maybe wrote the name down wrong, and I'm squinting, trying to decipher her handwriting, hoping like hell I didn't completely just butcher some poor guy's name. When I look back up, a guy in a cowboy hat is making his way through the crowd. "Sam? Come on up, you'll have to tell us the story about your na—"

Mason pulls the hat off as soon as he clears the crowd, and shoots me the most playful and proud smile. I haven't seen it since the days before he left for his tour, and I know he's up to something because the closer he gets to me, the tighter his lips have to fight not to break out into laughter. Once he reaches me, he puts the hat on my head and holds his hand out for the mic.

"May I?" he whispers, and I just shake my head at him and hand it over.

"You...are up to no good, aren't you?" I say, crossing my arms.

"Hey folks, let's hear it for Avery Abbot. I think she's doing a great job, don't you?" he says, walking the length of the stage and raising his hands encouraging people to get up from their seats and cheer for me. My face is on fire, I'm so embarrassed, and when he passes me again, I grab his arms and force them down, begging him to stop shedding the spotlight on me.

"All right, well...I'm not Sam. Sorry to disappoint everyone. I know a lot of you here tonight, and for those of you I don't know, my name's Mason Street..." and as soon as he says his name, the sound of screaming women takes over everything else. "Thank you...thanks."

He actually has to wait for the screaming to stop, shaking his head a few times and tossing his arms up to me, honestly a little embarrassed by the amount of attention he's getting.

"A'right, A'right...I've got more to say, so just hang on a bit, and then we'll start entertaining you all," he says, finally getting the crowd to break. "So here's the deal—it's not really an open mic night. This list you've got Avery? It's bogus."

He tosses the clipboard down to his mom and she gives him a wink and then smiles at me with a shrug. Holy damn! Barb Street pulled one over on me!

"We've got a few people here who *are* going to play for you tonight though. I'm going to kick things off, and then I'm going to pass the mic on over to an old friend—Stanley Richards," Mason says, and I pretty much fall on my ass. Stan played with my dad when I was a newborn—I've seen pictures of the two of them together, and my dad would tell me stories about watching Stan's career take off. He's become one of the best blues guitarists in the country—like multi-Grammy big.

I'm starting to realize that the room is filled with old friends of my father's, and the people who stumbled in here tonight just hoping for some drinks and a good show have no clue what a treat they are in for. Mason says a few more names, each one more amazing than the last, and some are people out on tour now, selling out to hundreds of thousands around the country.

"You see why we sort of had to keep this thing under wraps, huh? We're already turning people away," he laughs, waving his hands to the people lining the walls in the back. "Hope y'all can see back there!"

I'm absolutely floored by this tribute to my dad, and I make my way to the edge of the stage and slide off to take my seat by the bar so I can enjoy it for a while. "So what do you say we get this party started?" Mason says, raising his guitar in one hand and a beer in the other; the place erupts in applause again. I realize finally that Matt and Josh have joined him on stage along with

227

Mike Calloway, another longtime friend of dad's, on the drums. Mason plays two familiar chords—he's starting things off with Johnny Cash. Everyone. Goes. Nuts!

Mason mixes in two or three other songs, throwing in a new one he wrote, but keeping everything upbeat, really getting the crowd up and moving. I lean back to check the bar, and Cole and Derrick seem to have things handled, but the flow is constant. Dusty's is going to have a good night, and I feel a heavy blanket of stress leave my shoulders.

"You guys are awesome. Please, make sure you tip your waiters and waitresses—especially that sassy one with the short brown hair. I owe her a shitload of favors, so you'd be helping me out," Mason says, pointing and winking at Claire. She just takes a bow and blows him a kiss; I start to laugh. "All right, so one more song and then I'm going to pass this mic on over to the next guy."

He heads to the back of the stage, and I watch him flip open his guitar case, pulling a different guitar out and putting his away. When I realize what he's holding, I can't help the tears that drench my face. "Ray Abbot was the father I never had," he says, the entire room getting quiet now. "Ray gave me a lot of things—he gave me his guitar," he says, holding it up and waiting through a few whistles and applause.

"He gave me confidence when I had none," he continues. "He gave me advice, even when I thought I knew everything and clearly didn't. But there's one thing he gave me—*one thing*—that freakin' blows all that other stuff away."

I'm holding my breath, sitting on my hands and staring at Mason stand up there and take charge of this room. He looks down for a second, kicking his right foot against the base of the mic stand, sucking in his bottom lip, and then he looks at me. "Ray Abbot gave me his blessing to love his daughter. And he told me to be patient. Avery, he said, is *careful.*"

He smiles at me, his dimples deep, and his eyes focused on my every breath. "I love that Avery is careful," he says, situating his guitar around his neck and pulling the mic a little closer. "I love that she puts everyone else first. I love that she fights for her son. I love her son. And I love how she believes in me—even when I don't deserve it. But mostly, I just love Avery Abbot."

The tears are falling uncontrollably now, and I blot my eyes with the corners of my sleeve, knowing *everyone's* attention is on me again.

"I grew up at Dusty's. I know this place by heart. And I know there are a lot of things in your life that you're putting on hold," he says, looking right at me now, speaking to me and only me. "I'm thinking I might just make a good manager, run things around here—just for a while. And *I know* you're going to tell me I don't have to, and that I should go tour and live my dream, blah blah blah. But the thing is, Ave? You're sorta my dream. And being here—taking care of this place? I kind of don't think it gets any better than that. So, what I'm asking you is that you let me put *you* first—just this once. Whatdaya say?"

Mason is holding the mic in his hand, waiting, along with a thousand other people, for me to just take his offer—to give over some of the weight I carry, share the load with him. He wants me to choose me, and I'm frozen, my stomach weighted with the guilt that comes along with letting others into my life. What started as cheering is turning into light chatter and eventually whispering, and I'm looking side to side, waiting for someone to make my decision for me.

Then Mason starts to play. He's strumming slowly—his hands on my dad's guitar, the music conjuring every single memory I have in my heart. He plays "Tenderness," and he doesn't sing at first, but rather just plays the song, solo, on Ray Abbot's guitar. By the time he makes it through the song once, my eyes are puffy from crying, and Barb and Claire aren't far behind me. He moves closer to the mic the second time through, and pauses for a few seconds—long enough for a few women to scream out for him, and for me to break through the damn barrier inside my chest—and then he flashes me his smile, and sings about my grief and making it *easier to bear*.

He looks right at me when he hits the chorus; I shrug my shoulders, giving in completely. I look at Max, his face intent on the screen of my phone—he's still filming, even though I'm pretty sure his timer has run out by now. When I look back at Mason, he's started to climb down the steps of the stage, still playing the song, but getting closer to me. He lets the guitar rest over his shoulder finally, and Matt takes over the lead, keeping the song going.

I cry harder with every step he takes in my direction, but when he kneels in front of me, pulling my hands to his mouth and kissing them, then placing the small ring in my hand, I start to shake. I can't breathe, and my entire body is numb—the sound of the guitar in the distant background is coming in waves, and the room behind Mason is starting to sway out of focus. He can see the panic on my face, I know he can, but he holds strong, lifting my chin back up to face him and moving his hands to both sides of my face. He comes even closer to me, pulling my forehead against his, pulling me up to a stand in front of him, and my eyes shut while I force myself to drown out the noise in my head.

"I know you're scared," he whispers against me, soft enough that only I can hear. "I'm not going anywhere. And Ave, I don't *want* to go anywhere. Please…just say *yes*. Marry me?"

The whole thing feels like a dream. In fact, I'm sure I've had this exact dream—down to every detail. Only in my dream, my father was here. I was sixteen then, and Mason wasn't near the man he is now. But the one he's become? This one—the one standing here in front of everyone and asking to take care of me— is better than my make believe. I nod yes, and at first he doesn't feel it, so I nod stronger and whisper it to him.

"Yes?" he says, opening his eyes now and backing away from me just enough to slide the ring from my palm and onto my finger.

I nod again, and my core quivers with nerves, but happiness starts to flood my chest.

Mason doesn't go back on stage. He pulls me to him, his thumbs soft on my cheeks, and his fingertips deep in my hair; he kisses me so hard, he has to sweep my legs up and pull them around his waist to keep me from falling over. I can hear everyone around us start to whistle and cheer, but time stands still while Mason is kissing me, and soon I hear Stanley start to sing on stage.

The spotlight has finally gone back to where it belongs, and Mason and I slip to the booth in the corner, him on one side of Max and me on the other. Mason asks Max to show him what he's been working on, and without really answering, Max starts to flip through screens on my phone, showing him pictures and video clips, and Mason just watches in wonder, his face full of

230

contentment. All I can feel is the touch of his hand linked with mine on the booth top behind Max, his finger lightly running over the ring he's just placed on my finger. Subconsciously, I start counting in my mind, but rather than trying to survive until one moment ends and I can get to the next, I'm counting because I never want this one to end.

EPILOGUE

Mason

"This is stupid, I don't know why I even wrote this shit down," I say, shoving the list of people to thank back into my pocket. I wrote the list on a napkin at the diner we stopped at before the Grammys.

"It's not stupid, and I *know* you're going to need it," Avery says, snuggling up against my arm and tilting her chin up so she can kiss my cheek. I keep my eyes on her, watching her look up at me—not a doubt to be found on her face. Hell, I don't care if I win at this point, for me the best damn award in this world is earning that smile she's making right there.

Who knew Matt's words would be so prophetic. *There will be other bands.* He ended up sticking around Dusty's with me, and Josh hooked up with Stanley to make another blues album. Matt and I started working on some duets, refining a really cool country kind of folk-rock sound. We'd practice during the week, and perform on weekends at Dusty's; we ended up picking up another bass player and a drummer from those sessions—Jeremy and Nathan, just a couple of local guys who really dug our sound.

And that was enough. Then Kevin showed up one night for another show. I thought he was just passing through town, maybe staying at one of the fancy desert resorts. But then he stayed through the whole set, hung out until the place emptied, and waited at a table while I closed up for the night.

Seems my song "Perfect" was getting a lot of questions—and people started asking for it at Tenenbaum shows, wanting them to cover it or bring back the band that played it. Kevin offered me a recording contract that night—one shot at an album. It was two months away from Avery—away from Max. We had just gotten married, and Dusty's was just finding its groove again. But that woman of mine, she insisted. So the *new* Mason Street Band rented a house in LA, and I flew home every weekend until the album was done.

We called it *One Night at Ray's*—in honor of the man who will always be my father to me. Ray named Dusty's after his dad, and it just seemed fitting to me that I give him credit in my big break. And, yeah, it sounds arrogant as fuck, but I wasn't really surprised when "Perfect" hit the charts at number seven. People always loved that song on the road, and it had that emotional thing going for it.

When six other songs followed it though…one spending three weeks at number one? Yeah, that pretty much shot my surreal meter up to a million. My face was in magazines, and I even had to make some security changes to the house to keep out crazy stalker-types and paparazzi. I tried to talk Avery into moving; I'd made enough for us to move into one of those luxury, gated neighborhoods in the hills. But she's not quite ready to let go of her dad's place yet. I kinda don't think I am either. Besides, Max likes it there—and that's really all that matters to me.

Our category is coming up soon…best new artist. "Perfect" was up for song of the year, but I knew I'd lose that. Somewhere in the back of my head, though, I feel like we *might* win this one. I can't stop my knee from bobbing up and down, and Avery keeps sliding her hand over every thirty seconds to hold it still. She bought a new dress for tonight, a silky light pink one that hugs her amazing body—we took photographs together. *People wanted to take our picture!* I keep looking at her legs in that dress, and the more I do, the more I want to hunt down that photographer and get her photo back—I don't want people knowing how sexy my woman is.

"This is it," she says, holding my arm even tighter now. I smile at her, but I decide to keep my eyes on her, because I'd rather watch her face light up when they read the nominees. When they say our name, she screams and claps her hands close to me, still keeping her arm linked through mine. I don't miss any of it—from the quiver of nerves along her lips to the small side-glances she gives me just to see if I'm still looking at her.

"Mason Street Band!" I barely register it at first, but soon Avery's lips are on mine and she's practically sitting in my lap, hugging me, and talking in between kisses, her hands clinging to the sides of my face.

"You did it, Mason! Oh my god, you did it!" she says. "I'm so proud of you. So very proud!"

Somehow, I manage to get my legs to work, and I stand up and walk to the aisle, putting my arm around Matt, mostly because I need him to haul my numb ass up to the stage.

"Holy shit, man! We did it!" he says, shaking me with a side hug while we walk up to the front along with Nathan and Jeremy.

What they don't tell you about awards shows like this is that the awards are really heavy. It's not the one I'll actually take home, but it's a replica they use for the presentation—and it's really heavy! My hands are trembling, and I know I'm going to drop mine, so I hand it to Matt and look him square in the eyes while I reach into my pocket in front of the mic.

"Good thing Avery made you write that junk on the napkin," he says, laughing at me. I shake my head in disbelief and pull it out, turning back to the mic and adjusting it a little for my height.

"So…this is unexpected," I start, and the audience screams in response. "A year and a half ago, I was getting into bar fights and getting tossed from shows in two-bit holes in the wall in places like Norman, Oklahoma. Man…thank you guys for giving us a shot again."

I step back for a few seconds just to take it all in, but I know I don't have long, so I start rattling off the list of *thank yous* before time runs out. I get through the various agent and label types, and then I put the napkin away, because the rest of what I want to say is personal, and I'd never forget a word of it.

"Just a few more names…I promise. First and foremost, I need to thank my inspiration—Avery Street. Have you all seen how hot my wife is tonight?"

I throw that in mostly because I love watching her get embarrassed, and she does, shirking down in her seat, her eyes wide, but her hand quick to cover her face.

"I love you, Birdie," I say, letting those words linger out there for everyone to hear and remember. I started calling her Birdie again after our wedding—when she told me she liked my story about why I thought of that name, and the "Blackbird" song that inspired it.

"I also need to thank the man the album's named after. Ray Abbot was a silent warrior in the world of up-and-coming

234

musicians—and anyone who was ever touched by him was a thousand times better off as a human just for knowing him. I love you, Ray...this one's for you!" I say, taking my Grammy from Matt and holding it up to the sky. The rest of the guys do the same, and I can feel my eyes wanting to cry.

"Finally, there's one member of our band who's not up here. He couldn't make it tonight because his bedtime is eight o'clock. If you look on the credits for *One Night at Ray's,* you'll see the name Max Abbot. His name's actually Max Abbot-Street now. Max is my son—it became *official* four days ago when the judge signed the adoption order. Max has autism..." I say, and the crowd is quiet for this part.

"But he also has so much more," I say, smiling as I look into Avery's weeping eyes. "Max has fierce determination. He doesn't give up on things, and when he finds the answer, it's *always* right. He's also a very patient teacher. Technology comes pretty easily to him, and he taught me how to use the computer program we used to write all of our music for the album."

"Max is also a genius...and no, I'm not saying that because I'm biased as his dad. I'm saying it because he is. Before I left for LA to start recording, I sat in our music room working through melodies and various riffs and chords, looking for things that went together well so we had something to work with when we started recording. I'd play it once, and then it was locked away in Max's brain—permanently. By the next morning, he'd have every note written down and recorded on his iPad. So it just seems right that Max gets credit for this, too—he was a writer on the album. He's six, going on seven, so imagine what you all will get to see him do at twenty, thirty, forty."

I didn't expect the producers to let me go on so long, but I'm glad they did. And when the audience starts to clap and get to their feet for the words I just said, I feel overwhelmed. I hold up my award again along with the rest of the guys, and say one last "Thanks," into the mic. We all head back stage, and all I can think of is getting back to Avery. Some woman is telling us about picking up our final awards, and Matt's telling me he'll get mine, but I'm too busy pushing and shoving through people, just trying to find my girl.

Someone brings her backstage finally, and I kiss her lips just to ground myself. "Can you believe this?" I say, still in shock from everything.

"I knew you'd win," she says, her eyes still red from crying. "Mason, I can't believe everything you said. Oh my god, that was beautiful. Max...he's going to be so excited to see this in the morning. Oh, we have to get home...I want to show it to him!"

"Let's go then," I say, tugging her hand in mine, and tucking my award that Matt just handed to me under my arm.

"Mace, we can't just leave! You have to stay for parties and things," she says, giggling because she doesn't think I'm serious. But I am. I learned a lot of things from Ray Abbot, and first and foremost was that things like fame and attention don't add up to a hill of shit in the end. But Avery? And my life at home with her and Max? That's what I want my legacy to be. And when the guy getting the award after me gives a nod to Otis Redding in his acceptance speech, I know it's Ray's way of telling me I'm right.

So I get us a car, and we go straight to the airport, because clothes and things can be shipped. We'll be home when Max wakes up in the morning. And Avery loves me for it. And I love her...for *everything* else.

THE END

ACKNOWLEDGEMENTS

I've given a great deal of thought to this part of the book. The acknowledgements. There are *a lot* of people I want to acknowledge—people who have poured over my words with me, put up with my neurotic questioning, slapped my hand while I chewed my nails and worried that I was getting it *just right*. But the first words of acknowledgement need to go to the warriors on this earth—the parents, siblings, grandparents, aunts, uncles and friends of those with autism.

I came to understand autism fully years ago while working as a journalist. As with many things in my journalism career, it was a story assignment that educated me. I went into the assignment with some basic understanding, but I came away with open eyes—and a new passion. And over the years, I've volunteered my writing services for an organization here in Arizona—the Southwest Autism Research and Resource Center—and I've been blessed to meet amazing families, medical practitioners, therapists, volunteers and teachers who all work to pull on the strands of the puzzle that autism is with the hope of unraveling it just a little more for those living with it.

I have had family affected by diagnosis. I have had friends affected by diagnosis. And I have interviewed countless parents who, like Avery Abbot, are brave fighters in the face of a strong wind, traveling uphill every minute of every day. So this book is first and foremost for them, my humble way of honoring their story and spreading their mantra—hope.

I must also thank, as always, my husband and son, for believing in me more than I think I deserve. And this story would never have made it safely from my Mac to market without the assistance of my editors, Tina Scott and Billi Joy Carson, and my team of amazing beta readers who helped make sure Avery and Mason's story was honest, heartfelt and truly one of love. Thank you, Jen, Nikki, Shelley, Debbie and Brigitte.

And lastly, if you would like to learn more about the many amazing programs, services, research projects, resources, opportunities and more at the Southwest Autism Research and Resource Center, please visit them at www.autismcenter.org.

About the author

Ginger Scott is a journalist and writer from Peoria, Arizona. A proud Sun Devil, she is a graduate and associate faculty member of Arizona State University's Cronkite School of Journalism. When she's not typing feverishly on her MacBook during the wee hours or reading in the dark on her iPad, she's probably at a baseball diamond somewhere watching her son or her favorite team, the Arizona Diamondbacks, take the field.

Also by Ginger Scott

In addition to *How We Deal With Gravity,* Ginger Scott is the author of the powerful and character-driven coming-of-age romance series *Waiting on the Sidelines* and *Going Long* as well as the new-adult romance *Blindness.* She will have a new romance releasing in late summer 2014 titled *This Is Falling.* For the latest information on new projects, book signings and more, be sure to follow her on Facebook and Twitter or visit her online.

www.littlemisswrite.com
www.facebook.com/GingerScottAuthor
Twitter @TheGingerScott

Made in the USA
Lexington, KY
06 September 2014